One historical mystery series that never
gets these dull...

WHAT WOULD THE INSPECTOR DO
WITHOUT HER?

Even Inspector Witherspoon himself doesn't know—because his
secret weapon is as ladylike as she is clever. She's Mrs. Jeffries—
the charming detective who stars in this unique Victorian mystery
series. Enjoy them all . . .

The Inspector and Mrs. Jeffries
A doctor is found dead in his own office—and Mrs. Jeffries
must scour the premises to find the prescription for murder.

Mrs. Jeffries Dusts for Clues
One case is solved and another is opened when the inspector
finds a missing brooch—pinned to a dead woman's gown. But
Mrs. Jeffries never cleans a room without dusting under the
bed—and never gives up on a case before every loose end is
tightly tied.

The Ghost and Mrs. Jeffries
Death is unpredictable . . . but the murder of Mrs. Hodges was
foreseen at a spooky séance. The practical-minded housekeeper
may not be able to see the future—but she can look into the past
and put things in order to solve this haunting crime.

Mrs. Jeffries Takes Stock
A businessman has been murdered—and it could be because he
cheated his stockholders. The housekeeper's interest is piqued . . .
and when it comes to catching killers, the smart money's on
Mrs. Jeffries.

Mrs. Jeffries on the Ball
A festive Jubilee celebration turns into a fatal affair—and
Mrs. Jeffries must find the guilty party.

continued . . .

Mrs. Jeffries on the Trail

Why was Annie Shields out selling flowers so late on a foggy night? And more importantly, who killed her while she was doing it? It's up to Mrs. Jeffries to sniff out the clues.

Mrs. Jeffries Plays the Cook

Mrs. Jeffries finds herself doing double duty: cooking for the inspector's household and trying to cook a killer's goose.

Mrs. Jeffries and the Missing Alibi

When Inspector Witherspoon becomes the main suspect in a murder, Scotland Yard refuses to let him investigate. But no one said anything about Mrs. Jeffries.

Mrs. Jeffries Stands Corrected

When a local publican is murdered, and Inspector Witherspoon botches the investigation, trouble starts to brew for Mrs. Jeffries.

Mrs. Jeffries Takes the Stage

After a theatre critic is murdered, Mrs. Jeffries uncovers the victim's secret past: a real-life drama more compelling than any stage play.

Mrs. Jeffries Questions the Answer

Hannah Cameron was not well liked. But were her friends or family the sort to stab her in the back? Mrs. Jeffries must really tiptoe around this time—or it could be a matter of life and death.

Mrs. Jeffries Reveals Her Art

Mrs. Jeffries has to work double time to find a missing model *and* a killer. And she'll have to get her whole staff involved—before someone else becomes the next subject.

Mrs. Jeffries Takes the Cake

The evidence was all there: a dead body, two dessert plates, and a gun. As if Mr. Ashbury had been sharing cake with his own killer. Now Mrs. Jeffries will have to do some snooping around—to dish up clues.

Mrs. Jeffries Rocks the Boat
Mirabelle had traveled by boat all the way from Australia to visit her sister—only to wind up murdered. Now Mrs. Jeffries must solve the case—and it's sink or swim.

Mrs. Jeffries Weeds the Plot
Three attempts have been made on Annabeth Gentry's life. Is it due to her recent inheritance, or is it because her bloodhound dug up the body of a murdered thief? Mrs. Jeffries will have to sniff out some clues before the plot thickens.

Mrs. Jeffries Pinches the Post
Harrison Nye may have had some dubious business dealings, but no one expected him to be murdered. Now, Mrs. Jeffries and her staff must root through the sins of his past to discover which one caught up with him.

Mrs. Jeffries Pleads Her Case
Harlan Westover's death was deemed a suicide by the magistrate. But Inspector Witherspoon is willing to risk his career to prove otherwise. Mrs. Jeffries must ensure the good inspector remains afloat.

Mrs. Jeffries Sweeps the Chimney
A dead vicar has been found, propped against a church wall. And Inspector Witherspoon's only prayer is to seek the divinations of Mrs. Jeffries.

Mrs. Jeffries Stalks the Hunter
Puppy love turns to obsession, which leads to murder. Who better to get to the heart of the matter than Inspector Witherspoon's indomitable companion, Mrs. Jeffries.

Mrs. Jeffries and the Silent Knight
The yuletide murder of an elderly man is complicated by several suspects—none of whom were in the Christmas spirit.

Mrs. Jeffries Appeals the Verdict
Mrs. Jeffries and her belowstairs cohorts have their work cut out for them if they want to save an innocent man from the gallows.

continued . . .

Mrs. Jeffries and the Best Laid Plans
Banker Lawrence Boyd didn't waste his time making friends, which is why hardly anyone mourns his death. With a list of enemies including just about everyone the miser's ever met, it will take Mrs. Jeffries' shrewd eye to find the killer.

Mrs. Jeffries and the Feast of St. Stephen
'Tis the season for sleuthing when wealthy Stephen Whitfield is murdered during his holiday dinner party. It's up to Mrs. Jeffries to solve the case in time for Christmas.

Mrs. Jeffries Holds the Trump
A very well-liked but very dead magnate is found floating down the river. Now Mrs. Jeffries and company will have to dive into a mystery that only grows more complex.

Mrs. Jeffries in the Nick of Time
Mrs. Jeffries lends her downstairs common sense to this upstairs murder mystery—and hopes that she and the inspector don't get derailed in the case of a rich uncle-cum-model-train-enthusiast.

Mrs. Jeffries and the Yuletide Weddings
Wedding bells will make this season all the more jolly. Until one humbug sings a carol of murder.

Mrs. Jeffries Speaks Her Mind
Someone is trying to kill the eccentric Olive Kettering, but no one believes her, until she's proven right. Without witnesses and plenty of suspects, Mrs. Jeffries will see justice served.

Visit Emily Brightwell's website
www.emilybrightwell.com

Also available from Prime Crime:
The first three Mrs. Jeffries Mysteries in one volume
Mrs. Jeffries Learns the Trade

Berkley Prime Crime titles by Emily Brightwell

THE INSPECTOR AND MRS. JEFFRIES
MRS. JEFFRIES DUSTS FOR CLUES
THE GHOST AND MRS. JEFFRIES
MRS. JEFFRIES TAKES STOCK
MRS. JEFFRIES ON THE BALL
MRS. JEFFRIES ON THE TRAIL
MRS. JEFFRIES PLAYS THE COOK
MRS. JEFFRIES AND THE MISSING ALIBI
MRS. JEFFRIES STANDS CORRECTED
MRS. JEFFRIES TAKES THE STAGE
MRS. JEFFRIES QUESTIONS THE ANSWER
MRS. JEFFRIES REVEALS HER ART
MRS. JEFFRIES TAKES THE CAKE
MRS. JEFFRIES ROCKS THE BOAT
MRS. JEFFRIES WEEDS THE PLOT
MRS. JEFFRIES PINCHES THE POST
MRS. JEFFRIES PLEADS HER CASE
MRS. JEFFRIES SWEEPS THE CHIMNEY
MRS. JEFFRIES STALKS THE HUNTER
MRS. JEFFRIES AND THE SILENT KNIGHT
MRS. JEFFRIES APPEALS THE VERDICT
MRS. JEFFRIES AND THE BEST LAID PLANS
MRS. JEFFRIES AND THE FEAST OF ST. STEPHEN
MRS. JEFFRIES HOLDS THE TRUMP
MRS. JEFFRIES IN THE NICK OF TIME
MRS. JEFFRIES AND THE YULETIDE WEDDINGS
MRS. JEFFRIES SPEAKS HER MIND
MRS. JEFFRIES FORGES AHEAD
MRS. JEFFRIES AND THE MISTLETOE MIX-UP
MRS. JEFFRIES DEFENDS HER OWN
MRS. JEFFRIES TURNS THE TIDE
MRS. JEFFRIES AND THE MERRY GENTLEMEN

Anthologies

MRS. JEFFRIES LEARNS THE TRADE
MRS. JEFFRIES TAKES A SECOND LOOK
MRS. JEFFRIES TAKES TEA AT THREE
MRS. JEFFRIES SALLIES FORTH

MRS. JEFFRIES
FORGES AHEAD

EMILY BRIGHTWELL

BERKLEY PRIME CRIME, NEW YORK

THE BERKLEY PUBLISHING GROUP
Published by the Penguin Group
Penguin Group (USA) Inc.
375 Hudson Street, New York, New York 10014, USA
Penguin Group (Canada), 90 Eglinton Avenue East, Suite 700, Toronto, Ontario M4P 2Y3, Canada
(a division of Pearson Penguin Canada Inc.)
Penguin Books Ltd., 80 Strand, London WC2R 0RL, England
Penguin Group Ireland, 25 St. Stephen's Green, Dublin 2, Ireland (a division of Penguin Books Ltd.)
Penguin Group (Australia), 250 Camberwell Road, Camberwell, Victoria 3124, Australia
(a division of Pearson Australia Group Pty. Ltd.)
Penguin Books India Pvt. Ltd., 11 Community Centre, Panchsheel Park, New Delhi—110 017, India
Penguin Group (NZ), 67 Apollo Drive, Rosedale, Auckland 0632, New Zealand
(a division of Pearson New Zealand Ltd.)
Penguin Books (South Africa) (Pty.) Ltd., 24 Sturdee Avenue, Rosebank, Johannesburg 2196,
South Africa

Penguin Books Ltd., Registered Offices: 80 Strand, London WC2R 0RL, England

This is a work of fiction. Names, characters, places, and incidents either are the product of the author's imagination or are used fictitiously, and any resemblance to actual persons, living or dead, business establishments, events, or locales is entirely coincidental. The publisher does not have any control over and does not assume any responsibility for author or third-party websites or their content.

MRS. JEFFRIES FORGES AHEAD

A Berkley Prime Crime Book / published by arrangement with the author

PRINTING HISTORY
Berkley Prime Crime mass-market edition / May 2011

Copyright © 2011 by Cheryl Arguile.
Cover illustration by Jeff Walker.

ISBN: 978-0-425-24160-8

BERKLEY® PRIME CRIME
Berkley Prime Crime Books are published by The Berkley Publishing Group,
a division of Penguin Group (USA) Inc.,
375 Hudson Street, New York, New York 10014.
BERKLEY® PRIME CRIME and the PRIME CRIME logo are trademarks of Penguin Group (USA) Inc.

PRINTED IN THE UNITED STATES OF AMERICA

10 9 8 7 6 5 4

*This book is dedicated to Terry P. Waters,
who I agree with on most subjects,
except his well-meaning but misguided politics.*

CHAPTER 1

"Where on earth did she get that gown? It's too daring and bright a color for a married woman." Lady Emma Stafford sniffed disapprovingly as she stared at the lovely redhead in the emerald green evening gown sitting on the far side of the Banfield ballroom. "I'm sure she's wearing rouge as well. No one has cheeks that color; it can't be natural."

Geraldine Banfield exchanged a quick, amused glance with the other two women at their table, her houseguests Margaret Bickleton and Rosalind Kimball. Poor Emma's complexion was such a bright shade of red one could see her coming from half a mile away! The Staffords might be aristocrats, but poor Emma was not only cursed with a florid complexion but she had jowls so loose they draped over the top strand of her diamond choker. Her hair was white, styled in youthful ringlets that made her look absurd and held up by silver combs encrusted with sapphires. But even the most skilled of dressmakers couldn't disguise the fat threatening to burst out of the blue silk of her gown.

Lady Emma turned her attention back to her friends and gave Geraldine a condescending smile. "Oh dear, that was very unkind of me. I do hope you aren't offended. But we've been friends for such a long time, I thought I could speak freely."

Geraldine Banfield reached for her wine and took a sip before she responded. "I'm the first to admit that she's certainly not the sort of woman I expected my nephew to marry. But she is family now so I would appreciate it if you'd be a bit more circumspect with your opinions." She paused and leaned closer to her companions. "At least in public. You never know who is listening. The dark-haired man behind us is an old friend of hers."

Margaret Bickleton glanced over her shoulder at the laughing group sitting at the next table. She was a tall skeleton of a woman with deep-set eyes enclosed by dark circles, thinning gray hair worn in a tiny bun at the nape of her neck, and a long, sharp nose. "You mean the man who needs a haircut? Goodness, he is unkempt; I'm surprised you let him into the house." She picked a fleck of lint off the tight cuff of her beige chiffon sleeve.

"As I said, he's a friend of Arlette's," Geraldine responded dryly. "I thought I told you at breakfast yesterday that she insisted on inviting her artist friends."

"Artists indeed!" Margaret snorted delicately and gazed across the ballroom at the object of their conversation. "I'm surprised that Lewis allows her to mix with such people—and why is Lady Cannonberry sitting at her table? Surely those two aren't friends."

"But of course they are!" Rosalind Kimball exclaimed. She was a small, slender woman with stooped shoulders growing into a widow's hump, frizzy brown hair, and a thin, flat line of a mouth. "Ruth Cannonberry is a member of that society that's always agitating for something or other. I saw her outside of Parliament last year and she was marching with a bunch of other women and carrying a big sign about getting the right to vote. Honestly, voting, it's unthinkable." She glanced at Geraldine. "Frankly, I was surprised to see that you'd invited her tonight."

Geraldine gave her a sour smile. "I had no choice in the matter; Arlette specifically asked that she be put on the guest list."

"You could have refused," Rosalind snapped and then clamped her mouth shut as she realized what she'd just said. "Oh dear, I'm sorry. Sometimes I forget you're no longer mistress here."

"No, not anymore," Geraldine agreed with a shrug. "But I don't mind giving up the role of lady of the manor. Running a house this size was becoming very tiresome. Arlette, despite her unusual background, has enormous energy and is actually very intelligent. She's quite good at going over the household accounts."

"From what I've heard, that's not the only thing she's good at," Lady Emma said. The women laughed and continued staring at the table where Arlette Banfield was now taking a sip from a delicate blue champagne flute.

The Banfield ball was one of the premier events on the London social calendar, and everyone who was anyone in society was eager to be invited save for the woman sitting in a place of honor at the head table. Lady Cannonberry, or

Ruth, as she was known to her friends, was there because she hadn't been able to come up with a reasonable excuse to avoid the wretched thing and she'd not wanted to hurt Arlette Banfield's feelings. She glanced at the pretty red-head seated next to her. Arlette was leaning back in her chair, trying to get someone's attention on the far side of the huge room. Ruth sighed inwardly, she felt so guilty. She liked her hostess and found her to be kind, witty, and intelligent. But she really wished she were at home or having dinner with Gerald. There were times when a ball or a dinner party or a tea could be very useful, but as she wasn't "on the hunt" just now, she was bored.

Ruth turned slightly and studied the others at her table. Her host, Lewis Banfield, was discussing business with Sir Ralph Fetchman while Lady Fetchman gossiped with a lady at the next table. Sir Adrian Fortnoy was waving his empty glass at a waiter while his wife, Ellen, lifted her wrist closer to the candelabra so Nora Kingsley could see her bracelet. Rufus Kingsley, Nora's husband, was staring at the screens in front of the buffet and impatiently tapping his fingers on the tabletop. As she was sitting next to Rufus, she mentally decided to make sure she wasn't in his way when the barrier between him and the food was removed. He looked quite capable of bowling her over.

Her attention shifted to the room. Women in pastel ball gowns of yellow, coral, and blue, this year's favorite colors, moved between the tables, stopping here and there to chat while the orchestra members tuned their instruments. The French doors that led out onto the terrace were open, and the summer breeze sent the candles flickering but did little to cool the increasingly crowded room.

Her gaze fixed on the four women huddled around a table to the left of the terrace and, as if by magic, they all seemed to shift their heads at once and look back at her. Ruth didn't consider herself overly sensitive, but she could almost feel the disapproval coming from their direction. *Goodness gracious,* she thought, *with their sagging skin, hair in various shades of gray, and sour expressions, they looked like a coven of well-dressed witches.* But they were four of the most prominent women in the kingdom and apparently felt their social status and wealth gave them leave to be rude. Ruth lifted her chin and met their eyes. But their expressions didn't waver, and it took her a moment to understand that it wasn't she, but the woman sitting next to her, that was the real object of their scrutiny.

"Don't let them worry you." Arlette Banfield's whisper interrupted her thoughts. "They'll soon tire of staring at us and turn their attention to someone else. They remind me of the witches Macbeth met, except he only had three and we've got to put up with four."

Ruth tried to keep a straight face but failed. "You shouldn't say such things." She laughed. "But honestly, it was almost exactly what I was thinking. Why are they so miserable?"

"I don't know." Arlette shook her head. "You'd think that those who had every advantage this society has to offer would be a bit more cheerful, wouldn't you? I thought Geraldine was simply morose because I'd taken her place in the household, but her friends are just as long faced and disagreeable, and what's more, I've had to put up with them all week. Thank goodness tonight is almost over. As of tomorrow morning, the Mesdames Kimball and Bickleton will be gone. Then the only one I'll need to concern myself with is Geraldine." She took another sip of champagne and frowned as she put her glass down. "And that conversation isn't going to be pleasant."

"Oh dear, that sounds ominous," Ruth murmured. *Bang . . . bang . . .* She started as a crashing noise thundered so loudly everyone in the room suddenly stopped talking and turned toward the orchestra to see what had happened. *Bang . . . bang . . .* The sound continued.

A violinist, his instrument still in his hand, stood and watched helplessly as every music stand in the front row was sent crashing to the floor.

"Good gracious, the fellow knocked over his stand and sent the whole lot of them tumbling over." Sir Ralph laughed heartily. "I saw the whole thing. I'll bet he'd not be able to duplicate that again."

"Let's hope he doesn't try," Lewis Banfield replied.

The musician put his violin on his chair and began picking up the stands. When he reached the last one, he righted it, turned toward the ballroom guests and gave them a cheeky grin, and bowed. Everyone laughed and there was even a scattering of applause.

Ruth turned back to her companion and stared at her expectantly, hoping she'd continue with what she'd been saying before they were interrupted. She didn't like to think of herself as a gossipmonger, but it was only human nature to be curious.

"Tomorrow isn't going to be pleasant." Arlette glanced at her husband, who had gone back to his discussion with Sir Ralph Fetchman. "Lewis is going to suggest that his aunt might be more comfortable if she moved to the country house."

"Does Mrs. Banfield dislike London?"

Arlette shook her head. "She loves London, but she can't seem to understand that she's no longer mistress here. I've done my best to be sensitive about her situation and tried to allow her to have some say in the running of the household. But I cannot tolerate the way she treats the servants and neither can Lewis. My maid told me she was in the butler's pantry this morning bossing the staff about as if they didn't know what they were doing. Poor Michaels was run ragged. She insisted that all the glassware be washed again. But I know for a fact that every glass in that pantry was clean—I checked them myself yesterday. When I got home and heard what she'd done, I was furious." She paused and took a deep breath. "I told her that Michaels has been a butler for over thirty years and he certainly doesn't need her giving him instructions. She stomped off in a huff and didn't speak to me at luncheon, and obviously she told her houseguests to ignore me, because they barely spoke to me, either." She broke off and took another, deeper lungful of air. "But I didn't mind in the least. Geraldine has a mind so tiny it could sleep on a pincushion, and the less I have to do with her and her friends, the better. I've no idea why she invited them this week; she's barely spent any time with them at all."

"Oh dear, I'm sure the situation is most unpleasant." Ruth stared at her. Something wasn't right. "Are you alright? Your face is flushed."

"It's the champagne." Arlette's chest heaved rapidly.

"It seems quite strong tonight. It's gone straight to my head."

"But you've only had a glass," Ruth protested. She glanced at Lewis, hoping to meet his eye so she could signal her concern, but he was still involved in his conversation, so she turned back to Arlette. "And even the most potent champagne doesn't make you breathe the way you are now. It sounds like you can't get any air into your lungs. What's wrong? Are you ill?"

Arlette waved dismissively. "I'm fine. Really. It's just a touch of nausea and a bit of light-headedness, that's all." She reached for her drink, took another sip, and put her glass down. It landed with a thud loud enough to get her husband's attention.

He frowned at her. "Are you alright?"

But Arlette wasn't alright, not in the least.

Her face turned white and her eyes bulged as she grabbed her throat and gasped for breath. "I can't breathe," she rasped. Her body began to buck against the seat of the chair, and she'd have fallen to the floor if Ruth hadn't grabbed her around the shoulders.

"Get a doctor," Ruth yelled as she struggled to hold her friend on the chair. "Something is wrong."

"My God! Arlette, Arlette, what is it? Get a doctor, get a doctor!" Lewis screamed as he leapt up and threw his arms around his wife. Arlette was in full convulsions now, and the others at the table scrambled to their feet.

"Get her on the floor." Ruth shoved her hip against the rim of the table. The others understood her intent and they grabbed the edge, pulling it back out of the way as she and Lewis eased Arlette to the floor. Ruth took care to keep her hand under the woman's head to keep it from banging against the tiles.

"Is there a doctor in the house?" Sir Ralph yelled at the top of his lungs. "For God's sake, get a doctor."

"Arlette, Arlette, darling," Lewis crooned, his face a mask of shocked misery and pain. "What's wrong, what is it? Oh, my God, what can be wrong with her?" He looked at Ruth. "We must get her upstairs to a bed."

But Arlette couldn't move. Her body continued convulsing and foam came out of her mouth. She tried to speak but couldn't. Ruth's hand was being pounded by her head, but she barely noticed.

"Make way, I'm a doctor," a man cried as he shoved through the crowd. He knelt down beside them and grabbed Arlette's hand, snagging her wrist and feeling for a pulse.

Moaning, Arlette curled into a ball and tried to roll to her side but she suddenly went rigid, gave a gasp, and flopped onto her back.

The doctor put his nose to her mouth and sniffed at her lips, then he leaned back, made a fist, and smacked her hard in the chest.

Lewis screamed and grabbed at the doctor's arm as he started to do it a second time. "What are you doing?" he yelled.

"Let me go." He jerked his arm away and landed another blow on her chest. "I'm trying to start her heart and save her life. She's not breathing."

But despite the doctor's valiant efforts, Arlette Banfield wasn't going to be dancing at the ball tonight. She was dead.

* * *

The household of Inspector Gerald Witherspoon was settled in for the evening. Mrs. Goodge, the elderly, white-haired cook, had taken her cat, Samson, and retired to her room. Wiggins, the footman, had taken his notebook and gone upstairs to the attic room to write up his thoughts for the day, and Phyllis, the maid, who was the last to go up, asked the housekeeper, Mrs. Jeffries, if she might borrow yesterday's newspaper to read.

Mrs. Jeffries, who always encouraged the staff to better themselves, handed over the *Times*. After the housemaid had disappeared upstairs, Mrs. Jeffries went down the hallway to the inspector's study. She knocked lightly, opened the door, and stuck her head into the room. The inspector looked up from the stack of files on his desk. He was a dark-haired man in his late forties with a thin, bony face, a pale complexion, and a large mustache of which he was rather proud. His spectacles had slipped down his nose.

"I'm going to lock up, sir, and I wondered if you needed anything," she said.

Witherspoon smiled. "I'm fine, Mrs. Jeffries. But you go on up. I'll check the house locks before I retire." He broke off as they heard someone pounding on the front door. Mrs. Jeffries turned and started for the front of the house.

Witherspoon shot to his feet and raced after her. "Let me answer it, Mrs. Jeffries," he ordered. "It's dark now and we don't know who is out there."

Mrs. Jeffries slowed her steps and he pushed past her to the front door. His words made sense. Inspector Gerald Witherspoon had arrested more murderers than anyone in the history of the Metropolitan Police Force, and even killers had friends or family that might want a bit of vengeance.

The inspector opened the door an inch or so and peeked through the crack. "My goodness, it's Constable Griffiths. Come in, Constable."

"Thank you, sir." Griffiths took off his helmet and tucked it under his arm as he stepped inside. "I'm sorry to disturb you but I'm afraid it's urgent." He spotted Mrs. Jeffries and nodded respectfully. "Good evening, ma'am."

She smiled in return as her mind raced through the possibilities that would have brought him to the house this late in the day.

"There's been a murder in St. John's Wood, and they want you there straightaway," Griffiths said.

Witherspoon grimaced. "St. John's Wood isn't my district." He hated it when he got called out to another district. It tended to annoy the local police no end, and the inspector hated discord among his fellow officers.

"Yes, sir, I know, but the orders came from the chief inspector himself. He sent a telegram asking for you. The address is number eleven Wallington Square, St. John's Wood. I'm to go with you, sir."

Witherspoon sighed inwardly and hoped the superintendent for that particular police division wouldn't hold it against him. It wasn't his fault he was constantly summoned to murders outside his district. He'd no idea why he had a talent for solving homicides, but he did, and now he was always getting stuck with the difficult ones. "Has anyone notified Constable Barnes?" He and Barnes always worked together.

"He's being notified to meet us at the murder scene, sir," Griffiths replied.

Mrs. Jeffries glanced up the stairs, hoping against hope that Wiggins had heard the commotion and would come down, but the staircase was empty. She went to the coat tree and grabbed the inspector's hat. "Here you are, sir." She handed it to him as he straightened his tie. "Should I get your suit coat? I believe I saw it on the back of your chair."

"Thank you, Mrs. Jeffries, that would be most kind of you."

She hurried back to the study, her mind working furiously as to what could be done on such short notice. *Drat,* she thought, *it was too bad that Smythe no longer lived in the house.* Having him available to get to the murder house would be very useful. But when he and Betsy had married, they'd moved into their own flat.

Grabbing Witherspoon's coat, she raced back to the front door. She decided that it would be best to send Wiggins to get the others. At least she had the address at the ready so the men could get over there and see what they could learn.

"Here you are, sir." She helped him into the garment. "I take it you'll be very late getting home?"

"I imagine so." He nodded to the constable and they started out the door. "Don't wait up for me, Mrs. Jeffries."

As soon as they were gone, Mrs. Jeffries took the stairs two at a time. She was out of breath when she reached Wiggins' room but she could tell he was still up by the light under his door. She knocked softly.

Wiggins stuck his head out. He was a round-faced

young man in his early twenties. He had brown hair, blue eyes, and fair skin. "Mrs. Jeffries, is everything alright?"

"We've got a murder," she said. "You'll need to go and get the others."

One of the reasons that Gerald Witherspoon was so very good at solving murders was because he had a great deal of help. Of course he'd no idea that his entire household, under the leadership of Mrs. Jeffries, actively assisted him on each and every case.

Wiggins grinned widely. "It's about time. I thought we'd never get us another one. Sorry, Mrs. Jeffries." His smile disappeared as she scowled in disapproval. "I know it's not right to be happy when some poor soul gets done in, but we've not had one for almost three months."

"Yes, I know," she replied. She'd frowned to remind him that it was morally wrong to rejoice in the death of another human being, but the fact was, she was a bit of a hypocrite. She'd been thrilled when Constable Griffiths had announced there was a murder. It had been a long dry spell for them and the truth of the matter was, they loved helping the inspector. It was far more interesting than dusting furniture, making beds, or doing the household accounts. "But we've got one now. I'll wake Mrs. Goodge and you go get Betsy and Smythe . . . oh dear, perhaps that's not such a good idea, considering Betsy's condition."

"Cor blimey, Mrs. Jeffries, she'll be madder than a drenched cat if we try to keep her out of this," Wiggins exclaimed. "You know what she's like."

"True. But we'll all have to keep reminding her that she's to be extra careful."

"The little one isn't due for some months yet, so it

should be alright," Wiggins murmured. He hated the idea that Betsy wouldn't be on the case. It wouldn't be right if she wasn't part of it.

"Even so, it might cause a bit of friction in the household," she warned. "And it will be our task to ensure that Smythe knows we're all helping to keep an eye on her so she doesn't overdo it."

"What about Phyllis?" Wiggins asked. He ducked back into his room to grab his change purse, but as the door was wide open, he could hear her reply.

Mrs. Jeffries sighed. She'd known this day was coming, but they'd not decided what to do about it. Phyllis had come to the household as a day maid before Smythe and Betsy were married. She'd only moved into the house when the inspector's last case had been solved, and she didn't know about their activities. Yet now that she lived here, it would be impossible to keep her in the dark.

"We'll have to tell her something," the housekeeper replied. "But we can deal with that in the morning."

"Should I get Luty and Hatchet as well?" He closed the bedroom door and they started down the stairs.

"No. I'll send a street lad early tomorrow morning with a message. I just want Smythe and Betsy here as soon as possible. I've got the address of the murder house, and it might be useful if you and Smythe went there and had a look around."

Witherspoon paid the hansom driver and stared across the road at number 11. Behind the tall wrought-iron fence, the huge Georgian house was ablaze with light. An oval-shaped driveway led to a portico where people in formal evening dress were clustered together in small groups. Neighbors and passersby crowded along the pavement and peeked through the fence spokes, many of them standing on tiptoes to get a view of the proceedings. A good half dozen policemen stood guard across the two driveway entrances, and there was another standing in front of the gate.

"Looks like we'd better go in, sir." Constable Barnes' voice came from behind him.

The inspector whirled around and smiled gratefully. "You made very good time getting here, Constable."

Barnes grinned broadly. He was a tall, craggy-faced man close to retirement. He had a florid complexion, a ramrod-straight spine, and a headful of wavy, iron gray hair under his policeman's helmet. "The department has gotten clever, sir; they sent a telegram to the local station just around the corner from us and one of the lads brought me the message that I was needed." He'd been staring toward the house as he spoke. "Good gracious, sir, I believe I see Lady Cannonberry waving at us. She's by the front door."

"Lady Cannonberry?" Witherspoon frowned in confusion. "Oh, that's right, she said she had a social obligation tonight, but I'd no idea it was here." He glanced at Constable Griffiths as they crossed the road and started toward the house. "Stay with us, Constable. You're familiar with my methods and I'll need you to round up witnesses."

Ruth rushed down the driveway and pushed past the constables guarding the entrance. "Thank God you're here, Gerald." She halted in front of the inspector. "I can't get anyone to listen to me. All sorts of evidence is being overlooked and trampled and everyone wants to leave. You must do something."

"Are you alright?" he asked quickly. "Yes, of course you are. Now, before I can do anything, you must tell me what's happened."

"Our hostess, Arlette Banfield, has been poisoned." Ruth tugged on his sleeve, urging him toward the house. "And I don't think the family quite realizes this is no longer a private matter but a criminal investigation. They don't seem to want to do things properly and they tried to clean up everything in the ballroom."

As they crossed the portico, people broke off conversations and stared at them with both hostility and curiosity. The constable standing guard at the entrance opened the door, and they stepped into the foyer. Ruth took the lead, dashing down a hallway and ushering them into a huge room filled with white-clothed tables, flowers, candles, and a long buffet table at one end.

Barnes pointed in the opposite direction, toward the terrace. "Those doors are open, but I can see several constables out there." He smiled in approval. "That's good. I think I'll go have a word and make sure they haven't let anyone leave the premises." He started toward the terrace.

"And who might you be?" a woman's voice boomed from one of the tables by the deserted orchestra.

Witherspoon turned and saw a group of people in elegant evening clothes clustered together. Only one was seated, a dark-haired man; his head was down and an expression of disbelief was on his handsome face.

Next to him was a tall woman with silver gray hair and a very stern countenance. "I asked who you were," she repeated.

Barnes halted in his tracks and glanced at Witherspoon.

"I'm Inspector Witherspoon and this is Constable Barnes. Who might you be?"

"Geraldine Banfield. My nephew owns this house," she snapped and then turned her attention to Ruth. "You had no right to drag the police here. My family won't stand for this kind of public humiliation . . ."

"I'm afraid I insisted the police be sent for as well." Another man spoke up. He stood on the other side of the table and jerked his chin down to where the lower half of a woman's body could be seen lying on the floor. "I've good reason to believe a crime has been committed. I'm almost certain Mrs. Banfield has been poisoned, so that makes it a police matter." To Witherspoon he added, "I'm Dr. Phineas Pendleton."

"They wanted to move the body, Gerald," Ruth hissed into his ear as they moved toward the doctor. "But Dr. Pendleton and I wouldn't let them. We wouldn't let them touch the dishes, either, and they've all been raising a fuss about that as well."

"This is most undignified," one of the other women clustered around the table muttered. "I shall make sure the Home Secretary hears of this."

Ruth stepped back as the two policemen turned their attention to the victim. The inspector forced several deep breaths into his lungs as he crossed the small space to where the doctor stood. To give himself a few more seconds before he'd have to look at the corpse, he looked at Dr. Pendleton. The fellow was short and burly and had thick dark brown hair. "Why are you so certain she's been poisoned?"

"Her breath, Inspector; it smells of almonds," Pendleton replied. "That generally indicates that cyanide, usually in the form of prussic acid, has been ingested."

"That's absurd. No one we're acquainted with would do such a thing," the Home Secretary's friend exclaimed.

"It's alright, Rosalind," Geraldine Banfield said to her. "All of them are going to pay for this humiliation."

"Oh, for God's sake, Geraldine," the man who'd been sitting dejectedly suddenly blurted out. "My wife's just died and these men are doing their jobs, so I'll thank you to hold your tongue. If you or your friends say one word to the Home Secretary, you'll have to remove yourself from this establishment. Do I make myself clear?"

"Lewis, you've never spoken to me like this before." Geraldine's voice trembled. "I've lived here all my life . . ."

"Yes, but it's my house, isn't it?" he retorted. "My wife is dead and you've done nothing but concern yourself with the family name."

She stared at him in stunned silence, then drew herself up and said, "I'm sorry, Lewis, of course I'm upset that Arlette is dead. Please forgive me. Now, if you'll excuse me, I'll wait for the police in the morning room." Straightening her spine and holding her head high, she left the room. Two other women left the group and followed after her.

As soon as the ladies had disappeared, Lewis got up and extended his hand toward the inspector. "I'm Lewis

Banfield. Arlette was my wife." His eyes filled with tears as the two men shook. "And now she's gone and I've no idea what to do next."

"I'm so sorry for your loss," Witherspoon replied. "And I assure you, sir, if your wife was indeed murdered, we'll do everything in our power to find the culprit. You have my word on that."

An older man with an enormous mustache came over and draped his arm over Lewis' shoulder. "Come away, Lewis, and we'll let the police do their job." He glanced at the two policemen. "I'm Sir Ralph Fetchman. I'm sure you've a number of questions for those of us who were at the table when . . . when it happened. But there's no reason for us to stay in here, is there? We'll be in Lewis' study."

"Yes, of course. We'll be there in a few moments to take your statements."

When the last of the group had left the ballroom, Witherspoon said to Constable Griffiths, "Constable, except for household members and the people sitting with the victim, everyone else can leave. Just ensure that we have everyone's name and address. You'll probably need to get some other lads to help with that chore, and if anyone refuses to cooperate, come and get Constable Barnes."

In his experience a murder like this one appeared to be wasn't a random occurrence but was almost always committed by someone close to the victim. As long as he could speak with everyone connected to the Banfield household, there was no point in keeping the guests here any longer.

He turned his attention to the doctor. "I would appreciate it if you would stay until the police surgeon arrives. As you are a physician, he might have some questions for you."

"Actually, I am the police surgeon for this district," he replied. "I hope that isn't awkward. After all, I could well be a suspect. I was here as a guest this evening."

"Did you know Mrs. Banfield?"

He shook his head. "No, I've never met the lady. I was invited here tonight because my great-uncle is one of Mr. Lewis Banfield's business associates."

"Then I see no reason why you shouldn't continue as the police surgeon."

"What about me, Gerald?" Ruth tugged at his sleeve. "I was sitting at the table when she was poisoned. Won't you need to take my statement as well? I don't want any special treatment because we're . . . er . . . friends."

Witherspoon smiled gratefully, touched that she was trying to make his task easier. But then again, that was one of the reasons she was so special to him. "If you could wait out on the terrace, I'll come and take your statement as soon as we've finished here."

Ruth nodded and hurried off toward the open doors.

Witherspoon stepped around the table and looked down to where the victim lay. He was very squeamish about corpses, but more than anything else, this one made him sad. She was so very young to have died.

Arlette Banfield was on her back, eyes open, mouth gaping slightly, and hands lying neatly at her sides. The inspector knelt beside her. He studied her for a moment. "Where was she sitting?" he asked.

"In this chair here." The doctor pointed to a chair a few feet away. "It got knocked away from the table when we put her on the floor."

"Was she sitting at this table?" Barnes pointed to the one nearest the body. The pure white of the cloth was marred by a huge stain were a decanter of red wine had overturned. Two crystal glasses had smashed into the ornate centerpiece and shards of glass now glistened atop the lily petals. A blue champagne flute was lying on its side next to a crumpled serviette.

"Yes, I believe so," the doctor replied. He glanced at Witherspoon. "Your friend Lady Cannonberry wouldn't let them clear this table. She didn't want any evidence destroyed and I must say, I agreed with her."

Witherspoon nodded and kept his gaze on the body. "Are you certain she was poisoned?"

"She was greeting guests in the foyer when I arrived this evening and there didn't appear to be anything wrong with her then. Healthy young women don't generally die for no apparent reason, Inspector. As far as I could tell, she didn't have a heart attack or stroke. The symptoms I observed are consistent with poisoning," he explained. "But I'll be able to tell you more after the postmortem."

"Could it have been accidental?" Barnes asked.

"It's unlikely." Pendleton shook his head. "We're in a formal ballroom, and I can't think of any reason why anyone would have prussic acid or cyanide here when there's a houseful of people."

"Did you witness her actual death?" Witherspoon asked.

The doctor pointed to a table on the far side of the room. "I was sitting over there, so I didn't have a completely unobstructed view, and frankly, I'd not been paying any attention to Mrs. Banfield until after they began shouting for a doctor. I was chatting with the others at my table. By the time I got here, Mrs. Banfield was already having convulsions and she couldn't breathe. Seconds after I got to her, her heart stopped. I tried reviving her but it didn't work."

"Thank you, Doctor," Witherspoon said. "If you could supervise the removal of the body, I would be most grateful. The mortuary van should be here shortly." He turned to Barnes. "Get someone to take all the items off the table into evidence and then we'll interview witnesses."

Barnes waved a constable over and relayed the message. Then he said to Witherspoon, "Did you want to have a word with Lady Cannonberry now?" Barnes knew her observations and information would be valuable, but he couldn't say as such to the inspector.

Ruth Cannonberry was one of the Witherspoon household's special friends, in that she helped them when the inspector had a murder. Barnes had worked with the inspector ever since they'd solved those horrible Kensington High Street murders when Witherspoon was still in charge of the Records Room. Over the years, he'd realized the inspector had a good deal of assistance on his cases and it hadn't taken him long to realize that the inspector's servants, under the lead of the housekeeper, Mrs. Jeffries, were the ones doing the helping. They were out in the streets finding clues, following leads, and collecting the sort of gossip a copper couldn't get close to in a million years. But the inspector's staff went to great pains to keep Witherspoon in the dark about their activities. For the longest time, Barnes had pretended he didn't know what they were up to, but eventually he'd let Mrs. Jeffries know he knew what they were up to and that he approved.

The constable was no fool. Witherspoon's remarkable success as a homicide detective had made the man a legend in the department, and much of that glory had spilled the constable's way. But more important, he felt he'd done more for the cause of justice in these last years with the inspector than in all his previous years on the force put together. That meant more to him than anything. He'd admit to a bit of vanity, but it was justice that was really important. So he kept their secret and aided them when he could.

"That's a good idea. I'll have Constable Griffiths take her formal statement so there's no hint of impropriety in the investigation. But there's no reason I shouldn't have a word with her as well."

Not wanting to wake Phyllis, Mrs. Jeffries warned everyone to keep their voices down. They were huddled around the kitchen table. Mrs. Goodge, the white-haired, portly cook, had made tea, and Betsy, the blond-haired maid, and her husband, Smythe, the coachman, had arrived from their flat, which was less than a quarter of a mile away.

Mrs. Jeffries looked at Smythe. "How fast can you get to St. John's Wood?"

He was a tall, powerfully built man with dark brown hair, harsh features, and a ready smile softened by the kindness in his brown eyes. "If we can get a hansom, it shouldn't take more than twenty minutes. This time of night the traffic isn't bad. But we'd best get goin'."

"Drink your tea; it might be summer but it can get nippy out there." Betsy patted his arm. She was as protective of her husband as he was of her. They had been married since Christmas. Theirs had been a long and rather awkward courtship. He was fifteen years older than her, and their marriage had been put off twice by circumstances beyond their control. "And you don't know how long you'll be out."

Smythe laughed and picked up his mug. He drained it in one long gulp. "Come along, Wiggins." He pushed back from the table and stood up. "Let's see if we can find out anything useful. We'll be back as soon as we can." He bent over and gave Betsy a light kiss on the cheek.

Fred, the household's mongrel dog, got to his feet as the two men headed for the back hall. He wagged his tail hopefully. "Sorry, boy." The footman paused to stroke the animal's head. "We'll go walkies when I get back. You stay here and guard the ladies."

Betsy snorted delicately. "Guard us, indeed! We can take care of ourselves."

The men laughed and disappeared down the hallway.

"But Fred has come in handy a time or two," Mrs. Goodge pointed out.

"True," Betsy agreed. "But it galls me that the men get to go off and have all the fun while we're stuck here twiddling our thumbs."

"We're not twiddling our thumbs," Mrs. Jeffries declared. "We're coming up with ideas and strategies to solve this case. The first thing we must decide is what we're going to do about Phyllis."

Betsy tapped her finger against her chin. "Well, we've become fairly good friends and she's got a good head on her shoulders. She's quite smart."

Mrs. Goodge and Mrs. Jeffries exchanged amused glances. When Phyllis had first come to the household, Betsy hadn't been very nice to the poor girl.

Betsy was now a lovely matron in her twenties, but she had arrived at the Witherspoon household by collapsing on the inspector's doorstep when she was just a lass. He'd insisted they nurse the girl back to health and, even though she was completely untrained and had no references, when she'd recovered he'd offered her a position as a housemaid. Betsy would do anything for the inspector. He'd saved her from living on the streets. When she'd first married Smythe and they'd moved into their own flat, she'd felt that she was being pushed out and had taken her misery out on poor Phyllis. But since she'd come to her senses, the two young women had become fast friends.

"So you think we should tell her what we're doing?" Mrs. Jeffries commented.

"Yes, she can help," Betsy said. "Mind you, she's a bit of a nervous Nell; she's always worrying about losing her position. But she's ever such a sweet girl. It isn't right to keep her out of everything."

"I agree," the cook added.

Mrs. Jeffries nodded. She knew they didn't really have

any other option. "But you do understand that once we bring her 'on board,' so to speak, we'll have to make sure she knows that our work is a secret. Oh dear, I'm not explaining this very well. It's just that with Luty and Hatchet helping and Lady Cannonberry as well as Dr. Bosworth, well, it seems as if half of London knows our little secret."

Luty Belle Crookshank and her butler, Hatchet, had been witnesses in the inspector's second case. Luty had figured out what the household was up to and had come to them when she needed help. Ever since, the two of them had insisted on helping. Dr. Bosworth was a physician who worked at St. Thomas' Hospital and he assisted them as well. He had some very advanced ideas about what one could learn by studying the corpse and the scene of a murder. To date, only a few of his colleagues and the household of Upper Edmonton Gardens appreciated his theories.

"I know what you're sayin'," the cook agreed with a sigh. "But Betsy's right, it wouldn't be right to keep her out of it. Besides, we don't know that she'll want to help. She might want to stay out of it. Not everyone wants to dash about asking questions and hunting clues."

The cook got all of her information without ever leaving the kitchen. Mrs. Goodge had spent a lifetime working in some of the finest and most aristocratic households in the country. She had a vast network of former colleagues she could call upon to find out what she needed to know. Luckily, most of her old acquaintances were more than willing to come around for a long natter over a cup of tea and plate of sweets. If she couldn't find anything useful from her old friends, she had another source to tap.

Everyone who set foot in her kitchen was fair game. Mrs. Goodge believed that everyone had ears and heard things. Delivery boys, rag and bone men, street vendors, the butcher's lad, tinkers—all of them were fed tea and treats as she ruthlessly pumped them for bits and pieces about victims and suspects. Sometimes she was amazed by how much she learned. But then again, a lifetime in service had shown her that most of the upper classes didn't consider servants to be people, so they rarely guarded their tongues in their hearing.

That, of course, was of great value to her and the others who pursued justice.

"I suppose you're both right," Mrs. Jeffries said. "We'll tell her tomorrow before Luty and Hatchet get here. Let's just hope that Smythe and Wiggins are able to get us a few bits of information."

"They will." Betsy patted her rounded belly. "And then we can get out and about. I can't wait! It's been ages since we've had a case."

CHAPTER 2

It was a lovely evening in June and dozens of people milled about in Wallington Square. They pressed up against the wrought-iron gates, craning their necks and standing on tiptoe to gawk at the house where a murder had been committed. As soon as the first constables had arrived on the scene, the news of the crime had spread across the neighborhood. To avoid being spotted by any police constables that might recognize them as members of the Witherspoon household, Smythe and Wiggins stayed at the back of the crowd.

"What's 'appening now?" Wiggins hissed at Smythe. He couldn't see over the crush of people in front of him.

"It looks like everyone is leavin'," Smythe replied. Well-dressed gents and ladies in evening dress poured out the front door and stood about on the portico, waiting for their carriages while butlers and footmen scurried off in all directions looking for hansom cabs.

Wiggins didn't want to waste any more time—he wanted information. He sized up the group surrounding him and then grinned at two middle-aged ladies standing to his right. "Cor blimey, looks like something excitin' 'as happened 'ere."

"There's been a murder," the one closest to him replied. She was a plump woman with black hair pulled back into a fat bun at the nape of her neck. "The lady of the house was killed right in the middle of their fancy ball."

"It wasn't the lady of the house," her friend corrected. "Geraldine Banfield is still among the living."

"She's not the lady of the house," the first woman rejoined. "Mrs. Lewis Banfield is the lady of the house and she's the one that got done in."

"Cor blimey, news must travel fast round 'ere," Wiggins exclaimed.

"No faster than anywhere else, especially when the coppers aren't botherin' to keep their voices down," she replied. "You can hear them shoutin' orders at each other plain as day."

"Fancy there bein' a murder in this kind of posh neighborhood. But 'ow could someone get murdered in front of a roomful of people? Did they catch who done it?"

"'Course they didn't," the second lady said. "But I overheard one of the coppers sayin' Mrs. Banfield was poisoned, so I reckon they'll never figure out who done it."

"If it was Mrs. Banfield the younger who were killed," the dark-haired woman added, "then it was probably one of the master of the house's former paramours, if you get my meaning. There was more than one nose put out of joint when he up and married that model. That's who she was, you know, an artist's model. That sort of thing didn't used to be done in my day, but things have changed, haven't they?"

Inside the house, Witherspoon wasn't having an easy time of it. He'd had a quick word with Lady Cannonberry and then instructed Constable Griffiths to take her formal statement before seeing her safely into a hansom cab. Constable Barnes had gone to interview the only other family member who lived in the household.

Witherspoon sighed inwardly and motioned for the constable standing guard in the hall to open the door.

He stared at the group assembled in the Banfield study. Ruth had given him quick but concise descriptions of everyone who had been at their table. Lewis Banfield slumped in a leather chair in the far corner of the room. He had dark, curly hair, a well-trimmed mustache, and unremarkable, rather even features. Sir Adrian Fortnoy, a tall, white-haired man, stood next to him. Lady Fortnoy, a slender woman with graying brown hair, sat on the sofa. Another couple, Rufus and Nora Kingsley, were next to her. Sir Ralph and Lady Fetchman were on the love seat across from the sofa.

Sir Adrian looked at him. "Inspector, how much longer is this going to take? Mr. Banfield is on the verge of collapse."

"I'm alright, Adrian," Lewis muttered. "I'm sure the police have some questions for me."

"Yes, sir, I do. I'll try to be as quick as possible; I

know this has been a terrible ordeal for you. As to the rest of you, as you are all potential witnesses, I will need to interview you as well. However, it's getting late, so if you will please give the constables your preliminary statements, I'll speak with you at a later time." He wasn't particularly comfortable with letting them leave; any one of them could have the poison hidden in their clothing, but as he had no grounds for forcing them to submit to being searched, there was no point in making them stay here. Besides, sometimes people spoke a bit more freely when they were in their own homes.

"I insist on being present when you speak with Mr. Banfield, Inspector. I'm his adviser," Sir Adrian said. "If you like, I can send a message to the Home Secretary. I'm sure he wouldn't mind."

Witherspoon smiled slightly. He was used to people trying to bully him with hints about how close they were to the HS. "Are you his solicitor?"

"Well, no, but—"

"Then I'm afraid I do need to speak to Mr. Banfield alone," he interrupted. "It is police procedure to take witness statements without others being present. When you give your individual statements before leaving tonight, the constables will speak with you separately."

"But it's ridiculous to suspect either Mr. Banfield of any of us," Lady Fortnoy objected.

"No one is a suspect, but all of you were at the table when Mrs. Banfield died," the inspector replied bluntly. "I understand that Mr. Banfield has had a terrible shock, but it's important I take his statement immediately." Ye gods, didn't these people understand? As every copper on the force knew, the person most likely to have killed Arlette Banfield was her husband. The inspector thought it sad, but that didn't make it any less true.

Lewis stood up. "Of course you must, Inspector. Let's go into the library. Your constables can use this room and the drawing room."

"But, Lewis," Sir Adrian protested, "you should at least let me send for your solicitor—"

"There's no need," Lewis said, cutting him off and starting for a door on the other side of the desk. "I didn't kill Arlette. Come along, Inspector, we can get to the library through here."

The inspector motioned for the constable to take over and followed after him.

Bookshelves filled with volumes of all sizes and shapes covered three of the walls; a huge rug in an intricate pattern of reds, golds, and greens lay on the floor; and heavy, rose-colored velvet curtains hung from the windows. Lewis closed the door and gestured toward two overstuffed maroon chairs by the fireplace. "We might as well be comfortable, Inspector. Please sit down."

Witherspoon, delighted to have a chance to get off his feet, smiled gratefully as he sank into the seat. "I realize this is very difficult for you, Mr. Banfield, but can you tell me exactly what happened here tonight?"

"Where would you like me to begin?" he asked. He leaned forward, his whole body poised as if to leap up. "One moment we were all at the table laughing and having a jolly time, and the next, she was gasping for air and going into convulsions. She died right before my eyes." He broke off on a sob and looked away.

"Perhaps it would be best if I simply asked questions," the inspector offered. He'd seen killers who could cry at the drop of a hat, so he knew how easy it was to pretend, but for the life of him, if Lewis was faking his reaction, he ought to be on the stage. The poor fellow seemed utterly devastated. "You were having a ball tonight, is that correct, sir?"

"Yes, it's our annual summer ball." He swiped at his cheeks and turned to face Witherspoon. "We used to have it at our country house in Buckinghamshire, but these days most people don't leave London as they used to during the summer. So about ten years ago, the family decided to have the ball here. We've a proper ballroom at the summer house, but not here. We have to open the connecting doors between the two main reception rooms to get the space we need, so it's a bit of a nuisance—oh, God, I'm blathering on like a madman. You don't want to know all this nonsense . . ."

"But I do." Witherspoon knew that letting people ramble on a bit was an excellent way to get them to speak freely and perhaps reveal more than they intended. "Where exactly is your summer house, sir?"

Lewis took a deep breath and leaned back in the chair. "Just outside Aylesbury; it's called Banfield Hall."

"You say this is an annual event, sir?" Witherspoon looked at him inquiringly.

"My family has had a summer ball every June for over a hundred years." Banfield couldn't keep the note of pride out of his voice.

"And you generally invite the same people every year?"

Banfield nodded. "Yes, of course this year we added a number of my wife's friends and I added quite a few of my business acquaintances to the guest list."

"Does your wife have any enemies, sir?" He always felt silly asking this question. Of course the poor woman had an enemy; someone murdered her, and you don't do that sort of thing to a friend.

Banfield hesitated before he answered. "What do you mean by 'enemies'? There were certainly people who didn't like her very much, but I hardly think they'd murder her."

"But someone did murder her, sir," he pointed out, his expression sympathetic. "And it is my task to find that person. I'll need the names of anyone who may have disliked your wife."

The younger man slumped back in his seat. "My wife was from a very different background than myself," he said. "She's from a family of artists and she was an artist's model before we married. Some of my family and friends weren't happy when we announced our engagement."

"Which family members?"

"My aunt Geraldine and several of my cousins were vocal in their opposition to our match and a number of our friends made it obvious they didn't approve of our marriage, but I made it quite clear that Arlette was my wife and that anyone who was disrespectful wouldn't be welcome in my home."

"So your aunt opposed your marriage?" Witherspoon pressed.

Lewis shook his head. "No, not when she realized I wasn't going to change my mind just because my relatives might not approve. Besides, Arlette is from a family of some distinction. Her father is Crispin Montrose, the painter. He's exhibited at the Royal Academy. Her mother is Elizabeth Montrose, a sculptress of some renown. So it wasn't as if I was marrying a beggar maid. When we married, Aunt Geraldine accepted Arlette and treated her decently."

"Who ran the household?"

Banfield looked surprised by the question. "The housekeeper and the butler, of course."

Witherspoon smiled. "I meant, who gives them their instructions, who sets the meal menus, who makes the decisions about social engagements, that sort of thing."

"My wife does, of course." He broke off and closed his eyes. "I mean, she did. But out of respect for my aunt, she frequently consulted with her on household manners."

"Your aunt made household decisions before you married Mrs. Banfield, is that correct?"

"Yes, but Arlette was a very artistic person; she often deferred to Aunt Geraldine because she didn't have much interest in running the house."

"So she left it to your aunt?" he pressed.

"More or less."

Witherspoon decided to change tracks. "Can you tell me what happened from the time you entered the ballroom to when your wife collapsed?"

"We greeted the guests as they arrived, of course."

"Where? In the ballroom or the foyer?" He wanted to get a clear picture of the evening.

"In the foyer," he replied. "We were all there—myself, Arlette, and Aunt Geraldine—oh, and her friend Mrs. Bickleton. She's staying with us this week. She stood with us in the receiving line."

"Who was in the ballroom while the guests were arriving?"

"The servants, of course, and the musicians, because they were setting up their instruments."

"Were the doors to the terrace open or closed at this time?"

He frowned. "I think they were open. Once the guests begin to arrive it gets very warm in there."

"How long did you greet guests?"

"Probably fifteen or twenty minutes; then I took Arlette's arm and we joined everyone. There was to be a buffet supper and the dancing was to begin afterwards. When we entered the ballroom, the servants poured the wine and everyone milled about, chatting and having what I hoped was a good time while we waited for Michaels to signal that the buffet was ready."

"So the food hadn't been served when your wife collapsed?" Witherspoon clarified.

"It wasn't ready."

"When did Mrs. Banfield begin to show symptoms of being ill?" he asked. He wanted to make sure she hadn't been ill earlier in the day.

"When we were sitting at our table waiting for supper."

"You're certain that it wasn't earlier than that, perhaps earlier in the day?"

Lewis pursed his lips. "I'm sure. She was fine at luncheon today and she seemed well enough when I arrived home from my office."

"Where is your office, sir?"

"The East End, Inspector; I've offices near St. Catherine's Dock. My family has been in the shipping business for over two hundred years. I know that part of London isn't very fashionable, but we own the building and it's very comfortable. There was nothing wrong with Arlette until tonight," he insisted. "She'd drunk her champagne and put the glass down. Everyone else at the table was having wine."

"I don't recall seeing a champagne bottle on your table." Witherspoon frowned. "Was it taken away?"

"Arlette always drank champagne; she couldn't drink wine, as it gave her terrible headaches. The butler always kept her bottle in the pantry. It was kept in a tub of cool water so it would stay chilled . . ." His voice trailed off as Witherspoon suddenly leapt to his feet.

"Where is the pantry?" he cried. "You must show me immediately."

Banfield realized instantly what he was being asked. He shot out of his chair and the two men charged out into the corridor. They ran past startled servants, police constables, and a few lingering guests down the hallway, past a half dozen closed doors, and finally into a large pantry.

Banfield skidded to a halt and pointed to a tall, narrow pewter jar sitting on a table. "It should be in there. That's where her champagne was always kept."

But when they looked inside, there was nothing but water. The champagne bottle was gone.

Barnes smiled at Geraldine Banfield. "I realize this must be very upsetting for you, ma'am, but it's important we ask these questions."

"I don't see why this can't wait until tomorrow," she snapped. "I really should be with my nephew. He's most distraught."

They were sitting in front of an unlighted fireplace in a small room on the east side of the house. The walls were a pale pink color, the curtains white muslin, and the furniture was made of intricately carved wood upholstered in pink-and-white-striped satin. Barnes was miserable; his chair was as stiff as a plank and his backside was going numb. "I'll try to make this as quick as possible, ma'am." He flipped open his little brown notebook. "Did you notice anyone tampering with Mrs. Banfield's food or drink?" He'd decided to get right to the heart of the matter.

"Supper hadn't been served," she replied.

"Then did you see anyone tampering with Mrs. Banfield's drink?" he shot back.

"Of course not. If I had seen such a thing, I would have put a stop to it immediately." She stared at him as if he were a half-wit.

Barnes was in no mood to put up with her. He glared right back at her. "Where were you sitting when Mrs. Banfield took ill?"

Her eyes widened at his implication. "I was with some friends on the far side of the room."

"You weren't sitting with the rest of your family?"

"No, I stopped to speak with some of my friends and by the time we entered the ballroom, the head table was full, so we took seats at another table. I must say, I was surprised to see Lady Cannonberry at my nephew's table. I'd no idea she was so close to either Lewis or Arlette. But then again, perhaps she simply sat down without being invited."

Barnes felt his hackles rising. "It was Lady Cannonberry that kept you from removing the evidence, wasn't it? She's the one who insisted you leave both the table and the body alone."

She gasped. "What do you mean, 'removing evidence'?

We don't know that Arlette didn't die of natural causes! Lady Cannonberry and that stupid doctor insisting on bringing in the police was what kept us from treating poor Arlette decently. We had to leave her lying on the floor. I thought that was going to break poor Lewis' heart. Removing evidence, indeed."

"The doctor seems certain she didn't die of natural causes." Barnes watched her carefully. "So if you'd had your way, a great deal of evidence would have been destroyed."

Surprised by his bluntness, she blinked. Then her eyes filled with tears as an expression of confusion crossed her features. "Oh, please, Constable, you can't possibly think that I'd do anything like that. I honestly had no idea that a crime had been committed. I wasn't trying to hinder your investigation, I was trying to protect poor Arlette."

Barnes stared at her curiously. Her entire demeanor had changed. She was no longer the imperious matron, but instead, her shoulders sagged, her lips trembled, and her hands were shaking. "I don't understand. Protect her how? By helping her murderer?"

"No, no." She clamped her hand over her mouth to hold back a sob. Then she took a long, deep breath. "Forgive me, Constable, I'm not explaining this very well. But I acted as I did because I feel so guilty. I was trying to make up for what I let happen earlier."

"What do you mean?"

Her eyes flooded with tears again. "You don't understand. Just moments before poor Arlette died"—she broke off as a sob escaped—"moments before she died, my friends were making some rather unkind remarks about her. They didn't mean anything by it, it was simply the sort of catty comments that women often make. But Lady Stafford never has anything nice to say about anyone, so I let her witter on about how Arlette's dress was too bright for a married woman. But then Margaret and Rosalind joined in with their remarks and I should have interrupted and reminded all of them that she is my nephew's wife." She closed her eyes and shook her head. "But I didn't; I let them go on and on."

"Were any of the remarks threatening?"

"No, not at all. They were simply unkind." She swiped at her cheeks. "They said her dress was cut too low for a matron and they all thought she must be wearing rouge. It was that sort of nonsense. But I should have stopped them immediately and I didn't. Then when poor Arlette was lying there on the floor with all and sundry staring at her, I simply couldn't bear it. After the way I'd let them talk about her, I didn't want them seeing her in such an undignified manner. I didn't realize I was doing something wrong. I'd no idea she'd been murdered."

"Did Mrs. Banfield have any enemies?"

"Not as far as I know," she replied. "But I can only speak about her since she's been my nephew's wife."

"And how long has that been?"

"They married last July. Before that, she was an artist's model. Her parents are artists. Her father is a painter and her mother is a sculptress or a craftsperson of some sort. Arlette modeled for both of them and for many of their friends as well. There were a number of those people here tonight—Arlette insisted on adding names to the guest list—so perhaps one of them had a grudge against her. But despite my friends' silly comments, Arlette has made no enemies of anyone of our circle."

Barnes knew good and well that people like Geraldine Banfield didn't open their arms or their hearts to anyone except one of their own. But just because they didn't like Arlette Banfield didn't mean they'd murder her. They might snub her, they might ignore her, but he sincerely doubted they'd kill her just because she had the temerity to marry outside of her class. "How was she received by the rest of the Banfield family and friends?"

"I'm not certain what you're asking."

"I think you know exactly what I'm asking." Barnes smiled cynically. "Once she and Mr. Banfield married, how was she treated? Did the invitations to tea come readily, was she accepted by the other wives in your circle, did other ladies come calling?"

"She was accepted because Lewis made it known we had to accept her," Geraldine blurted out. "Not that it made one whit of difference to her. She didn't care what anyone thought of her and she certainly didn't sit around worrying about whether or not she received any social invitations."

"What did she worry about?" he pressed.

"Arlette thought the rest of us were philistines." Geraldine smiled grimly. "She didn't give a toss about how one ought to behave in society. She certainly didn't care about setting a good example or taking one's proper place in society. She only cared about art and music and books. She considered herself an intellectual and I once overheard her telling Lewis that she'd done him a favor by marrying him, that it had saved him from interbreeding with one of the half-wits from his own class."

Barnes stifled a laugh. He had a feeling he'd have liked Arlette Banfield. "So she wasn't bothered by the lack of social invitations?"

"I've just told you, there was no lack of social invitations," Geraldine said impatiently. "Lewis can be very ruthless and he'd made it quite clear that no one was to slight his wife, so, whether Arlette accepted them or not, the invitations kept coming. Back in my day, that certainly wouldn't have happened, but whether we like it or not, times change."

"Yes, ma'am." He decided to change tactics. "So you weren't anywhere near Mrs. Banfield when she began to show poison symptoms?"

"We don't know that she was poisoned," Geraldine declared. "But no, I was all the way across the room with my friends. I was sitting with Lady Stafford, Mrs. Bickleton, and Mrs. Kimball."

"Did you see Mrs. Banfield before the ball began?" He shifted slightly, trying to get comfortable.

"Of course I saw her today; we live in the same house." She uncrossed her arms and sat up straighter. "She was out this morning but she came home for luncheon and she was here for tea this afternoon."

"Do you know where Mrs. Banfield went this morning?"

She thought for a moment. "I'm not certain; she wasn't the sort to report her comings and goings to anyone. Mrs. Banfield was one of those feminists. She thought it proper to be independent."

"So you've no idea where she went?"

"I didn't say that," Geraldine corrected him. "I said she wasn't one to report her comings and goings to anyone. I overheard her tell her maid that she had an appointment on Blecker Street and then she was going to see her parents. They live in Chelsea. But she was back in time for luncheon."

"Mr. Lewis Banfield didn't object to her coming and going as she pleased?" he asked curiously. Even the most enlightened and liberal of husbands usually wanted to have some idea of what their wives might be up to.

"Lewis found her behavior charming; he fancied himself a bit of an intellectual as well. He was always complaining that he only took over the family business because he'd no choice and that he really wanted to be a naturalist." She snorted derisively. "'Just look at the trouble Mr. Darwin's book has caused, and Lewis walks around quoting it as if it is the gospel. Survival of the fittest, indeed; it's that sort of nonsense that gives the lower classes ideas. It's dangerous notions like that which make everyone and their brother think they've the right to do as they please and that true superiority isn't in birth or class, but in what one can actually do. As if accomplishment was any sort of measurement of breeding. Rubbish, I say. Absolute rubbish."

Ruth Cannonberry knocked softly on the back door of Upper Edmonton Gardens. She'd seen that the lights were on and she was fairly sure the household would be up.

The door opened a crack and then Mrs. Jeffries said, "Ruth, how wonderful. Do come in."

"I'm so sorry to come this late." Lady Ruth Cannonberry smiled and stepped inside. "But we've a murder and I wanted to get here and give you the details as quickly as possible."

"Yes, we heard. Constable Griffiths came to get the inspector, but we don't know much more than that."

Ruth was the daughter of a country parson who took the admonition to love one's neighbor as oneself very seriously. Consequently, she tended to see every human being as her equal and didn't have the class consciousness of most women of her social stratum. She'd become involved with the Witherspoon household and insisted they call her by her Christian name, at least when the inspector wasn't present. She knew they'd be uncomfortable addressing her in that fashion in front of him. Like the others, she loved working on the inspector's cases but she took great care to ensure he didn't find out he had so much assistance. "I'd gone to the Banfield ball, you see, because Arlette had invited me and even though I'm not fond of that sort of occasion, I couldn't think of an excuse not to attend. We were sitting at the table together, chatting and gossiping, and all of a sudden, she couldn't breathe . . . oh, it was dreadful to witness, absolutely dreadful. Gerald is there now, but then, you know that, don't you? Oh dear, I'm babbling. But it's been a trying evening. Watching the life go out of another human being is horrible and I never want to do it again."

By this time, they were in the kitchen. Betsy and Mrs. Goodge had heard every word. "You poor thing." Betsy got up. "You need a good strong cup of tea."

"No, get the whiskey, that's what she needs," Mrs. Goodge ordered. "She's had a shock. There's a bottle in the cupboard by the cooker. I used it to make a trifle the other day."

"You put whiskey in the trifle?" Betsy yanked open the cupboard. "My cookery book says you should use sherry."

"I use both," the cook replied. "Mine is an old and wonderful recipe and if I do say so myself, there's never so much as a crumb left when I put it on the table. Besides, a splash of good Scots whiskey makes anything taste better."

Grateful they were trying to distract her, Ruth smiled wanly as she sank into her chair.

Betsy poured a generous shot and handed her the glass. "Drink this, it'll do you good. You're pale as a ghost."

"I tried very hard to keep my head and do what was right, but it was most distressing." She chugged the alcohol and sighed in relief. "Thank you." She smiled at the cook. "This was exactly what I needed."

"Alright, now tell us what happened," Mrs. Jeffries said softly. "Smythe and Wiggins are at the murder scene now to see what they can find out from the neighbors."

Ruth said nothing for a moment. "I'm not sure where to begin. I suppose it would be best to start from the moment I arrived at the Banfield house."

"That is a very good idea. I take it you're well acquainted with a member of the Banfield household." Mrs. Jeffries had observed that it was often easier for people to recall events if one led them with comments or questions.

"Oh yes, I've known Arlette Banfield's parents for years. They are artists. Her mother is a member of my women's suffrage group. I'm also acquainted with the

Banfield family through my late husband. He and Lewis Banfield had some business dealings. The two families have known one another for years. We were always invited to their annual summer ball, but after my husband died, the invitations stopped, so I was rather surprised to get an invitation this year."

"Did you find out why you were back on the guest list?" Betsy asked curiously. "You've been widowed for a long time now."

"Arlette insisted I be sent one." Ruth smiled sadly. "That's what she told me this evening. We were having a discussion about the true nature of what society's rules and etiquette actually meant to the individual when she told me she'd added my name to the guest list over the objections of her husband's aunt, Geraldine Banfield. Apparently, once I no longer had a husband to answer to and could do as I pleased with my life, I was no longer fit to be a guest in that house."

"That's absurd," Mrs. Jeffries murmured. "But not surprising. You wouldn't be the first lovely widow to be struck off the social roles."

"You flatter me." Ruth laughed. "But rest assured, it isn't my physical form that annoys Geradine Banfield and her ilk, it's my politics."

"There's nothing wrong with your politics," Mrs. Goodge exclaimed. "Your efforts to get women the right to vote and have a bit of control over their person and their purses should be applauded."

"Thank you, it's good to know there are people like you who support our efforts, but I don't think your attitude extends to most of the ladies who were at the Banfield ball tonight. I suspect that the main reason Arlette invited me and made certain I was seated at the head table was because she wanted to annoy her husband's family and friends. As a matter of fact, I'm sure of it. But I digress. You need to know the facts of the evening, not a lesson in London social history." She paused and took a deep breath. "When I arrived, the family was lined up in the foyer to greet their guests. Arlette and Lewis were at the head of the line with Geraldine and a friend of hers who is staying at the household at the end."

"What's the name of the friend?" Betsy asked.

"Margaret Bickleton," Ruth replied.

"Bickleton, Bickleton," the cook muttered. "I know that family name. They're from Buckinghamshire."

"And their estate is right next to the Banfield summer house," Ruth added. "The families have been close friends for years. After I passed through the receiving line, I went into the ballroom. The buffet was still screened off, so people milled about and chatted. I started to take a seat near the terrace when a footman came and told me that the Banfields had requested I sit at their table. So I did. It was a bit awkward as there were three other couples at the table and I was on my own, of course. The tables seated ten and because I was alone, we had an empty chair, but no one seemed to mind."

"Who else other than you and the Banfields were sitting there?" Mrs. Goodge asked eagerly.

"The Fetchmans—Sir Ralph and Lady Henrietta—Nora and Rufus Kingsley, and Sir Adrian and Lady Ellen Fortnoy," she replied. "I'm certain I'd not have been sitting with them if I'd not bumped into Arlette last week as she was coming out of an office building off Oxford Street. I'd met her on previous occasions and I didn't really know any of the others at the table."

"Why would your accidental meeting have to do with this evening?" Mrs. Jeffries asked.

"Because I'd never really talked with Arlette before last week. It started to rain and so we went into a Lyons tea shop to wait till it stopped. We started chatting and before you knew it, we were debating women's rights, books, music, and even art, of which I know very little. As I was leaving, Arlette commented that running into me had brightened her day enormously. Of course I was flattered and told her we must get together again soon, you know, the sort of thing you say in social situations. She laughed and said her mother was right and that I wasn't an aristocratic old stick in the mud. It made me laugh. Tonight the same thing happened; we were having a very interesting conversation before poor Arlette . . ." She broke off and looked away, then she brushed at her cheeks and turned back to them. "Investigating the murder of a friend is very different from when it's a stranger, isn't it? I was starting to like her enormously and I think she was the kind of person who could have made a real difference in this world."

"I'm sorry, Ruth," Mrs. Jeffries said. "If you'd rather do this tomorrow . . ."

"No." She held up her hand. "The best thing I can do for her now is to help catch her killer." She drew a breath. "And that's what I'm going to do."

"Do we know for certain we've got a murder?" Mrs. Goodge asked. "It seems to me that figuring out if someone is poisoned should take a bit of time. How did you know to send for the police? Don't they have to do tests and that sort of thing during the postmortem to be sure?"

"When she had trouble breathing, Lewis and Sir Ralph called out that we needed a doctor, and luckily, one of the guests is a physician. Arlette was still breathing when Dr. Pendleton reached the table, but she died a few seconds later. The poor fellow did his best—he even tried to restart her heart by giving it a great, whopping thump with his fist—but it was no use; she was gone."

"Dr. Pendleton?" Mrs. Jeffries murmured.

Ruth nodded. "Phineas Pendleton. Why? Do you know him?"

Her brows drew together in thought. "I think I met him at St. Thomas' Hospital. He's a colleague of Dr. Bosworth."

"He's also a police surgeon," Ruth said. "He examined her and then I heard him mutter that healthy young women didn't drop dead for no reason. Then he sniffed her breath, looked into her throat, and said to me that we'd best call the police, that he thought she'd been poisoned."

"Did anyone at the table object?" Betsy asked.

Ruth shook her head. "Lewis Banfield was in shock and the others were too far away to hear what was being said. I was close because I'd been sitting next to her and I'd cradled her head in my hand to keep her from banging against the floor."

"Tell us about what Mrs. Banfield ate and drank," the housekeeper suggested.

"But that's just it, the supper buffet hadn't been served, so she had nothing to eat, unless she ate before the ball, which I hardly think is likely."

"What was she drinking, then?" the cook asked.

"She had champagne and the rest of the table drank wine. Lewis teased her that she was lucky she married him and that he could afford to give her what she liked, otherwise she'd have had to drink water. Arlette replied that he knew good and well she couldn't drink wine, as it gave her terrible headaches."

"Who served the champagne?" Betsy asked. "I mean, did someone bring her a glass of it or was it on the table?"

"It came from the pantry," she explained. "After everyone at the table had been served wine, I saw Lewis Banfield signal a footman. The waiter came with the champagne glass on a silver tray. I remember it vividly because the flute was a lovely pale blue glass and Arlette commented that her mother had made two champagne glasses for her and Lewis as one of their wedding presents. Elizabeth Montrose, her mother, is quite a well-known sculptress. Arlette told me that two years ago she went to Italy to learn glassblowing as well."

"Did·she drink the champagne immediately?" Mrs. Jeffries asked.

"She took a sip right away," Ruth said. "I remember because she laughed and told Lewis it was delicious. We chatted for a good five minutes and she took a few more sips, then we were both distracted. We started talking again when she noticed her husband's aunt and her friends staring at our table from across the room. We both laughed about them, and just then, there was a loud crash and the entire ballroom came to a halt as everyone turned to see what had happened. One of the musicians knocked down his music stand and it went over in such a manner as to send the entire row of stands tumbling to the floor. They made a frightful noise, but the fellow handled the situation nicely. He righted them, gave us a big cheeky grin, and then did a nice bow as though we were his audience. Everyone laughed."

"How long were people distracted?" Betsy glanced at Mrs. Jeffries as she asked the question and was rewarded with a knowing nod from the housekeeper.

Ruth tapped her fingers against the tabletop. "Ten or perhaps fifteen seconds. No, it was a bit longer; because of the show the lad put on for us, it was closer to twenty or thirty seconds."

Mrs. Jeffries leaned forward. "What instrument did he play?"

Ruth looked surprised by the question. "Oh, let me see, I think it was a violin. Why? Is it important?"

"Only if she was poisoned by someone at your table while the musician distracted everyone. In which case, we'd best find out if he was paid to draw everyone's attention away," Mrs. Goodge responded.

"But we only turned away for a few seconds," she protested.

"Twenty seconds is long enough for someone to have slipped something into the victim's glass," Mrs. Jeffries declared.

"But they would have had to have brought the poison with them and had it at the ready," Ruth mused.

"A small vial or jar of poison is easy to hide." Betsy ran her hands over her arms and torso, picking up folds of material and the pockets in her voluminous loose dress. "I could probably put half a dozen tiny pillboxes or tins on my person."

"But wouldn't it have taken a few moments to find the container and either get the stopper off or remove the lid?" Ruth argued as she played the devil's advocate.

Mrs. Goodge held up her hands. Her fingers were gnarled and swollen. "I've got rheumatism in these," she said, "but when they are really hurtin' and I'm desperate for a bit of relief, I can get the stopper off my little medicine bottle and the medicine poured into a mug in two shakes of a lamb's tail. So believe me, if our killer had a strong enough reason for wanting that poor woman dead, it would have been child's play to do it."

She glanced toward the window at the far end of the kitchen as they heard the clip-clop of a horse pulling a hansom cab outside.

Betsy reacted first. She shoved her chair back and leapt up. "I'll see if it's the inspector." She flew across the room.

They weren't concerned about being caught gathered together; the inspector knew that despite his admonition to the contrary, the household wouldn't retire for the evening while he was out on a case. Nor would he be surprised by Ruth's presence. She was very much at home in this kitchen, especially tonight, as she was the one who'd raised the alarm about the murder. The only fly in the ointment would be explaining Betsy being here at this time of night without Smythe. But they'd come up with something that sounded reasonable—they always did.

At the window, Betsy stood on tiptoe, reached up, and shoved the curtain to one side. She peered out into the darkness. "It's hard to see," she mutttered. "But it's Smythe and Wiggins. Wiggins is talking a mile a minute. I'll bet they've found out something!"

* * *

"We searched the house as best we could, sir," the young constable said to Barnes, "but it was difficult. There were servants everywhere and some of the guests took their time leaving the premises even after we told them they could go. Besides, sir, we weren't sure what we ought to be looking for." Constable Long was a strapping, red-haired lad with a baby face that made him look about twelve.

Barnes wasn't sure what they ought to be looking for, either, but when it came to murder, it always paid to follow procedure. He and Constable Long stood in the middle of the dance floor and surveyed the ballroom. "Don't fret, lad, I've had a hunt around the room myself and I didn't see anything out of the ordinary." He stifled a yawn and looked at the spot where the body had been. "Was everything from that table taken into evidence?"

"Yes, sir. There wasn't much, just their glasses and two decanters of wine." Long cleared his throat. "Uh, Constable Barnes, can I speak freely? The other lads asked me to have a word with you."

Barnes turned and met his gaze. "You may. What's the matter?"

Long took a deep breath. "A few moments ago, the inspector was in the pantry with Mr. Banfield. He seemed a bit upset, sir. He actually raised his voice, but none of us could hear what he said. Inspector Witherspoon is known for having an even temperament so when we heard him, we were a bit alarmed. The other constables wanted me to find out if he was agitated because of any perceived dereliction of duty on our part." He took another breath, but before Barnes could say a word, he started talking again. "We did everything as instructed, Constable Barnes. The grounds were searched, we got everyone's name and address, and as I told you, we even looked about the house as best we could. Mind you, there is a nasty old lady upstairs who chased Constable Perry out of her room with an umbrella. That was uncalled for, sir; Perry had no idea the lady was even in there. He knocked but she didn't answer, so he went in the room."

Barnes was amused but did his best not to let it show. Metropolitan Police constables generally didn't worry overly much about what their superiors thought of them, but then again, most superior officers weren't as highly regarded as Gerald Witherspoon. "Inspector Witherspoon rarely gets annoyed, but it is late and we're all tired, so he did raise his voice." He shifted his weight off his sore knee. "The doctor who attended Mrs. Banfield happens to be a police surgeon. Against his express instructions, someone removed what might be an important piece of evidence from the butler's pantry. The bottle of champagne that was served to Mrs. Banfield is gone. We've some men looking for it now, but I don't think it's likely to turn up."

Long sighed in relief. "Oh, thank goodness. We were all worried it was something one of us had done."

CHAPTER 3

Barnes stifled a yawn as he trudged down the hallway. The Banfield household was now eerily quiet and he hoped they could call it a night. He tucked the sheaf of statements and reports under his arm and stepped into the foyer. Witherspoon was sitting on the bottom of the staircase; his eyes were closed, his tie loosened, tufts of his hair stood straight up, and his spectacles had slid to the end of his nose.

The constable cleared his throat and the inspector's eyes flew open. When he spotted the constable, he grabbed the banister spindle and hoisted himself up. "Oh dear, you've caught me. I know one oughtn't sit down on the job, so to speak, but I had to have a rest. It feels as if I've been on my feet for days. I imagine you're just as tired as I am."

"That I am, sir," he admitted. "But I was able to sit down while I interviewed Mrs. Geraldine Banfield and, truth to tell, I had a bit of a breather while the constables did another search of the terrace and ballroom. Speaking of the lads, they were a bit worried." He handed the stack of statements to Witherspoon.

"Worried?" He shoved his glasses back into place, folded the documents in half, and stuffed them into the long inner pocket of his jacket. "Gracious, what about?"

"Well, sir, they heard you earlier this evening when you were in the butler's pantry. Some of them were concerned you raised your voice because you thought they'd been derelict in their duty," Barnes replied. Despite what he'd told Constable Long, he knew that the inspector wouldn't lose his temper because he was "tired." He was concerned himself and this was a good excuse for finding out what was wrong. He could count on the fingers of one hand the number of times the inspector had lost control of himself. "They wanted me to assure you that they'd followed both established procedures and your 'methods' in gathering statements and evidence and searching the house."

"Of course I don't think anything of the sort. They all appeared to be doing their jobs quite admirably, especially under what was less than ideal circumstances," he replied. "Why on earth are they so concerned? Except for tonight, none of them are under my command. With the exception of Constable Griffiths, they're all from the local precinct."

"They know you by reputation." Barnes smiled wanly. "And I imagine they were rather hoping to impress you or, at the very least, ensure you didn't think ill of them. I don't think you understand just how much the rank-and-file lads respect you, sir." He was speaking the truth.

The inspector wasn't just famous on the force because

he'd solved so many murders, he was greatly admired because he had a habit of giving credit where credit was due. Unlike many high-ranking officers, when Witherspoon wrote his reports, he included the name of every constable who'd contributed to the solution of the crime. If the constables were from another district, as was often the case, he took extra care to make sure their superiors were aware of how much the men had contributed. If someone had done something outstanding or if they'd put themselves in harm's way, Witherspoon would put their names in for a commendation.

"Oh dear, please tell everyone that my lack of civility had nothing to do with any of them. Generally, I've far more self-discipline than I exhibited this evening."

Barnes crossed his arms over his chest and regarded him steadily. "What's wrong, sir? We've worked many a late night and I've never heard you start shoutin' like you did."

Witherspoon said nothing for a moment and then sighed heavily. "I'm worried. Really, really worried."

"About what, sir? The case has just started and I know the powers that be expect you to solve it quickly; they always do. But even the Home Secretary himself knows he's got to give you time to investigate properly."

"That's not why." The inspector shook his head. "Don't you see, Constable, I don't know what to do about Lady Cannonberry."

"Constable Griffiths took her statement, sir," Barnes pointed out. "You followed proper procedure."

"That's not the point. Lady Cannonberry was sitting right next to Arlette Banfield when she was poisoned.

That makes her a suspect," Witherspoon cried. "Yet we've a close relationship." He blushed and looked away. "And I'm wondering if the honorable thing to do would be to excuse myself from this case."

"You can't possibly think she had anything to do with the murder." Barnes couldn't believe his ears.

"Of course I don't, but I'm going to have to treat her as I do any other suspect and I don't think I'm capable of behaving in such a manner. She's very dear to me and I can't bear the thought of questioning her as if she were a criminal." He looked down at the floor.

"You won't have to, sir," Barnes said dryly. "To begin with, you're always respectful of everyone when you're taking statements and asking questions. The only time you speak harshly to anyone is if they refuse to cooperate or they try to bully one of your men. Secondly, sir, unless we find evidence that Lady Cannonberry had a motive to want Arlette Banfield dead, all we'll have to do is ask her the same questions we ask everyone else. If you let me handle all the interviews with her, that should avoid any hint of impropriety or favoritism."

Witherspoon looked up, his expression hopeful. "Do you think so, Constable? I should hate to hurt her in any way."

"Just let me take care of it, sir. Besides, I'm sure we'll find that Lady Cannonberry was the one person at the Banfield table who didn't want the poor woman dead."

"That's an excellent solution, Constable." Witherspoon smiled. "I should have thought of it myself, but, frankly, from the moment I saw her here and heard what had happened, I've not been able to think clearly."

"None of us are at our best at this time of night, sir." Barnes yawned. "It's now almost one a.m."

"Let's call it a night, shall we? We can continue taking statements tomorrow morning. "Make sure there are two constables posted out front and we'll ask the local lads to double their patrols in the area. I think I'll have one more look at the crime scene before I leave."

Barnes nodded and hurried off to relay the instructions to the local constables. The inspector yawned and went back to the ballroom. He paused just inside the huge double doors.

The cavernous room had an air of despair about it. The food from the buffet had been cleared away, but the servants hadn't had time to clean the room properly. There were still tablecloths on the tables; crystal wineglasses, many of them still holding drink, were everywhere; and the white carnations in the centerpieces were wilting.

The inspector went toward the table where Arlette Banfield had sat and tried to envision what it would have looked like before she drank the fatal potion. According to what he'd been told, Lewis Banfield had sat with his back to the butler's pantry entrance and Arlette had sat directly across from him. He made a mental note to find out where everyone else had been sitting. Perhaps he'd ask Ruth to draw him a diagram.

Witherspoon studied the room for a few more minutes, trying to get a sense of where everyone was and if they could see one another clearly or how they might have been moving about. But it was no use. Staring at the empty room didn't help him one bit.

* * *

Back at Upper Edmonton Gardens, the only person awake was Mrs. Jeffries. Wiggins and Smythe had come back and reported what little they'd found out, and, after they'd discussed it thoroughly, Smythe and Betsy had escorted Ruth to her house across the communal garden before going home themselves.

Mrs. Jeffries sat at the kitchen table with a covered tray in front of her. She hoped the inspector would get here soon; even with the three cups of tea she'd drunk, she was getting very sleepy. But she was determined to have something for the others tomorrow morning. They'd be here for their breakfast meeting and by then, if she was very lucky, she'd have a bit more information.

She heard the telltale jingle of a harness as a hansom rounded the corner and then the clip-clop of the horse's hooves as it drew up in front of the house. She grabbed the tray and flew up the back steps and down the hall, stopping just long enough to deposit the tray in the drawing room. She reached the entryway just as the inspector unlocked the front door and stepped inside.

"Good gracious, Mrs. Jeffries, you shouldn't have waited up for me. It's dreadfully late." He hung his bowler hat on the coat tree.

"I don't need as much sleep as I used to require, sir," she said cheerfully. "And I thought you could do with a hot mug of tea and a snack before you retired. I know it is very late, sir, but sometimes a few minutes relaxing helps one get to rest easier." She held her breath, hoping he had enough strength left to spare her a few moments before going upstairs.

"That is very thoughtful of you, Mrs. Jeffries. Shall I come down to the kitchen?"

"I thought you'd be more comfortable in the drawing room," she replied. "I've brought up a tray."

"Excellent." He took off down the hallway and she was right on his heels.

He sat down in his favorite chair.

"Lady Cannonberry very kindly stopped in and told us some of what happened, sir," she said.

"We're lucky she was there and had the presence of mind to insist they leave things alone. We've got the glass the victim was drinking out of tonight. Between Ruth and Dr. Pendleton, they kept most of the evidence from being cleared away." He settled back further in the chair and yawned.

"Was it awful, sir?" She put the tray cover to one side, poured him some tea, and placed a bun on a plate. She was one of the few people who knew how squeamish he was about bodies. She handed him his food.

He leaned forward, put the tea on the side table, and held the plate on his lap. "This is wonderful," he murmured as he stuffed a bite of food into his mouth.

She waited patiently while he chewed.

"It wasn't as bad as some I've seen," he replied. "Mrs. Banfield was poisoned, so there wasn't an excess of blood. Poor woman, what a terrible way to die; but then again, I suppose the only good way to pass on is in one's bed at a very advanced age. Her name was Arlette Banfield and she was a young woman in the prime of her life."

"Yes, Lady Cannonberry gave us a few details," she

admitted. She wasn't sure how much to reveal. "She said the doctor who happened to be there was a police surgeon."

"That's correct." He nodded. "But he was at the Banfield house as a guest." He continued on, giving her the details of his evening.

She listened carefully, not asking questions but simply listening. When he paused to take a sip from his cup, she said, "Was the doctor absolutely sure she'd been poisoned?"

"Well, one can't be one hundred percent certain until the postmortem is finished." Witherspoon reached for another bun. "But he was fairly sure of it. He told one of the first constables on the scene there was a harsh, chemical smell on Mrs. Banfield's breath. That almost always indicates poison." He popped the last of the bun into his mouth.

"Was he able to identify the poison?"

Witherspoon shook his head as he swallowed. "He suspects cyanide but he wants to do the postmortem to be certain."

"Who else lives in the Banfield household?" She already knew, of course, but she didn't want him to think that Ruth had told them too much.

"Aside from the victim's husband, there's only his aunt, Geraldine Banfield, who is a permanent resident of the household. But there have been two houseguests staying for the past week, a Mrs. Bickleton and a Mrs. Kimball."

"Two houseguests?" she repeated. Ruth had only mentioned Margaret Bickleton. Perhaps she didn't know about the second guest.

"Yes, but I didn't have time to interview them." He sighed. "It got so late that people sort of drifted off. But I don't think I'll have any problem speaking to either of these ladies; even if they've left the Banfield house, we've got their addresses." He put his cup down and rose to his feet.

She stood up. "I'll lock up, sir. You must get your rest. Shall I let you sleep a bit later than usual in the morning? It is very late."

He shook his head and stretched as he moved toward the hallway. "No, get me up at my usual time. We've much to do tomorrow and Constable Barnes will be here to fetch me just after breakfast."

A mug of steaming hot tea was sitting at his spot at the table when Constable Barnes came into the kitchen behind Mrs. Jeffries.

"We thought you'd like something to drink before you and the inspector got about your business," the cook said.

When they were on a murder case, Barnes always stopped and had a quick chat with the housekeeper and cook. He'd learned he could trust them with information and, more important, the household had a knack for hearing gossip, facts, and speculations that a copper wouldn't. They passed what they'd learned to him and oftentimes it was these small bits and pieces that enabled the case to be solved.

Barnes grinned broadly and sat down. "Thank you, ladies. I don't have much to tell you as yet—the case has barely started—but we did learn a few interesting facts." He glanced at the housekeeper. "I take it you had a word with Lady Cannonberry?"

"She came by and told us what she knew," Mrs. Jeffries confirmed. "And I had a quick word with the inspector when he came home."

"Then it sounds as if you know the basics," he said. "But I did find out something interesting from Geraldine Banfield. It seems she wasn't all that happy to have Arlette come into the family and marry up with her nephew." He gave them the particulars of his interview with the woman.

"Good for Lewis Banfield," Mrs. Goodge exclaimed. "He did right in making it clear they couldn't snub her."

"It doesn't sound as if she much cared whether they accepted her or not," Mrs. Jeffries murmured.

"Before Lewis Banfield married, it was Geraldine that ran the household." He took a sip from his mug.

"Being displaced could be a motive for murder," the cook muttered. "I once worked at a household where the old mistress locked herself in the wine cellar with all the household keys rather than hand them over to the young master's new bride."

"But Lewis Banfield told the inspector that his wife frequently deferred to his aunt in household matters," Mrs. Jeffries added.

"My instincts are that they didn't like each other very much, despite what Mr. Banfield may have thought. I'm going to be interviewing the servants today," Barnes said. "We'll see what they say about the relationship between the two women. So far, all we know is that Geraldine Banfield is a snob, not a killer. There's no evidence that she had anything to do with the murder, and she was sitting across the room when Arlette was poisoned. So she couldn't have added anything to the woman's drink. But it's early days yet and we've a long way to go."

They heard footsteps clomping down the back stairs.

"That must be Phyllis," Mrs. Jeffries murmured.

They'd still not decided what to do about her. "Wiggins is out. We sent him to fetch Luty and Hatchet."

Barnes drained his mug and stood up. "I'll be in again tomorrow morning and we'll trade information," he whispered as the maid came into the kitchen.

The maid stopped at the entryway and blinked in surprise. "Good morning, Constable." Phyllis was as plump as a pigeon and had a round face, brown eyes, and blonde hair tucked up in a neat bun under her cap. She had a porcelain complexion and a straight nose, and she wore a pale lavender maid's dress covered with a white apron.

"Good morning," he replied.

She gave him a curious glance as she continued on toward the pine sideboard.

"Is the inspector up yet?" Mrs. Jeffries asked.

"Yes. I was going to take his tea up to the dining room." She opened the bottom cupboard, leaned down, and pulled out a wooden tray.

"Take an extra cup for the constable," Mrs. Jeffries said. "Have you had breakfast, Constable?" she asked.

"I've eaten, but another cup of tea would be welcome."

Phyllis nodded, finished arranging the tray, and went upstairs. Barnes followed her.

As soon as they'd disappeared, the cook crossed her arms over her chest and stared at the housekeeper. "You've got to decide what to do. We've a meeting starting here in less than an hour."

"I know, I know." Mrs. Jeffries sighed. She didn't know why she had to make this decision; it involved all of them.

Phyllis had only worked in the Witherspoon household

since December. On their previous cases, the girl had
lived out. She'd come in only after their morning meetings, and Mrs. Jeffries had made sure the girl was either
given an errand to run or had left for the day when they
had their afternoon meetings. But now she was here and
it was time to bite the bullet, as Luty would say. "We're
going to have to tell her and invite her to be a part of it."

"We don't know that she's any talent for snooping,"
the cook pointed out. "She's a bit awkward with people
and she's not the friendliest lass I've ever seen."

"She's shy." Mrs. Jeffries felt it her duty to defend the
girl. "And we won't know what her talents might be when
it comes to our cases unless we give her a chance. Besides,
short of coming up with an errand every morning and
every afternoon to get her out of the house, I don't see
what else we can do. Betsy thinks she could do it."

"That's true enough." The cook went to the stove and
put the skillet on, then grabbed two eggs off the top of
the bowl she'd brought in earlier and put them on the
counter. A plate of crisp bacon was draining on last
week's newspaper and the toast was cooling in the rack.
She checked to ensure there was enough fat in the pan,
and then, when it was sizzling, she cracked the eggs in.

Five minutes later, the inspector's breakfast had been
duly served and the girl was back in the kitchen to set
the table for the household's morning meal. Mrs. Goodge
glanced at the housekeeper and said, "I'm going to the
dry larder to get my supplies." She started down the hallway to the back of the house. "I've a lot of baking to do
if I'm going to feed my sources today."

As soon as they were alone, Mrs. Jeffries said, "Phyllis,

come and sit down for a minute. There's something I need to tell you."

Phyllis' eyes widened and she dropped the stack of plates on the table with a heavy clatter. "I'm not being sacked, am I? If I've done something wrong . . ."

"No, no, that's not it at all," the housekeeper said quickly. A wave of compassion washed over her. She'd never seen anyone who worked so hard to please, who was so frightened of being without a position. "You're doing a fine job. Come sit down."

"But what about breakfast?" She jerked her chin toward the second batch of bacon draining on the counter. "Are we not eating this morning?"

"We'll eat later," Mrs. Jeffries said as she took her seat. The others wouldn't be arriving for at least a quarter of an hour, so they had plenty of time. "There's something important I must tell you, but, before I do, you must give me your word of honor you'll not repeat what I've said."

Phyllis, looking even more alarmed than before, slipped into the chair next to Mrs. Jeffries. "I promise."

"You know, Phyllis, everyone here in the household has the highest regard for Inspector Witherspoon."

"Oh yes, and I share that regard as well. He treats us decently, like we were people and not just here to do his bidding. He's the best master I've ever had. I want to stay here forever," she declared.

"That's excellent. I'm sure the inspector very much appreciates your loyalty. But there is something else the household does for him, something we work very hard to make sure he doesn't know about."

"What would that be?"

"His cases, Phyllis, we help him with his cases."

Her mouth gaped open. "You what? But I thought you said you made sure he didn't know . . . I'm confused. What does it mean? How do you help?"

"We do many things, and our efforts have contributed greatly to the inspector's success as well as the cause of justice," Mrs. Jeffries replied. She watched the maid carefully as she went over what each member of the household did for Witherspoon. The girl wasn't reacting at all as she'd expected. "Betsy is especially good at getting shopkeepers to talk about the suspects on a case, and Smythe has a number of sources he uses for information," she explained. "He's also very good with hansom drivers. Wiggins is talented at getting servants to chat and, uh, we've other friends who contribute as well."

"Other friends," she repeated. Her eyes were the size of Mrs. Goodge's fat mince tarts and her face had gone paler than usual. "You mean other people go out and snoop, too?"

Mrs. Jeffries drew back slightly. "I wouldn't put it like that."

"I'm sorry." Phyllis bit her lip. "It's just this is makin' me right nervous. You say the inspector doesn't know you're doin' this for him?"

"That's correct." Mrs. Jeffries decided it would be best if she didn't mention any additional details.

Phyllis looked as if she'd gone into shock. She said nothing; she simply stared at the housekeeper.

"You do understand what I've told you," Mrs. Jeffries finally said when the silence had lengthened considerably. "We're helping Inspector Witherspoon and I'm asking if you'd like to join us in our endeavor."

"But I don't think I can do any of those things," Phyllis said in a voice so soft Mrs. Jeffries had to lean close to hear her. "I'm not good with people. I've never gotten anyone to tell me any secrets and I don't think I could follow someone if my life depended on it."

"You don't have to do any of those things," Mrs. Jeffries assured her. As she was confiding their secret to the girl, she'd realized she'd made a horrible mistake. Phyllis would be quite content to stay completely out of their cases. This was such an odd turn of events, she didn't quite know what to make of it. "But the one thing we will require of you is to keep our secret. When the inspector is on a case, we gather twice a day to share what we've learned. You'd be welcome at these meetings or you could continue with the chores. It's your decision."

She looked uncertain. "I don't understand. You mean I don't have to do it?"

"That's right."

"And the inspector doesn't know what any of you are up to," she pressed.

"Correct."

Phyllis took a deep breath and lifted her chin. "So you want me to keep it a secret from the inspector?"

"That's what I've just said." Mrs. Jeffries struggled to keep the impatience out of her tone.

"But what if he finds out and then gets annoyed that I knew what you were doing and I didn't tell him?" she cried.

Mrs. Jeffries didn't like the way this conversation was going. "I doubt very much that such a thing would happen."

"But what if it does?" Phyllis insisted stubbornly. "I don't want to lose this position—it's the best one I've ever had. I don't want to risk Inspector Witherspoon getting angry at me . . ."

"He won't get angry at you," Mrs. Jeffries interrupted. She was going to put an end to this nonsense. But more than anything, she was annoyed with herself. Trusting Phyllis was obviously a mistake. "Inspector Witherspoon has given me complete authority over the household. I'm in charge of the household affairs."

"But the inspector had to approve my getting hired in the first place," Phyllis argued. She shook her head in confusion.

"I go to him as a courtesy, but he doesn't really like being bothered with staffing concerns. If anyone has the authority to give you the sack, it's me."

Phyllis' eyes widened. "I meant no disrespect, Mrs. Jeffries, I'm just frightened of losing this job. Please don't be annoyed with me . . ."

"I'm not annoyed," she reassured the girl with a tight smile as she got to her feet. She wasn't angry at Phyllis, she was furious at her own lack of judgment. She'd forged ahead without thinking this situation completely through. She should have realized that the only thing in life Phyllis wanted was to stay working here. She wasn't in the least concerned with truth or justice or any other abstract notion she felt might threaten keeping a roof over her head. "And you won't lose your position. No one is forced to help us. Please, just forget I said anything, alright?"

"I guess that's alright," she replied.

"Thank you. After breakfast, you can start in the drawing room. All the furniture on that floor needs a good polish. There's a new tin of Adam's Furniture Polish in the cleaning cupboard and some clean rags."

"I'm sorry, Mrs. Jeffries, I've said the wrong thing, haven't I?" She stood up. "I do that all the time and I don't mean to, but I'll not say a word to anyone about what the rest of you are doing, I promise."

Mrs. Jeffries wasn't sure she believed her, but it was too late now. "Thank you, Phyllis, I appreciate that. Now let's get breakfast on the table."

Lewis Banfield waited for the inspector and Barnes at the bottom of the staircase. He looked as if he'd aged ten years in a single night. His eyes had sunken into his head, his shoulders were slumped, and he'd not shaved.

"I didn't expect you back quite so early in the day," he muttered.

"I'm sorry, I know it's distressing having the police about the place, but we've a number of people to interview today. We need to speak to every member of your staff that was here last night."

"I'm aware of that, Inspector," he replied wearily. "I've already instructed our housekeeper to give you any assistance that is needed. Mrs. Peyton has some rooms ready for your use."

"We appreciate that, Mr. Banfield," Witherspoon replied. "We'll also be needing to speak with your houseguests."

His brows drew together in confusion. "Oh, you mean Mrs. Bickleton and Mrs. Kimball. That's right, they've been here this week." He rubbed his hand over his face.

"Forgive me, Inspector. For a moment I couldn't think. The two of them are probably in the dining room at breakfast. Now, if you'll excuse me, I must go make myself presentable. Arlette's parents will be here in an hour. We've got to make the funeral arrangements."

He turned on his heel and trudged up the stairs.

A middle-aged woman wearing a black bombazine dress stepped out of the hallway into the foyer. "I'm Mrs. Peyton, the housekeeper. If you'll come with me, I'll show you to the rooms that have been set aside for your use."

"Thank you," Witherspoon said as he and Barnes fell into step behind her.

She led them down the corridor and stopped at a door near the end. "You can use the morning room, Inspector." She pointed to the one across the hall. "And that room has been set aside for you, Constable. It's Mrs. Banfield's dayroom."

"I was there last night," Barnes replied. He didn't relish the thought of sitting on that miserably uncomfortable furniture again.

She turned to the inspector and said, "Who would you like to speak with first?"

"Mrs. Bickleton and then Mrs. Kimball."

She looked at the constable. "And who should I fetch for you?"

Barnes smiled. "I'd like to begin with you."

"Howdy, everyone," Luty Belle Crookshank called out as she burst into the kitchen in a whirlwind of bright colors. A peacock blue hat festooned with lace, feathers, and yards of veiling was perched at a jaunty angle on her white hair. She wore a matching jacket over a high-necked pale blue blouse and a long strand of jet beads dangled around her neck.

Her butler, Hatchet, came behind her at a more sedate pace. He was dressed in his usual black suit jacket, white shirt, cravat, and black trousers. He took off his top hat. "Good morning, everyone." He put the hat on the coat tree.

Luty and Hatchet were old friends of the household. They'd been witnesses in one of the inspector's first cases, and Luty, with her sharp eyes, had figured out what the inspector's household was up to when she'd spotted them asking questions of her servants. After that case had been solved, Luty had come to them for help with troubles of her own. Ever since, both Luty and Hatchet insisted on helping out on every one of the Witherspoon murders.

Luty was an elderly American who had more money than the Bank of England and could find out almost anything about anyone. She had access to cabinet ministers, aristocrats, bankers, financiers, and just about anyone else of consequence in London. She had no qualms about using her money to bribe a clerk or a crooked lawyer into revealing the contents of a will. She'd been born poor, but married an Englishman who was in the American West seeking his fortune and they'd struck silver, literally.

Hatchet, a tall, white-haired man, was devoted to his elderly employer and had sources of his own he could tap for information. He had a mysterious past but he was good, true, and honest. Both Luty and Hatchet were devoted to the cause of justice.

"Ruth should be here any moment," Mrs. Jeffries said as the two newcomers took their seats. "I'd like to wait for her before we begin."

"But we do have us a murder, don't we?" Luty interrupted. "Wiggins said we did but when he mentioned poison, I wasn't so sure. There's lots of poisonin' death about from just eatin' plain old bad food."

"Ruth was there and she said the doctor who examined the victim was quite sure of his diagnosis. She was deliberately poisoned," Mrs. Jeffries said. She broke off as she heard a knock on the back door. "Ah, that'll be Ruth. You'd best hear the details from her."

"I'll get it." Wiggins shoved back his chair and got up. He disappeared down the back hall. They heard the door open and a few seconds later he escorted Ruth into the room.

"I'm so sorry to be late," she apologized as she took her seat. "But I had an unexpected visitor this morning. Mrs. Stadler from across the street came over to complain about the gas lamps again. She wants me to write a letter to the council. It took ages to get away."

"That's alright, we don't mind waiting," Mrs. Jeffries replied. "Now, would you tell what happened last night. I know you've already told it once, but I'd like Luty and Hatchet to hear it from you as well."

Ruth nodded her thanks as Mrs. Goodge handed her a cup of tea. "First of all, let me say that when you're actually sitting at the same table with someone who dies, it's very, very upsetting. I didn't sleep very well last night, but that's neither here nor there. I'll not do Arlette Banfield any good by having an attack of nerves.

Here's what happened." She told them everything she could remember from the time she arrived at the Banfield house until the moment she left. When she'd finished, she took a deep breath, picked up her tea, and took a drink.

No one spoke for a moment, then Luty said, "It must have been awful for you."

"It was," Ruth admitted honestly.

"But if you'd not been there, there's a good chance that whoever killed Arlette Banfield might have gotten away with it," Betsy added. "After all, you kept them from clearing off the table and getting rid of the evidence. So perhaps you were meant to be there, for her sake."

Under the table, Smythe squeezed his wife's hand and then gave her a quick, proud smile. She always knew just the right thing to say.

"Thank you, Betsy, that does make me feel a little better about the whole situation, but I will tell you all this, I'll never be cavalier about the inspector's cases again. There's too much pain and misery for those left behind when someone's life is deliberately taken by another."

Luty tapped her finger against the top of the table. "Banfield, Banfield, I know I've heard that name before."

"Of course you have," Mrs. Goodge said. Last night, as she'd fallen asleep, she'd realized why that name had sounded so familiar and then she'd remembered where she'd heard it before. One of the few good things about aging was that sometimes you couldn't remember who was the current prime minister, but as the years went by, it became easier and easier to recall the past. "They're one of the richest, oldest families in the country. My old

colleague Thomas used to say they walked about with
their noses in the air so high you'd think a Banfield came
over on the boat with the Conqueror."

"Cor blimey, not another aristocratic lot," Smythe
muttered. "That sort is always a bit of trouble for the
inspector and for us."

"They're not aristocrats," the cook said quickly. "But
they've served the crown for hundreds of years. Thomas
worked for them at their country estate. He was the butler,
then he got offered a better position here in London—this
was many years ago, mind you. I was cook in the house
where he came to work and he used to tell us how the
Banfields considered it a point of honor to serve without
getting any reward for it."

"That's something you don't hear very often." Luty
snorted in disbelief. "From what I've seen, them that
works hard like to get a title for it."

Mrs. Goodge shook her head. "That's usually true;
that's why the Banfields are so highly regarded. Titus
Banfield was the old head of the family in those days
and he was one of the Queen's ministers. His grandfather had served as adviser to one of the Georges, I forget
which one, but Thomas told us how old Mr. Banfield
would lecture his grandchildren that there was no honor
in taking a reward or a title for doing one's duty. Honor
was everything in that family."

"So there's not any lords, ladies, or sirs among the
bunch." Wiggins grinned cheerfully. "That'll make it a
bit easier."

From upstairs, there was a series of thumps against
the ceiling and everyone looked up.

"Don't be alarmed, it's just Phyllis moving the side table out from the wall so she can polish the furniture in the drawing room," Mrs. Jeffries explained. "It always makes that noise. Now, time is a-wasting, so let me tell you what I found out from the inspector last night and what Mrs. Goodge and I heard from the constable this morning."

When she'd finished, Luty said, "Well, we've not got much to go on."

"I know," Mrs. Jeffries said. "But then, we never have very much information at the beginning of a case. I suggest we start where we usually do."

"You mean find out who benefits the most from her death," Mrs. Goodge muttered. "Let's hope it'll be that simple. Maybe someone murdered the poor woman just because they hated her."

"That's a possibility," she replied.

"If Arlette Banfield wasn't rich in her own right, I can't see why killin' her would help anyone. But you never know, so I'll go and have a word with some of my friends in the City. Let's see if the Banfields are as rich as everyone seems to think." Luty turned to Hatchet. "What are you goin' to do?"

Hatchet smiled craftily. "I'll keep that as a surprise, madam. But I do have something interesting in mind." He and Luty were very competitive with one another when they were on a case. He also had a connection that would serve him well.

Smythe glanced at Betsy. He didn't quite have the nerve to order her to stay home and put her feet up because he knew she simply wouldn't do it. "Are you goin' to be chattin' with the shopkeepers near Wallington Square?"

Betsy tried not to look surprised by the question. She'd been certain they were going to have words over her going out. "Of course, but I'll be very careful." She patted her tummy. "I'll not tire out the wee one. I'll stop and rest often, I promise."

"Betsy, if you'd prefer to stay in, I can speak with the shopkeepers," Ruth offered. "I'm not as good at it as you are, but I might learn something."

Betsy shook her head. She wasn't going to give up their cases just because she was having a baby. "Thank you for offering, but I'd just as soon be out in the fresh air and walking about. I feel better when I've had a bit of exercise. Besides, with your connections, don't you think you'd learn more by asking . . ." She broke off, not sure how to phrase what she was trying to say.

"People that I see socially about the Banfields," Ruth finished for her. "You're right, of course. I'm going to a luncheon today with one of Lord Cannonberry's aunts. I'll see what I can find out there. I'll also try to speak to some of the ladies from the suffrage group. As I told you, Arlette's mother is one of our members. Perhaps I'll hear something useful from that source. Oh dear, I'm never quite sure what to ask . . ."

"We don't know, either," Mrs. Goodge assured her. "I've got two or three people comin' by today and I've no idea if I'm going to find out anything that will end up being useful to catch this killer. But we just start asking whatever comes into our heads and see what happens. It's often the bits that you don't think make any difference that end up bein' the clues that point to the killer, isn't it, Mrs. Jeffries?"

"That's very true," she replied. "But however confusing this case may be now, there is one thing we do know. Whoever murdered Arlette Banfield must have been desperate to do it in such a public place. If the doctor's assumption is correct, the fatal dose was probably in the champagne she was served at the ball."

"Why would that mean the killer was desperate?" Luty asked. "From what you told us, everyone knew that Arlette Banfield only drank champagne. Seems to me that dropping poison in a champagne bottle is pretty danged easy."

"Only if no one sees you do it," the housekeeper said. "And remember, according to the inspector, not only were there dozens of guests, but there were dozens of servants, and the champagne bottle was kept in a cooler in the butler's pantry.".

"That doesn't mean anything, Mrs. Jeffries," Hatchet argued. "The sort of people who get invited to a Banfield ball wouldn't have any qualms about walking into a butler's pantry and doing their worst. With a large social gathering like that, there would be plenty of time when no one was in the pantry at all. The servants would have been out on the floor serving the guests."

Mrs. Jeffries thought about it for a moment and nodded. "You're right. But still, I think the killer took an awful risk." She glanced at the footman. He was staring off into the distance with a dreamy, unfocused expression on his face. "Wiggins, are you alright?"

He started. "Oh, sorry, I was just thinkin' . . ."

"And what were you thinkin'?" Smythe asked.

"I was thinkin' that if Arlette Banfield didn't bring any money to the family when she married her husband, then maybe the person who killed her is someone she knew before she married. I'll try to find one of the Banfield servants and see what I can find out."

"Right, then, if we're finished, I'll get out and about." Betsy stood up. She didn't want Smythe to have second thoughts about her going out and start nagging her to stay here.

Smythe shoved back his chair and rose as well. "I'll walk you to the hansom stand."

"But I don't need a cab, I can take an omnibus . . ." Her voice trailed off when she saw the set of his jaw. "Fine, walk me to the hansom stand." Some battles simply weren't worth fighting. "But it's a waste of money."

Within a few moments, the kitchen was silent save for the ticking of the clock on the pine sideboard. Mrs. Goodge looked at Mrs. Jeffries, her expression quizzical. "I expected Phyllis to join us."

Mrs. Jeffries sighed. "It seems, Mrs. Goodge, that I may have made a mistake in speaking to Phyllis. Come on, I'll help you get the apples and the mince from the wet larder for your tarts. I'll tell you all about my little chat with her and you can tell me what a complete fool I've been."

CHAPTER 4

———

The walls of the morning room were papered in a cream color with a pattern of pink and green climbing roses. Pink silk curtains hung at the two windows and a carpet in various shades of green was on the floor. Margaret Bickleton sat on a chair upholstered in pink satin while Inspector Witherspoon was perched on the edge of a matching chaise.

"I didn't really know Mrs. Lewis Banfield very well," Margaret Bickleton declared. "I'm here as a guest of Geraldine Banfield."

"How long have you been here?" he asked.

"A week," she replied. "There were a number of social occasions I was expected to attend and I wanted to spend some time with Mrs. Banfield."

"Were you here at the Banfield house yesterday before the ball?"

She raised her eyebrows. "Where else would I be? As I told you, Inspector, I'm a guest."

"But even guests go out and shop, you know, that sort of thing," he replied. "Did you see Mrs. Lewis Banfield during the day?"

"I did; we had luncheon together. Everyone was here. Even Lewis was present, and he is usually at his office at that time of the day, but Arlette—Mrs. Banfield—apparently insisted he come home."

"Do you know why?" he pressed.

"Of course not." She gave a delicate snort. "It's not the sort of question one asks in polite society."

"If it is considered an intrusive question, Mrs. Bickleton, how did you become aware that it was Arlette Banfield who insisted her husband come home?" he asked. "Those were your words, Mrs. Bickleton."

A flush climbed her cheeks and she looked away for a moment before turning back to face him. "I overheard them arguing when I came down to luncheon. Lewis was angry at her for dragging him away from his business, but she kept saying she'd not sent for him in the first place. Apparently he'd received a message from her, asking him to come home immediately, but she maintained she'd done no such thing and that she wasn't some silly upper-class, empty-headed social—" She broke off and clamped her lips together.

"Go on," he urged. "Exactly what did she say?"

Margaret took a deep breath, as though it actually pained her to say the words. "She made it perfectly clear that she thought the women of his class were empty-headed fools and that she wasn't one of them and she certainly wouldn't call him all the way across town because of a case of supposed nerves."

"Where were you when they were having this argument?" He wasn't trying to get her to admit she'd been eavesdropping, but he did want to understand where the argument had taken place and who, besides Mrs. Bickleton, might have heard it. He wondered why Lewis Banfield hadn't told him this last night. At one point, he'd specifically asked the man if anything unusual had happened in the household that day.

"I was in the dining room waiting for the others; Lewis and Arlette were in the hallway. Arlette didn't mind if people overheard her words—she had no proper sense of decorum, but then, she wouldn't, would she?"

"And why would that be?" Witherspoon pressed. He sensed that Mrs. Bickleton's dislike of Arlette was more than just general snobbery on her part.

"Because of the way she was brought up, Inspector. She was raised to do and say exactly as she feels with no regard for what is right and proper," Margaret snapped. "And just because the Montroses are well-known artists, that doesn't mean they know how to behave in a civilized household, either! Why, two weeks ago, Arlette and her mother were screaming at each other like fishwives. The way they carried on was dreadful. Geraldine was so embarrassed, she shooed me out before we finished our plans for my visit here."

"What were they arguing about?" Witherspoon asked.

"How should I know?" she replied irritably. "All I heard was shouting. As I said, poor Geraldine was so humiliated by the incident she ushered me into a hansom cab. Which was decidedly inconvenient, as we'd not finished discussing my visit so I'd no idea what social events I was expected to attend. I had to bring an extra trunk, Inspector."

"An extra trunk?" he repeated. "Whatever for?"

"For my wardrobe." She stared at him as if he were a half-wit. "There are dozens of social events in London this time of year. If I don't know which ones I'm expected to attend with my hostess, I have to bring enough clothing to ensure I'm properly attired for any of them. As I said, Inspector, we hadn't finished our planning before Arlette and her mother's horrid behavior drove me out of the house. I'm sorry someone murdered her, but nonetheless, it doesn't change the fact that she had no sense of her proper role in society."

"And you've no idea why Mrs. Montrose and Mrs. Banfield were arguing?" he asked.

"No."

Witherspoon changed tactics. "Was anyone else in the dining room with you yesterday when you heard Mr. and Mrs. Banfield arguing?"

"Mrs. Kimball was there as well. She heard the argument, but she's slightly deaf so she kept asking me what they were saying," Margaret explained. "It was rather embarrassing; I kept having to shush her. People who can't hear don't realize how loud they speak and I didn't want Arlette or Lewis to think I was eavesdropping."

"I won't keep you long, Mrs. Peyton," Barnes said. "I understand you're very busy."

Mrs. Peyton gave him a wan smile. She was a small,

slender woman with red hair and light blue eyes. "Thank you, Constable, I appreciate your consideration. There is much to do. We've still to clean up from the ball last night and we've also to prepare the house for mourning."

"I take it you were on duty during the ball?" He paused and went on when she nodded assent. "Can you tell me who was in charge of the pantry? Namely, who would have had access to Mrs. Banfield's food or drink."

"Michaels was supervising the wine and champagne. I was in charge of the food, but, of course, the food was never served. But both of us were back and forth between the pantry and the kitchen."

"Who was doing the serving?" He began writing.

"Everyone, Constable." She sighed. "We had over two hundred guests, and Mrs. Banfield the elder had two houseguests staying here for the week. So everyone was pressed into service. We brought in some additional help from a domestic agency. But all they did was serve the guests."

Barnes glanced up from his notebook. "How many outside people were here?"

"Three young men were employed as waiters."

"Do you have their names and addresses?" he asked.

She seemed surprised by the question. "No, I don't. The arrangements were made through a domestic agency. We use Stannard's on Winslow Road when we need additional help. When Mrs. Banfield the younger died and it became apparent the ball was over, I sent them away."

"Was this before the police arrived?"

She thought for a moment. "Oh dear, I think it must have been. But when the tragedy first happened, we'd no idea that she'd been murdered. Those of us in the pantry and the kitchen only knew that she'd died. I told them they could go. I'm terribly sorry, Constable."

He stared at her for a moment. "Not to worry, Mrs. Peyton. As you said, you'd no idea a murder had been committed. I'm sure the agency will have their names and addresses." He wondered how often people dropped dead at Banfield social occasions. Then he realized that because of his work, he saw homicide everywhere. But to the average person, a death in the house usually meant natural causes.

"I'm sure they had nothing to do with it," she said. "We only decided we were going to need more help yesterday morning. When the footman came back from taking the message to Stannard's, he said they weren't even sure they could find anyone to send to us on such short notice. So those young men wouldn't have known they were going to be here until the very last minute."

He nodded in understanding. "Why did you wait so late to decide you needed extra help?"

"That wasn't how we usually do things around here, Constable." She sighed. "I kept trying to tell Mrs. Banfield we needed more people to do the serving—"

He interrupted. "Which Mrs. Banfield?"

"Geraldine Banfield," she replied. "The younger Mrs. Banfield had left the planning of the ball to her, except, of course, for the additions that she'd made to the guest list. She'd invited a few of her own friends. I suspect that's why Mrs. Banfield the elder was so stubborn about bringing in more help—she was annoyed because there were so many additional guests."

"She was annoyed at Arlette Banfield?"

"She was more annoyed at Mr. Banfield." Mrs. Peyton laughed and then caught herself. "Mrs. Banfield the younger only added a few names, while Mr. Banfield added over a dozen of his business acquaintances and their wives. Mrs. Banfield the elder was furious. I overheard her telling Mrs. Bickleton that she was disgusted with how the ball was deteriorating into a social occasion for art and commerce."

"But she gave in and let you hire more waiters," he commented.

"No, not really. I had a quiet word with Mrs. Banfield the younger—" She broke off and looked away, but not before Barnes saw her eyes fill with tears.

"So it was Arlette Banfield who came to the staff's aid?"

She swiped at her cheeks and turned back to him. "Yes, I didn't want to involve her, but I had no choice. It wasn't fair to expect our staff to try to serve over two hundred guests on their own. So I asked her to intervene. She asked Mr. Banfield to have a word with his aunt."

"Why didn't she do it herself?" he asked. "From what I've heard of Arlette Banfield, she wasn't in the least intimidated by anyone."

"She wasn't. But we were running out of time and I think she thought there would be less chance of an argument or a delay if the order came from Mr. Banfield."

"I see. So, let's get back to the ball itself. While the drink was being served, the food was being prepared and put out on the buffet table. Is that correct?"

"That's right."

"Was any of the food in the butler's pantry?"

"No, all the dishes came straight up from the kitchen to the buffet table. Michaels was overseeing the alcohol and that was coming out of the butler's pantry."

"Who would have had access to the butler's pantry?"

"Everyone in the household." Mrs. Peyton shrugged slightly. "The whole exercise is organized chaos and, frankly, I spent most of my time in the kitchen making certain the food was put into the proper serving dishes. Mrs. Geraldine Banfield is always very particular about that. God help us if a fish sauce is served in a gravy boat."

"But your food was never served," Barnes mused. "Only the drink. We've been given to understand that Mrs. Banfield only drank champagne, is that correct?"

"That is correct," Mrs. Peyton replied. "Wine or spirits gave her terrible headaches."

"And the drink was supervised from the butler's pantry, is that right?" The constable considered this a very important piece of information and he wanted to be certain that it was absolutely the truth.

"Michaels uncorked the wine and supervised the waiters," she agreed.

"How was the drink served?"

"Once the bottles were opened, the servers went from table to table, pouring either red or white. We had both."

Barnes frowned and cocked his head to one side. "I'm no expert on etiquette, Mrs. Peyton, but I was always given to understand that wine was generally served in accordance with the kind of food being served."

"That is correct, Constable," she agreed. "But this was a buffet and therefore a bit more casual than the usual dinner party. Besides, there wasn't a fish dish on the menu, and that is generally the only dish that requires a white wine."

"What will you do with all the food from last night?" he asked curiously.

"We'll eat up as much as we can and save the hams for Mrs. Banfield's funeral reception." She sighed heavily. "Everyone liked Mrs. Banfield the younger. She was very solicitous and courteous to the staff. Personally, I'm going to miss her very much. She brought a breath of fresh air and laughter to this house. She loved champagne and she adored using that champagne set her mother had made for her. It was one of the few things she insisted upon: she was always to have her glass at the ready during any social occasion"—Mrs. Peyton leaned toward him and lowered her voice—"and she didn't give a toss that Mrs. Banfield the elder thought the set ostentatious. I think that's why she always insisted they be out; she liked irritating the woman."

Barnes wanted to make sure he understood. "Arlette Banfield only insisted her glass be used to upset her husband's aunt? Is that what you're saying?"

Mrs. Peyton laughed. "That's precisely what I'm saying. I overheard her telling one of her friends that she loved watching Mrs. Banfield the elder's face pucker up with disapproval every time they had a dinner party and the set was brought to the table."

"Who was the friend?"

"Mr. Julian Hammond. He's a sculptor. He came for luncheon last week."

"Did you notice anyone from the household, other than the servants, coming from or going into the kitchen or the butler's pantry?"

"I don't recall anyone but the servants coming into the kitchen and I can't comment on the butler's pantry. I wasn't there. You'll need to speak with Michaels about that."

He nodded. "You've said that Mrs. Banfield the younger was liked by all the servants—"

She interrupted. "Very much so."

"She hadn't had anyone dismissed? None of them had any sort of grudge against her?"

"Not at all," Mrs. Peyton said. "Take my word for it, Constable, if anyone in this household was going to be murdered by a servant, it wouldn't have been Arlette Banfield."

Betsy held her basket in front of her as she stepped into the grocer's. She'd come to the shops nearest Wallington Square and she hoped the Banfield household didn't do their shopping elsewhere. She'd gone up and down the street twice, peeking in through the windows and deciding which of them was most likely to be a good source of information. The grocer's shop had won: the clerk was homely, young, and male. The first time she passed by, she'd seen him laughing with his customers.

Holding her basket at an angle that she hoped both looked natural and hid her gently rounded tummy, she smiled and walked toward the counter.

"May I help you, ma'am?" he said politely.

"Yes, thank you, I need a packet of corn flour, a tin of Bird's custard powder, a bottle of vinegar, and some allspice." Betsy actually needed these items.

"Very good, ma'am." He turned to the row of shelves behind him and paced down to the end. He pulled a small bottle off the middle shelf and started back toward her.

"I was wondering if you knew of a family called Banfield that lives around here." She held her breath. This was always the moment of truth for her. From the expressions on their faces, she could always tell whether they were going to talk or shut up tighter than a bank vault.

"I do, ma'am." He smiled broadly and stopped again, reaching up and pulling off a tin from the top. "The Banfields are well known in the neighborhood. They live in the huge house just around the corner on Wallington Square."

Her spirits soared. She'd found a chatterbox. "Oh, good, I mean, that's wonderful. A friend of mine gave me a note to give to the housekeeper, but I was in such a hurry to get out and do my shopping, I left the address at home."

"Well, the house is easy to find, it's number eleven." He put the items on the counter in front of her. "But unless you're taking a letter of condolence there, I don't know that you'll be welcome."

She was further cheered. The news of the murder had already started to spread. "And why is that?" she asked innocently. She shifted her basket slightly.

He glanced toward the door and made sure no one

else was coming into the shop. "Because one of the ladies of the household was murdered last night. It happened right in front of everyone, in the middle of their annual summer ball. Suddenly, poor Mrs. Banfield the younger—she's the one everyone likes—had a fit and then toppled over. She'd been poisoned."

"Poisoned? My goodness!"

"I know that for a fact because my cousin works right next door and he's friends with the footman from the Banfield house," the clerk continued eagerly. "He overheard the doctor talking to the police and they said it was poison that killed her."

"My gracious, that is terrible," Betsy said. "Did they catch the one that did it?"

"No." He shook his head. "Jonny—that's my cousin—said the footman told him the police were there for ages last night, but no one's been arrested."

"Mrs. Banfield the younger." Betsy shifted her weight. "Why do you call her the one that everyone likes?"

He turned back to the shelves and went in the other direction, moving up the aisle till he came to a rack of seasonings. He scanned the rows, found what she'd ordered, and put it on the countertop and gave it a shove, letting it slide until it came to a stop next to the custard powder. "Mrs. Banfield the younger is nice to everyone," he explained. "Everyone liked her and the footman told Jonny that the servants are very upset that she's dead. She treated them decently." He came back to where Betsy stood. "She even encouraged one of the housemaids with her drawing. Mrs. Banfield the younger was one of those artistic sorts. When she saw that Winnie was good at drawing faces, she bought the girl a whole packet of paper. Can you believe it, a whole packet. I know because she bought it at the stationer's shop just down the road, and Horace—he's the lad who works there—told me Mrs. Banfield came in and picked it out herself."

"Mrs. Banfield the younger sounds like a very nice person." Betsy glanced over her shoulder and saw a well-dressed woman carrying a shopping basket crossing the road and heading directly for them. Drat. "I take it there's someone the staff isn't too fond of . . ."

"Indeed there is," he confirmed with a snort of derision. "Mrs. Banfield the elder is a hard one. The servants don't care for her at all." Leaning forward, he lowered his voice and said, "And we're not all that happy with her, either. We've had trouble over their account. Mrs. Banfield is always claiming that the household didn't receive the goods on our invoice and we know that isn't true because Mr. Allard—he owns this shop—always packs the Banfield order himself. It's gotten really difficult lately and now that they've had a murder, who knows when we'll get paid. Mr. Allard was going to send a letter to Mr. Banfield, the master of the house, but now that doesn't seem right, does it?"

Just then Betsy heard the door open and the clerk raised his gaze and focused his attention on the newcomer. "Good afternoon, Mrs. Gould, I'll be with you in just a moment."

Witherspoon sighed in relief as he closed the door behind Margaret Bickleton. He went back to his seat and pulled out his notebook. He usually relied on Constable Barnes to make notes, but as they had so many people to interview, they'd had to split up.

He took out his pencil and began scribbling, looking up as he heard voices in the corridor. A second later, there was a light knock and the door opened. A tall, dark-haired woman dressed in a simple black blouse and skirt entered and closed the door. She was a very attractive woman who appeared to be in her late fifties. There were a few streaks of gray at her temples, but her skin was smooth and clear. Her eyes were brown, her nose straight, and her cheekbones high. "I'm Elizabeth Montrose, Arlette's mother. I'd like to speak with you."

He shoved the notebook to one side and hurriedly got to his feet. "Of course, Mrs. Montrose. Please come in and sit down."

She crossed the small room and took the seat vacated by Margaret Bickleton. "I don't know why rich people have to have such ugly and uncomfortable furniture," she said. "Oh dear, forgive me, Inspector, I'm babbling because I'm at my wit's end. I can't believe my daughter, my beautiful, wonderful child, is dead." She pulled a black handkerchief out of the sleeve of her blouse as her eyes filled with tears.

"I'm so sorry for your loss, Mrs. Montrose," Witherspoon said softly. "But I assure you, I'll do everything in my power to bring whoever did this to justice."

She brushed the tears from her cheeks. "I'm sure you will, Inspector. I was so happy to hear that you were the one to head the investigation. You've a very good reputation amongst those of us in London who care about such things as justice. You've proved you won't be intimidated into letting a murderer go free just because he or she is a member of the upper class."

Witherspoon hoped he wasn't blushing. "Really, ma'am, you give me too much credit."

She took a deep breath. "No, I don't think so, Inspector, and in my daughter's case, I'm counting on your commitment to justice. The Banfields may not be encumbered with titles, but they are upper-class aristocrats all the same."

"Are you trying to tell me something?" he asked curiously.

"But of course. I'm trying to tell you that my daughter was murdered by someone of that ilk, someone from their circle."

"Are you saying that she was murdered by a member of the Banfield family?"

"Not just the family, Inspector," Elizabeth said quickly. "There were plenty of Banfield friends here last night who would have loved to see my daughter dead. The person you were just speaking with hated Arlette."

"You mean Margaret Bickleton?" he queried.

"The very same." She smiled grimly. "The cow had the nerve to stop me in the hallway to offer her condolences. It was only out of respect for Lewis that I didn't spit in her face."

Her bluntness shocked him. After all the murders he'd investigated, he didn't think there was much that could still surprise him, but he was wrong. Yet Witherspoon

understood all too well that grief frequently made people say and do things they wouldn't normally say or do.
"Mrs. Montrose, please tell me why you think Mrs. Bickleton would want to have harmed your daughter."

"I'm not saying she did it," she corrected, "I'm saying
she's capable of it and that she loathed Arlette."

"Would you please tell me why?" he pressed.

"Margaret Bickleton thought that Lewis was going to
propose to her daughter Helen, but then he met Arlette.
Right before their wedding, she accused Arlette of stealing the man away. But my daughter had nothing to do
with his ending his relationship with Helen Bickleton.
Lewis later told Arlette that the supposed engagement
had been in Helen's imagination. He was never in love
with her nor had any plans to offer for her in marriage."

"I see," he replied. "Mrs. Montrose, I'm no expert on
affairs of the heart, but I've observed that people of a
certain class marry for reasons other than love. So his
not being enamored of Helen Bickleton wouldn't be an
impediment to their marrying."

"Are you saying my daughter wasn't of their class?"
she charged.

"No, no, ma'am," he said hurriedly.

"But she wasn't, Inspector," she stated candidly. "Nor
would I wish her to be. The upper class in this country
is riddled with chinless wonders and idiots. I didn't want
my daughter to marry Lewis Banfield and neither did
her father."

"Is her father here today?" Witherspoon asked
quickly. He really should have a word with him as well.
Plus, he was hearing information so very fast that he

wanted to give himself a moment to absorb precisely what she was saying.

"My husband is overcome with grief. He's an artist, as am I. Artists are very sensitive. He's at home in bed. I'm making the arrangements with Lewis."

He nodded. "Did I understand you correctly when you said you didn't want your daughter to marry Lewis Banfield?"

"You heard correctly, Inspector. My husband and I were both opposed to the match and we let both Lewis and his family know of our objections. But Arlette was in love and she insisted they would wed whether we approved or not." She smiled sadly. "I must tell you, Inspector, Lewis and his family were quite shocked by our objections. I thought Geraldine Banfield was going to have an apoplexy attack when we told her."

"Why, exactly, did you disapprove of the match?" he pressed. "Surely it wasn't simply because you had such strong feelings about the upper class."

"No, of course not, but that was a big part of it," she admitted. She cocked her head to one side and studied him for a long moment. "Are you married, sir?"

He shook his head. "Sadly, no."

"Then this may be difficult for you to understand, but when two people fall in love and marry, as time passes, love changes. Our objection to Lewis was much simpler than a dislike of his class. We were both afraid that once the passion was spent they would find they had nothing, and I do mean nothing, in common with one another."

"And that was important to you and Mr. Montrose?"

Witherspoon asked. He wasn't sure what to make of this woman.

"Very," she replied. "Arlette wasn't raised to be an ornament on a man's arm. We brought her up to view marriage as a genuine partnership in every sense of the word. My husband and I are very close, Inspector. We share everything. We discuss everything and my opinions and ideas are just as important as his. My career as an artist is just as important as well, but that's not my point. Our daughter spent her life in a household where people discuss ideas, and not just about art, either. But about politics, books, music, food, interesting articles we've read in the papers and even scientific discoveries. We wanted Arlette to have the same sort of life. When she was growing up we spent the dinner hour having spirited debates on everything from women's rights to the theories of Mr. Jeremy Bentham. You have to spend your life with the person you marry, Inspector, and we didn't think Lewis was the right person for her. He is a very nice man, but the appreciation he has of art or music or literature is only social. That was very distressing to my husband and I."

He frowned. "I don't understand. What do you mean by 'social'?"

"I mean if the Banfields attend the opera, it isn't because they love the music; they go to be part of London's upper-class society," she explained. "If they go to an art show, it certainly isn't because they care about great works of art, it's because that sort of behavior is expected of that class. Frankly, despite how many books there are in the Banfield library, I don't think any member of the family has read any of them, except Arlette, of course."

"I see," he murmured.

"Do you?" She smiled skeptically. "We raised our daughter to be a free thinker and not to accept the dictates of a society that is entrenched in the past and that rewards people because of an accident of birth rather than achievement."

"But the Banfields are well known for not accepting any rewards in the way of titles or honors for their service to the country," he pointed out.

"True, and they wallow in their own self-righteousness like pigs in a sty," she retorted. She closed her eyes and caught herself. "That was very coarse, Inspector. Please forgive me, but I'm so upset over Arlette's death." She broke off and looked away, but not before Witherspoon has seen the tears pooling in her eyes.

"Of course you are, Mrs. Montrose," he said softly.

"If she'd never come here, she'd still be alive." Elizabeth flung her hands out in a wide arc. "They hated her, the Banfields and all their kind, and one of them murdered her."

"Are you making a specific accusation?" he asked.

She lowered her arms and closed her eyes, fighting for control. "No, of course not. Like any mother, I feel if she'd still been at home with her father and me, she'd have been safe."

"Did you notice any discord between your daughter and her husband?"

She smiled grimly. "No, despite our trepidation about their marriage, they seemed to love one another. Lewis adored her, and that wretched aunt of his had no reason to want her dead, but if she'd never married him, if she'd never become part of his circle, she'd still be alive."

Witherspoon wasn't sure that was true. "Mrs. Montrose, I understand you and your daughter recently had quite a loud argument with one another."

"We often argued." She glanced away, avoiding his gaze. "As I told you, Inspector, she grew up in a household where one was expected to have opinions."

"And exactly what was the disagreement about?" he pressed, wondering why she'd suddenly become evasive.

She said nothing for a moment and then she lifted her chin and looked him squarely in the eyes. "Forgive me, Inspector, I tried to avoid answering your question because I didn't think it had anything to do with her death and I was embarrassed. Arlette and I had a terrible argument and now that she's gone, it seems so foolish and petty I'm ashamed of the way I reacted."

"I'm sure at the time it seemed important," he said sympathetically.

Her eyes flooded with tears again. "But it wasn't, it was silly. A few months before she was married, Arlette posed for a bust of the goddess Diana. She wasn't nude but she was wearing a very diaphanous gown. The sculptor did a small statue in brass before doing a larger one in stone. He gave her the brass statue; the stone one was sold to a private collector in France for quite a handsome sum."

"You were angry because she posed in a diaphanous gown?"

"Of course not, Inspector. The human body is a thing

of beauty and Arlette was especially lovely," she replied. "Our quarrel had nothing to do with her posing for Julian; we disagreed over what she planned to do with the statue. She was allowing it to be reproduced by some awful factory and then sold. Mass-produced, Inspector. I was outraged and, frankly, so was Julian."

"Julian?" He thought her husband's name was Crispin Montrose.

"Julian Hammond; he's the sculptor. But there was nothing he could do about it, as he'd given her the piece, so he asked me to talk some sense into her. So we argued and she told me to mind my own business." The tears started up again and this time she let them fall. "She said there was no good reason bank clerks or schoolteachers couldn't have a decent piece of art in their homes and that, in my own way, I was as bad a snob as the Banfields and their kind." She broke off, sobbing.

Witherspoon cringed inwardly. Ye gods, he hated this part of police work. "Please, Mrs. Montrose, don't upset yourself. We all say things we don't mean when we're having a disagreement."

"But she was right, Inspector." Elizabeth Montrose mopped her cheeks with her handkerchief. "She was right and I was dreadfully wrong. We are as bad as the Banfields—we simply don't show it as much. But, as I said, we often had disagreements and we saw each other soon afterwards and mended fences. She was my daughter and I found it difficult to stay angry at her."

"Were you or your husband here last night?" he asked, hoping to distract her with a mundane question.

"We were invited, but we had a prior engagement,"

she replied. "Arlette was upset with me when I told her we couldn't come. She accused me of still being angry over the statue and I told her not to be childish. Oh, dear God, instead of taking the high road I let it degenerate into another quarrel and I'm sorry now that the last thing I said to her was that she was behaving like a selfish idiot. Oh, dear God!" Her voice broke and she buried her face in her hands, sobbing.

"All families have words every now and then." He glanced at the closed door, hoping that someone, anyone, would come in. This poor woman needed comfort, and he'd no idea what to say to ease her pain.

"You're trying to be kind, Inspector." She looked up at him with a face ravaged by grief. "But those were the last words my daughter heard from her mother and they will haunt me till the day I die."

Smythe stepped into the Dirty Duck Pub and paused in the doorway. It was a good, working-class pub on the river. Dockworkers, seamen, day laborers, counting clerks, and lorry drivers crowded around the bar and filled the benches along two walls. He craned his neck over the crowd, looking for his quarry, and then grinned as he spotted Blimpey Groggins at his usual table near the fireplace.

There were two men sitting with him and Smythe headed for the bar to wait. But just then Blimpey glanced his way and saw him. Groggins was a ginger-haired middle-aged man with a ruddy complexion. He was short of stature, big of heart, and dressed in his usual outfit of a checked jacket over a white shirt that had seen better days. Blimpey waved him over and then turned back to his companions. By the time Smythe reached him, the two men were on their feet and moving toward the door.

"I hope you didn't run 'em off on my account." Smythe slipped onto the stool. "I'd 'ave waited my turn."

"They were finished," he replied. "And your showin' up was a good excuse to get shut of 'em. Besides, it warms the cockles of me heart when you step through the door. You're one of my favorite customers."

Groggins had once been a thief. However, after a close encounter with two nasty guard dogs, together with a nasty fall from the second story of a London town house, he'd had second thoughts about his chosen profession and reassessed his talents. He'd always had an ability to recall details and once he heard something, it stayed in his memory forever. So, from that day forward, Blimpey became a buyer and seller of information. His clients ranged from fences wanting to know if a particular thief could be trusted (they usually couldn't) to insurance companies wanting to know whether a fire had been truly an accident or if the flames had had help.

Blimpey had sources everywhere: the courts, the hospitals, the newspapers, the City, and even the prisons. If someone wanted to know something about someone else in London, he was your man. But he had standards. He wouldn't trade information that harmed women or children and he tried to avoid situations that, in his judgment, had the potential to lead to violence. Everyone in London used his services and even the most vicious thug knew not to cross him. Blimpey wasn't a vicious sort himself, but he had lots of friends who'd slit a throat without a second thought.

"That's because I pay well." Smythe grinned.

"All my customers pay well or I wouldn't be doing business with 'em," Blimpey said with a laugh. "You want a pint?" Without waiting for an answer, he signaled the barman with a jerk of his head, then turned back to Smythe. "How are you and how is your good lady?"

"We're both fine," Smythe replied. "Marriage suits us."

"And you're goin' to be a father soon." Blimpey grinned from ear to ear. "I was right chuffed when I heard that bit of news."

Smythe started to ask him how he'd learned about the baby and then caught himself; of course Blimpey knew about their good news, that was the man's business and the reason he'd come to see the fellow. Blimpey made it a point to keep tabs on everyone, customers and criminals alike. "Thank you. The baby won't be here for a few more months, but we're ready for him or her."

"You wantin' a boy?" He nodded at the barmaid as she brought their beers and put them on the table.

"I don't care what it is as long as Betsy and the baby are both healthy," he replied.

"'Course, 'course, I don't blame ya, that's all that's important." Blimpey picked up his glass and took a sip. "Now that we've had the niceties, what do ya need?"

Smythe wasn't fooled. He'd bet his last penny that Groggins knew good and well why he'd come. "I'm lookin' for information about the Banfield family and anyone who might have wanted Arlette Banfield dead." He reached for his own beer. "Don't pull my leg, Blimpey, you know that the inspector caught that case."

Blimpey laughed again. "'Course I do. I just like playin'

about a bit. As a matter of fact, once I heard he'd got it, I figured you'd be by, so I've got a few bits for you now."

"Good, that'll 'elp some," Smythe said. It would be nice to go to their afternoon meeting with something useful. The others weren't aware that on most of their cases, he relied on Blimpey for information. It wasn't that he was lazy or stupid or anything like that, but he wasn't as good at getting people to talk as the rest of the household. He thought it might be because he was big and his face was on the hard side. Sometimes he thought people were a bit scared of him. Still, he liked to think he did his fair share. It shouldn't matter that he had to cross a few palms with silver to find out what he needed to know if it meant that the guilty were caught and the innocent didn't suffer. "What 'ave you got for me?"

"The Banfield family wasn't all that happy when Lewis Banfield asked Arlette Montrose to marry him, but that's to be expected. What was odd was that they might have objected a bit, but as it's Lewis that controls the lolly in the family, they all came around pretty quickly and accepted the girl."

Smythe shrugged. "That's interesting. Is there anyone in the household who might not have gotten over the fact he was marryin' beneath him, so to speak?"

"No, it was the Banfield circle that was more upset than the family. Lewis Banfield was one of the most eligible bachelors in town. He was rich, good-lookin', and smart. When he married Arlette Montrose there were howls of rage heard in fancy drawing rooms from 'ere to Edinburgh. But as I said, that was to be expected. What wasn't expected was that Banfield changed his will right before he wed."

"Changed it how?" Smythe asked.

"He fixed it so his new wife would be taken care of no matter what happened to him." Blimpey grinned. "He must 'ave been besotted with the girl—my source said he left everything to her."

Smythe's heavy brows drew together in a puzzled frown. "What's so odd about that?" He'd done the same thing himself. As a matter of fact, he'd hired a solicitor to write him his will as soon as they'd become engaged. He left everything to her, of course. Any man that didn't take care of his wife was no man at all, in his eyes. "I took care of my Betsy before we wed."

"And I took care of my Nell when we got married, too," Blimpey protested. "But the upper class don't do things like you and me. They don't leave any of it out of the family before there are children. But Lewis Banfield did; he willed everything to her, the house, the money, the estate, the business, everything."

"Maybe it was a marriage settlement of some sort," Smythe said. "That's common enough amongst the rich."

"This wasn't a marriage settlement," Blimpey explained. "This was giving the family property away before they even had children. It would have been one thing if he'd changed his will after they'd had offspring, but he did it before they married. Cor blimey, Smythe, if the fellow had dropped dead two weeks before the ceremony, she'd have gotten it all."

"I see what you're sayin'." Smythe crossed his arms over his chest. "And you're right, the rich ain't like you or me. When the family is old and prominent, they usu- ally make certain the wealth stays well within their own circle. Which makes me wonder why Banfield did what 'e did."

"Maybe that was the only way she'd marry 'im." Blimpey shrugged. "Some men will do anything for a woman before they're wed to 'em, if you know what I mean. But I'll give you this, it made me right curious as well, so I did a bit more checkin' and found out that he weren't the only one seein' a solicitor before the big day. Arlette did the same thing—she willed him all of her property."

"Did she have anything worth leavin'?" He took another sip from his glass.

"Actually, she did." Blimpey laughed. "You probably already know that she was a Montrose before she became a Banfield." He paused and then continued when Smythe nodded. "So you know the Montroses aren't just artists themselves, but as luck would have it, so are all their friends. Turns out, Arlette Montrose Banfield has some right valuable bits and pieces that will now go to Lewis."

Smythe leaned forward. "Like what?"

"For starters, she owns a Turner and a piece by one of them old Italian fellows whose name I can't remember. Her father's work fetches a hefty price and he's given her one of his paintings every Christmas since she was five, so that alone would be worth quite a bit of lolly. Strange, isn't it? Everyone thought Lewis Banfield was daft because he willed everything he owned to her, but she's the one who ended up dead and he'll be all the richer for it now."

CHAPTER 5

———

"And did you see anyone, anyone at all, come into the butler's pantry?" Barnes asked Winifred Jones, the housemaid. She sat across from him in a straight-backed chair with her hands folded neatly in her lap. She looked to be about sixteen. Her brown hair was tucked up under her maid's cap and she was as thin as a rail. But she gazed at him steadily out of a pair of dark brown eyes.

"No, sir, but I was only there for a few minutes. Mrs. Peyton asked me to bring up Mrs. Banfield the younger's champagne. I brought up the two bottles and gave them to the butler. Then I went back to the kitchen—we were bringing the food up, you see."

"The cooler, did you bring that up as well?"

"It was already in the pantry; Mr. Michaels takes care of that himself."

Barnes nodded. "Did you see either of those two bottles again?" he asked.

"I did, sir," she replied. "Later that night, after we knew poor Mrs. Banfield the younger was dead, I saw that someone had put the unopened bottle on the table just outside the wet larder. All the unopened bottles of wine had been put there."

"And you're certain this was one of the bottles you took upstairs?" He wished someone could tell him what had become of the one that had disappeared from the butler's pantry, the one with the poison it in.

"Oh yes, sir, it was one of the two I'd taken to the butler's pantry. When I was bringing them upstairs, I noticed that one of the bottles had a tiny tear on the label. This bottle had the same tear. It's probably still in the wet larder—would you like me to fetch it so you can see for yourself?" She started to get up but he waved her back to the chair.

"That won't be necessary. I'm sure you're very observant and that it's the same bottle. Do you happen to know what became of the other bottle of champagne?"

She shook her head. "I don't, and everyone in the kitchen is talking about how it up and disappeared. None of us took it, that's for certain."

Barnes drew back slightly. "Are you sure it wasn't one of the servants? Someone who thought they were doing their job and helping to tidy up?"

"None of us touched it."

He tried a different approach. "You don't have to be frightened; we'll understand that if someone took it away, they didn't realize it was evidence."

"None of us did it," she insisted. "Right after Mrs. Banfield died, Mrs. Peyton told the kitchen staff to stay downstairs. We found out the bottle had been taken away when Mr. Banfield and that other policeman came downstairs looking for the ruddy thing. But it weren't there."

"And you only took the two bottles up to begin with, is that right?"

She nodded. "Mrs. Peyton always sent two bottles for Mrs. Banfield."

Barnes raised his eyebrows. "That's a lot of champagne."

"Mrs. Banfield didn't drink it all," the girl said defensively. "We always brought the extra bottle in case one of the other guests wanted a glass."

"Of course," he agreed, but he deliberately kept his expression skeptical.

"It's true," she cried. "Mrs. Banfield wasn't a drunkard. She never had more than a couple of glasses out of the bottle. If you're interested in who is a secret drinker, you ought to look to those friends of Mrs. Banfield the elder. If you don't believe me, you can ask Mary. She does the table serving and she said that after dinner the other evening, Mrs. Kimball crept into the pantry and helped herself to the rest of the champagne when she thought no one was lookin'. But Mary saw her, saw her as plain as day, pouring the stuff into a water tumbler and then creepin' off to her room. So if anyone says that Mrs. Banfield the younger drank too much, they're lying."

"You sound as if you liked her," Barnes pressed.

"I did, we all did. She was decent to us." Winifred paused and glanced at the closed door. "She treated us like human beings, not like the others in this house. She bought me a packet of paper for my birthday last month." Her eyes filled with tears. "And no one has ever done such a nice thing for me. But she saw me drawing on a scrap of paper I'd pulled out of the dustbin and she said I had talent. She said I ought to have art lessons." She swiped at the tears that rolled down her cheeks. "Now that she's gone, I'm goin' to start looking for another position. I don't think I can stand working here without her. Most of the others want to leave, too; we even heard Mrs. Peyton telling Cook she might go as well."

"Apricot jam," Wiggins exclaimed as he sat down. "Cor blimey, Mrs. Goodge, 'ow'd you know I was goin' to be needin' a nice treat today? I've spent the day dodgin' constables who might recognize me and, what's worse, not one ruddy 'ousemaid or tweeny so much as set foot on Wallington Square. I've nothing to show for my efforts."

"Oh, good, I love that jam," Betsy agreed as she took her chair. "And I'm hungry enough to eat a bear!"

Mrs. Goodge shoved a plate of buttered brown bread toward the maid. "I'm glad to see someone smiling. The rest of you have such long faces I'll wager that Betsy is the only one to have anything useful to report, and I got the jam out because I needed a bit of cheering up. I've not found out anything."

"I learned a thing or two." Smythe planted a quick kiss on his wife's cheek.

"I didn't," Luty complained.

"Nor did I," Hatchet admitted glumly.

"Oh, good," Ruth said cheerfully. "I was afraid I was

going to be the only one without anything to report. Oh dear, that isn't precisely what I meant to say . . ."

"We understand." The cook laughed. "And I know just how you feel. I've had two tradesmen here today gobbling up my apple tarts like they'd not eaten in a week and neither of them had even heard of the murder. I don't know what this world is coming to when people can't be bothered to keep up with the latest news."

Betsy looked at Mrs. Jeffries. "Where's Phyllis? I thought she'd be joining us."

"She's at the ironmonger's," the housekeeper replied. She picked up the big brown teapot and began to pour the tea into the semicircle of cups in front of her. "I sent her there to get the handle on the housemaid's box repaired."

Betsy started to say something, but thought better of it and reached for her tea.

"Should I start, then?" Smythe asked. He was a bit mystified as to what was going on with Phyllis not being here, but he sensed that it was best not to ask too many questions. He could tell by his wife's serene expression that she'd figured out what was going on and she'd probably tell him later. Probably. But sometimes he'd discovered that women didn't appreciate men poking their noses too far into domestic matters.

"That's an excellent idea, Smythe," Mrs. Jeffries said as everyone reached for their tea.

Smythe told them what he'd learned from Blimpey. When he'd finished, he reached for a slice of brown bread.

"Cor blimey, you mean Lewis Banfield is actually benefitin' from his wife's death?" Wiggins scooped a heaping spoonful of jam onto his plate.

"That's what it sounds like."

"But his benefiting could be relative," Hatchet interjected. He knew something about the art world. "We've no idea which, er, 'Italian painter' it might be, and Crispin Montrose's work sells very well, but it's not museum quality."

"What about the Turner?" Luty charged. "They fetch a pretty penny. I know, I bought one a few years back and it cost me an arm and a leg."

"As you have all your extremities, madam, you are, as usual, exaggerating," he replied. "However, your statement is correct. Turners don't come cheap."

"But even if she has art worth a lot of money, does it come anywhere close to what she'd have inherited if he'd been the one murdered?" Ruth mused. She reached for a slice of bread and the jam pot.

"Probably not in this case," Luty said dryly. "Okay, I'll admit, I did learn a thing or two today, but it wasn't much so I was savin' it. One of my sources confirmed that Lewis Banfield ain't broke."

"Is that the same as being rich?" Betsy asked. "Besides, what I think is really interesting isn't that she had something to leave him, but that they changed their wills before they got married and had children."

"I agree," Mrs. Jeffries said. "And as Smythe pointed out, this wasn't just a marriage settlement. If one of them had died before they married, their family would not have inherited the deceased's property. That's very unusual."

"That's it for me." Smythe looked at Ruth, who'd managed to get the jam pot from the footman, and said, "Could you pass the apricots, please?"

She pushed the pot toward him.

"I'll go next then," Betsy said. "I didn't learn much but I did find out a tidbit or two." She told them what she'd heard from the clerk. "So that leads me to wonder if the Banfields are as rich as everyone thinks," she concluded. "After all, if they have so much money, why does Geraldine Banfield always argue over their bill?"

Witherspoon yawned as Mrs. Jeffries handed him a glass of sherry. She'd taken the liberty of pouring both of them a glass of Harvey's, as she knew he fully expected her to have one with him. "You look exhausted, sir." She smiled sympathetically as she took her own seat. "Did you have a tiring day?"

"Truth to tell, it was," he replied. "And the odd thing is, no matter how hard we tried, it was difficult getting people to actually sit down and talk to us."

"Oh dear, sir, was the Banfield household very uncooperative, then?" she said. That was usually the reason for a dour mood on his part.

"Well, one could say that, I suppose. I interviewed Margaret Bickleton and I wanted to have another word with Mr. Banfield and his aunt, but both of them were tied up planning Arlette Banfield's funeral. Then when I went to have a word with the other houseguest, Mrs. Kimball, none of the servants could find hide nor hair of her, either."

Mrs. Jeffries looked at him over the rim of her sherry glass. "Was she deliberately avoiding you, sir?"

"I don't think so," Witherspoon replied thoughtfully. "It was more that the household was chaotic. For instance, when I went to ask Lewis Banfield for the whereabouts of either his aunt or Mrs. Kimball, the butler and a footman were lugging a great huge old trunk down the staircase. Just then, Mr. Banfield appeared and asked them what on earth they were doing. The butler replied that Mrs. Banfield had ordered them to bring down the mourning cloth and begin draping the mirrors and windows. Mr. Banfield told them to take it right back upstairs, as his wife would have hated that sort of thing. Right at that moment, his aunt suddenly appeared on the first-floor landing and began shouting that just because Mrs. Banfield the younger wouldn't have liked the custom, they had traditions and standards to uphold. I felt very sorry for the servants; they were just standing halfway down the staircase, hanging on to this trunk, while Mr. Banfield and his aunt shouted at one another. Finally, when Mr. Banfield directly ordered the butler to take the trunk back to the attic, she turned on her heel and stomped off. Well, as you can probably guess, when I asked Mr. Banfield about the whereabouts of his aunt's houseguest, he said he'd no idea where Mrs. Kimball might be and that as far as he was concerned, she and every other old lady in the household could go to the devil. He then stomped off as well."

"Oh dear, what did you do then?"

"I went and found Constable Barnes." He sighed and took a quick sip from his glass. "He'd spoken to most of the servants." He told her what the constable had shared with him and about his own interview with Margaret Bickleton.

"So you only really spoke with Mrs. Bickleton?" Mrs. Jeffries queried.

"Oh no, I also spoke at some length with Elizabeth

Montrose, Arlette Banfield's mother. The poor woman is in utter agony. Usually I can distance myself somewhat from the grief of the family, but today I saw just how utterly devastating losing a loved one can be."

"That must have been dreadful for you, sir," she murmured.

He smiled grimly. "It was far more dreadful for Mrs. Montrose. You know, it's odd, but when I was growing up, except for my mother, I didn't really have a circle of people I cared deeply about. It was just the two of us, except for my aunt Euphemia, of course. But I didn't really know her. She was merely a nice lady I wrote to twice a year thanking her for my wonderful Christmas and birthday presents. But now that I've a household of my own and Lady Cannonberry as my dear friend, I find myself wondering how I would feel about losing any of you."

Surprised, Mrs. Jeffries stared at him. "But surely you were upset when your mother passed away. You've spoken of her so often I felt certain that the two of you were very close to one another."

"Of course we were; I loved her dearly. But she died of natural causes, after a long illness," he explained. "She wasn't snatched from me by the hand of another at the prime of her life. It's bad enough to lose someone you love, but losing that person to a murder must be a living hell. It's a terrible, terrible thing and I'm only now beginning to understand the rage and bitterness those left behind must feel."

She had no idea what to say, so she said nothing. But he didn't seem to notice and continued speaking.

"It makes one wonder what keeps more people from

committing the same grave crime to avenge their dead."
He cocked his head to one side, his expression puzzled.
"Do you suppose it's because we have a system of justice
that tries to punish the guilty so the survivors of that
particular kind of horror don't feel they have to?"

"I suppose that could be the case, sir."

"But that in and of itself is rather amazing, isn't it?
That an individual who has lost someone and is absolutely devastated by that loss is content to see that justice
is done by their society and not themselves?"

"Most of us are civilized people, sir, and even a terrible loss doesn't mean we wish to have blood on our
hands," she replied. Gracious, what on earth had got into
the man?

"I'd like to think you're right, but after speaking to
Elizabeth Montrose, I'm not as certain about that as I
used to be. I don't think catching her daughter's killer
will give her any consolation whatsoever. As she put it
to me, she'll never see her child again and nothing will
ever make up for that. It seemed to me that she'd be quite
happy to loop the noose around the guilty party's neck
and pull the hangman's lever herself."

Mrs. Jeffries found the inspector's reaction curious,
but it was getting on and they didn't really have time
for a philosophical discussion on the ramifications of
homicide.

"Was it only Elizabeth Montrose who appeared to be
devastated?" she asked.

"Oh no." He shook his head. "Mr. Montrose is so
upset he's taken to his bed, and as I've already mentioned, Lewis Banfield seems genuinely distraught. Of

course, they could all be acting a part, we've certainly had that happen before. But somehow I don't think that is the case in this instance."

"If everyone is so upset over the woman's murder, who could possibly have killed her?" Mrs. Jeffries mused. "I don't suppose Lewis Banfield is going to inherit anything from his wife, is he?" she said casually.

He tipped back his glass, drained it, and stood up. "We're going to speak to her solicitor as soon as the funeral is over."

The next morning, they had a quick meeting and Mrs. Jeffries shared all the information she'd learned with the others. "Constable Barnes told Mrs. Goodge and me that the housemaid was certain that none of the servants had removed the champagne bottle," she concluded. "So I think we can assume the killer must have gotten to it."

"It's probably at the bottom of the Thames," Luty observed as she shoved back her chair.

"Perhaps not," Hatchet remarked as he helped her to her feet. "Despite all the chaos that ensued with Mrs. Banfield's death, the servants would have noticed if one of the guests had tried to sneak off with the thing. There would have been no place on their person to hide it. It's far too warm this time of year for long cloaks or heavy shawls, and a bottle of champagne isn't easy to hide."

"Then where is the danged thing?" Luty cried. "It didn't just git up and waltz away on its own."

"I think Mrs. Jeffries is right," Betsy said. She was standing by the coat tree, putting on her hat. Smythe was next to her. "I think the killer took it and hid it somewhere in the house until he or she can sneak back and get rid of it."

Mrs. Jeffries refrained from pointing out that she'd not exactly said those words. It was actually an interesting idea. From what they'd learned thus far, it had only been the public, downstairs rooms that had been thoroughly searched on the night of the murder. Perhaps she'd have a quick word with Constable Barnes when she saw him the next morning and suggest another search might be in order.

"Let's 'ope the rest of us find out something today," Wiggins muttered. He was still smarting over having nothing to report at the previous day's meeting. "I'm going to work double 'ard to find a servant from the Banfield house. Somebody is bound to stick their nose out of the place today."

"Do the best you can, lad." Mrs. Goodge smiled. "It's still early days. She was only murdered two days ago."

Lady Cannonberry patted his arm in commiseration as they started for the back door.

"And you aren't the only one that hasn't found out anything," Luty told the footman as she and Hatchet fell into step behind them. "I haven't had any luck, either. But I will today, that's for danged sure."

As soon as the kitchen was empty, Mrs. Goodge went to her work counter and pulled out her big brown bowl. "I'm going to make another batch of scones," she announced.

"Will there be enough left for our tea today? Everyone dearly loves your scones," Mrs. Jeffries said. She went to the coat tree and pulled down her jacket and matching bonnet.

"There ought to be, I'm making a double batch. Where are you off to, then?"

"St. Thomas' Hospital." She put on the hat and slipped her arms into the coat. "I want to prevail upon Dr. Bosworth to help us. They still haven't given the inspector a full report, so we don't know the exact kind of poison that was used to kill Mrs. Banfield. Now that Dr. Bosworth is an official police surgeon for his district, he might be able to get us that information."

Dr. Bosworth was another of their special friends and his expertise was very useful to them.

"What about Phyllis?" Mrs. Goodge pulled out her flour tin from the shelf and plonked it next to her bowl. "Do you want me to keep an eye on her?"

Mrs. Jeffries sighed heavily. "No, let's leave her alone. I've thought long and hard about what to do about the situation and I've decided we must trust the girl unless we see that she's not to be trusted, if you know what I mean."

The cook nodded in agreement. "I do. I've been watching her when the inspector is around the house and there's not been any indication she wants to say anything to him about us."

"That is my conclusion as well." Mrs. Jeffries walked over to the pine sideboard and opened the top drawer. Reaching inside, she pulled out her good purse and tucked it into her pocket. The purse was always kept in this drawer and always had a minimum of two pounds in it. She'd instructed the household that it was to be used if any of them needed money for a cab or any other expense that might crop up when they were "on the hunt."

"I think we were so surprised by her less than enthusiastic response to our invitation to include her that we assumed she might be less than trustworthy. Generally, people are most eager to help us."

"She would be, too, if she wasn't such a scared little rabbit." Mrs. Goodge opened the flour tin. "Phyllis won't do anything that she thinks might threaten her job. Mind you, I think she's had some very hard times in her past and she likes it here."

"We all like it here. Even if the inspector did find out what we were doing, I don't think he'd sack us." As she stepped into the hall and walked briskly toward the back door, she wasn't certain, but she thought she heard Mrs. Goodge say, "I'd not be too sure of that."

Witherspoon and Barnes' first interview of the day was with Sir Ralph and Lady Fetchman. The Fetchmans lived in a huge white Regency-style house on a side street near Hyde Park.

"I'm sorry to have kept you waiting." Sir Ralph, a tall, balding man with a huge gray mustache, swept into the drawing room with his hand extended. "But when Vinner told me you were here, I dashed upstairs to tell Henny to hurry up and come down. My wife is always fussing about something and I knew you wanted to speak with both of us. This is a terrible business, isn't it?"

"Yes, sir, it is," Witherspoon agreed as he shook hands. "I'm Inspector Gerald Witherspoon and this is my colleague Constable Barnes."

Barnes stood just a bit straighter as he shook Fetchman's

hand, pleased that his superior officer had introduced him as a "colleague." That was another reason the rank-and-file men admired the inspector so much, he always treated them with respect in front of civilians. "Pleased to meet you, sir."

"I know who you both are. You introduced your-selves the other evening. Let's sit down." Sir Ralph gestured toward a pale gold sofa and two matching chairs in front of the fireplace. "We might as well be comfortable. Would you like tea?"

"Not for me, sir," Barnes answered quickly.

"Nor for me, sir, but it was kind of you to offer." Witherspoon took a seat on one end of the sofa as Barnes settled down at the other and whipped out his notebook. Fetchman took a chair.

"Sir Ralph, can you give us an account of what happened at the ball?" Witherspoon asked.

Fetchman closed his eyes briefly. "It's not something I·like to think about. That poor woman struggling to breathe has given me nightmares, Inspector. But I know my duty. Where would you like me to begin?"

"Start from when you arrived and don't be afraid to mention anything, no matter how trivial it might seem, that struck you as odd or out of place," he said.

Fetchman nodded in understanding. "Henny and I took a hansom to the ball. The carriage clapped out this winter and, frankly, a horse and four or even two is such an expense in the city that we didn't bother getting another. But you're not interested in our domestic arrangements." He smiled self-consciously. "We went inside and went through the receiving line to greet the Banfields. Arlette looked lovely and Lewis, of course, was gracious. Geraldine Banfield and her friend Mrs. Bickleton were in the line as well."

"What about the other houseguest, Mrs. Kimball?" Witherspoon asked. "Wasn't she in the line?"

"No, she wasn't."

"What happened after that?" Barnes prompted. Out of the corner of his eye, he saw the drawing room door open a crack.

"We passed through and went into the ballroom. The buffet wasn't ready as yet and there were servants going back and forth from behind the screens to the halls, but there were waiters serving wine, so I got Henny and myself a couple of glasses of Bordeaux and we went out to the terrace. Henny loves red wine."

"I'm not the only one." A short, plump, dark-haired woman wearing a mint green skirt and white blouse stepped into the room. She smiled as she came toward them.

As she approached, Witherspoon could see that she was older than he'd initially thought. There was a substantial amount of gray in her dark hair and laugh lines deeply etched around her eyes and mouth. He, along with the other two men, started to rise.

She waved them back to their seats. "I'm Henrietta Fetchman. I know why you've come and I want to do everything I can to help. Ralph, as usual, has left out some very important information."

"What have I left out?" Her husband frowned at her.

She took no notice but kept her attention on Witherspoon as she sat down in the chair next to him. "Quite a bit, darling. To begin with, you didn't mention that not only wasn't Rosalind Kimball in the receiving line, but she snubbed Arlette when she came into the ballroom. She walked straight past her and Lewis to his aunt and Margaret Bickleton. For God's sake, Ralph, the woman was right in front of us. I can't believe you didn't notice her. Don't you remember when I poked you in the ribs? I could see that Lewis was furious over the breach."

"My gracious, was that why you were poking me? I thought it was because I stepped on your dress," he exclaimed. "And she was right ahead of us in the receiving line?"

"Yes, dear, and she didn't bother to say hello to us, either." Henrietta sighed in exasperation. "Men don't notice anything."

Witherspoon would have liked to argue that point, but in all fairness, she might be right. He, however, made it a point to observe as much as possible regardless of where he was at any given moment. But then, he was a trained police officer. "How did you come to your conclusion that Lewis Banfield was upset?"

"He clenched his jaw and his fist," she replied. "And Arlette squeezed his arm and whispered in his ear. She knew he was riled, but he managed to get hold of himself by the time he greeted us."

Barnes looked up from his notebook. "Was she angry over the breach as well?"

Henrietta shook her head. "If anything, she was amused. After she calmed Lewis, she looked at Rosalind Kimball, who, by this time, was looking in our direction. Arlette stared her down and it was Rosalind who looked away."

"Do you know of any reason why Rosalind Kimball would dislike Mrs. Banfield?"

Witherspoon knew he was probably wasting his breath by asking the question. No doubt the animosity sprang from the fact that Mrs. Banfield wasn't of the same class and background as the Kimball family.

"She didn't dislike her, Inspector; Rosalind hated her," Henrietta said.

"Now, Henny, you mustn't exaggerate," Fetchman warned his wife. "We don't know that for a fact."

"Yes, we do," she charged, giving her husband a good glare. "I was there when it happened and I saw and heard it with my own eyes and ears."

"Saw and heard what?" Witherspoon said sharply.

She turned back to him. "Rosalind Kimball threatened Arlette and, what's more, she did it in front of everyone."

"Mr. Widdowes can see you now, Mrs. Crookshank," the young man said as he crossed the elegant foyer toward Luty.

"Why, thank you, young feller." She got up from the straight-backed chair she'd been occupying while she waited in the outer office of Widdowes and Walthrop, Merchant Bankers. She hadn't waited long. Her large diamond brooch and the pearls around her neck, coupled with her expensive, flamboyant clothes, American accent, and general air of friendliness to everyone who came within ten feet of her, guaranteed that the clerk would let John Widdowes know she was here and waiting to see him.

"It's right this way, ma'am." He grinned and led her across the foyer. Just then the door in front of them opened and a middle-aged, rather handsome man with thick, graying blond hair, a neatly trimmed beard, and dark eyes stepped into view.

"Luty, what a delightful surprise. Now that you've finally come to see me, I hope you've brought all your money." He smiled broadly and stepped toward her, his hands outstretched to grasp hers.

Luty laughed and grabbed his fingers. "Not all of it, John, but maybe I'll give you some of it to play with." Of all the merchant bankers she knew, she liked Widdowes the best.

"Bring us a pot of tea, please," Widdowes instructed the clerk as he ushered Luty through the door and into his office.

"Right away, sir," the lad replied.

Luty gasped as she entered the office. Directly in front of her were three wide windows opening the room to a panorama of the river. "My goodness, John, how the dickens do you get any work done with that view?"

"That's why I've got my back to it, Luty. If I saw it every time I looked up, I'd spend the whole day watching it."

Barges, fishing boats, ferries, and steamers all plied up and down on the wide green-gray ribbon of water. The Thames was a rich and vibrant slice of life, constantly moving and changing shape as the river traffic moved in each direction.

Widdowes helped Luty into a chair in front of his wide desk and then stepped behind it and sat down.

She took a moment to adjust her voluminous skirt so that she was comfortable. When she'd finished fidgeting with the material, she looked up and saw that he was staring at her speculatively. "I'll bet you're wonderin' why I'm here."

He smiled slowly. "I think I might have some idea." He turned his head as the door opened and the clerk came in carrying a tea tray. "Put it just there." He pointed to an occasional table next to the window and got up. He went to the table and poured the tea into elegant blue and green china teacups. "Do you take cream or sugar?"

"Both: one lump of sugar and a smidgen of cream," Luty replied. She'd forgotten how smart Widdowes was; unlike most of the bankers she knew, he'd actually worked his way up in the financial world. He wasn't going to be an easy mark. Dang. Maybe she should just ask him for some investment advice and go somewhere else. But where? John Widdowes knew more about the financing of manufacturing companies than anyone in London and that's where the Banfields made their money. They owned two factories right here in London. "It's right nice of ya to take the time to see me," she began.

He handed her a cup of fragrant tea and put a plate of biscuits within easy reach on the edge of his desk. "Help yourself." He picked up his own cup and went back to his chair. "And of course I wanted to see you. Not only are you one of the richest women in the country but I find you one of the most delightful people I've ever met.

Now, the more important question is why you wanted to see me."

Luty took a sip from her cup. She had to be careful here. She wasn't going to insult the man by underestimating his intelligence. "I was wonderin' if you could give me some advice. I'm thinkin' about investing in a factory that makes railway equipment for export. I understand they make a lot of money."

He said nothing for a moment; he simply looked at her, his expression thoughtful. "You're aware there are already two facilities manufacturing railway supplies and material here in London?"

"And I hear they're doin' real well." She shifted uncomfortably. "Besides, the one I'm thinkin' of investin' in is goin' to be in Baltimore. There ain't nobody manufacturin' that in the States."

He burst out laughing. "Oh; my God, you are shameless."

"What are you talkin' about?" she charged. Blast it all, she shouldn't have come here. That was the trouble with people who'd worked their way up in this world; they were like her—too smart to be easily fooled. She decided to go on the offensive. "I'll have you know I came to see you in good faith, thinkin' you was a decent man that would help a poor old woman manage her . . ." She trailed off as he began to laugh so hard tears formed in the corners of his eyes. She slammed her cup down so hard she was afraid she'd cracked the china and leapt to her feet. "Well, if you're goin' to insult me, maybe I ought to just git out of here."

He brought himself under control. "Oh, for God's sake, Luty, sit back down and we'll talk," he ordered. "Poor old

woman, my foot. I'll wager you know more about business than anyone in the country and could probably teach
me a thing or two about running this bank."

Luty couldn't help it, she started to laugh. "Well, alright,
maybe that was goin' a bit far. But I do need your advice."

"Of course you do, but you don't have any intention
of opening a railway equipment factory in Baltimore;
you want to find out what I know about the Banfields."

"How'd you come to that idea?" She frowned and picked
up her teacup. It was good tea and she was thirsty. He was
good. Next time she'd stick to one of her aristocratic upper-
class financial friends; they were lots dumber than this one.

"Come now, Luty, your reputation precedes you. When-
ever your good friend Inspector Gerald Witherspoon has a
murder case, you and your butler start asking questions."

"Now, that ain't—"

He interrupted with a wave of his hand. "Don't panic,
your activities aren't common knowledge, but there are
those of us in the financial world that keep our ears and
our eyes open. We hear things." He stopped and cocked
his head to one side. "Is it true you got Angus Fielding
drunk on homemade whiskey?"

Luty winced. God, how had that story got out? "It
wasn't homemade whiskey, it was white lightning. It
come straight from the hills of Webster County, West
Virginia, and it was fine stuff. I didn't get him drunk,
I offered him a taste because he was always braggin'
about bein' a connoisseur of the world's alcoholic bever-
ages. He's the one that kept wantin' more."

Widdowes chuckled. "Do you have any left? I'd like
a taste myself."

"I've got some down in my wine cellar. It's usually kept in glass jars but that woulda been hard to transport all the way here so my friend put it in little kegs. You come on over to my house for supper soon and you can have all ya want. But it's a strong brew."

"I'll hold you to that," he replied. "Now, what do you want to know about the Banfields and their factories?"

Luty studied him for a moment, not sure how far she should go. But Widdowes had a reputation for fairness and honesty. A rare commodity in the rough-and-tumble business of money. "What kind of financial shape is the family in? Mind you, I'm not admitting that I'm askin' questions because my friend is a police inspector . . ."

"No, of course you aren't," he agreed. He looked amused. "And the Banfields are in good financial shape, at least from what I've heard. The factories are doing well and as far as I know they've paid off all their loans, none of which were with my bank so that's why I can talk about them so freely." He held Luty's gaze. "I'm happy to help you as long as you don't ask me questions about my clients. Understood?"

"I understand." Luty nodded. "You won't break confidence with those you do business with." Right then she decided to switch some of her financial business here. "What do you mean that they've paid off their loans?"

"Garrett Banfield, Lewis' uncle, borrowed heavily and used the factories and most of the property as collateral for the debts. Five years ago, Garrett died of a heart attack and Lewis took over. He might be young but he's a good head for business and he made some excellent investments that allowed them to pay off their debt very quickly."

"So they were in debt?" Luty frowned. "I thought the Banfields prided themselves on . . . on . . ." She didn't know precisely what word to use.

"On being honorable and doing their duty to Queen and country," he finished for her. "They do. Which is why it was such a surprise when Garrett began to borrow so heavily. Not that being in debt is dishonorable; if it was, half the families in town wouldn't be able to hold their heads up. But the Banfields had never been the sort of people to borrow against their assets."

"What did Garrett do with the cash he borrowed?" she asked curiously.

"Supposedly, he was investing in various enterprises in the Far East," John replied. "I know he went to Singapore a time or two during this period."

"And did those investments eventually pay off?" Luty pressed. "Was that the reason Lewis Banfield was able to get out of debt so fast?"

"No, no, Lewis Banfield liquidated the Far East holdings and used the money to invest in mining. He had tremendous success with a gold mine in southern Africa. That's supposedly the investment that gave him the cash to pay off the creditors so quickly."

Luty thought for a moment. "Was Garrett married to Geraldine Banfield?"

"He was, and by all accounts it was as good a marriage as any other." He shrugged slightly. "I never heard any rumors that he wasn't a good and faithful husband."

* * *

"You'd gone to get us a glass of champagne," Henny said to her husband, "so you weren't there when it happened. You didn't see Rosalind's face. She was so angry I thought she was going to scratch Arlette's eyes out right there in the middle of the gallery."

"What happened?" Barnes asked quickly.

"We were at Gillette's on New Bond Street. Arlette had invited us to the opening of a show featuring her mother's glasswork and an exhibit of her father's paintings. Crispin Montrose is quite a well-known artist. His work sells for thousands of pounds, not that money is the only criterion to judge the worth of a piece of art, of course."

"Henny loves art," Sir Ralph interjected. "She's a painter herself. Her landscapes are lovely enough that she could have a showing if she wanted. I've encouraged her to give it a go, but she's far too modest."

Henny laughed gaily and reached across the small space separating them to pat his hand. "You're far too kind, my dear. At best, I'm a talented amateur, but I appreciate your faith in my abilities. I do love art, though, which is why we were one of the few people from Lewis' circle that Arlette invited to the opening." She focused her attention on Witherspoon. "Have you been to Gillette's?"

"I've never had the pleasure."

She smiled in amusement. "I do have a reason for asking, Inspector. Gillette's is a very large gallery and even with the showing going on, the front part of the establishment carried on doing business as usual. That is pertinent to what happened." She took a deep breath. "The showing was in the back part of the gallery and it was lovely. The pieces were showcased perfectly and there was some excellent champagne being served. Arlette and I were standing in front of an exquisite glass bowl her mother had made, when all of a sudden Rosalind Kimball swooped in like an avenging angel from the pits of hell."

Barnes smiled at the colorful language. "I take it she was furious about something?"

"She was indeed, Constable. She charged over to Arlette and said she had no right to interfere in her husband's business."

"Whose husband, hers or Arlette's?" Witherspoon asked quickly.

"As it turned out, she was speaking about Lewis, but it took a few seconds before I realized what she was actually trying to say."

"And what was that?" Barnes asked. "It would be helpful if you could recall her exact words."

"Let me see." She thought for a moment. "She said, 'Who do you think you are? How dare you interfere in your husband's business affairs?' Then Arlette said something like, 'When I see the old guard trying to take advantage of him, it's my duty to speak up and tell him what I know.'" Henny smiled apologetically. "At this point I wasn't quite sure what they were talking about, but it was clear that Rosalind was furious and Arlette started to lose her temper as well. Arlette told Rosalind that the Kimballs had no right to use their friendship with the Banfields to pressure Lewis into giving them a loan on that dilapidated old house of theirs. Those were her exact words. Then she said that Rosalind's husband was a disgusting old reprobate who used every penny he could lay his hands on to indulge in horrid practices and that she wasn't going to allow her husband's money to contribute to the ruin of any more young girls." She broke off and glanced at her husband, who was gaping at her with a shocked expression.

"That's when Rosalind really got angry," she continued. "Her eyes narrowed and she started calling Arlette names, saying she was no better than a jumped-up guttersnipe who was going to get what was coming to her if she couldn't learn to stay in her place."

"She actually used those words?" Barnes pressed.

"She did," Henny replied. "Then she turned on her heel and stormed out. I was very shocked."

"Really, Henny, why didn't you tell me this?" Sir Ralph exclaimed. "Why, I'd not have spoken to the woman at the ball if I'd known she'd behaved in such a manner."

Henny smiled at her husband. "She was gone by the time you returned with our champagne and Arlette asked me not to say anything about the incident. She didn't want her parents' showing ruined."

"What did she mean about contributing to the ruin of any more young girls?" Witherspoon asked. He was embarrassed to ask a lady such a question, for he suspected he knew what had been meant. But he had to learn all the facts, no matter how uncomfortable it might make him feel.

Henny flattened her lips into a thin, disapproving line and glanced at her husband again. "Cover your ears, dear, I'm going to tell them the truth."

"No, I'll tell them." Sir Ralph smiled grimly. "It's

an ugly subject, but I want Arlette's killer caught." He looked at the inspector. "Gregory Kimball likes young girls, very young girls, and he's also a drug addict."

"He drinks to excess as well," Henny added.

"The gossip we've heard is that the Kimballs are now broke because he's spent every pound they have feeding his habits."

"And it appears as if Arlette Banfield stopped her husband from lending him more money?" Witherspoon guessed.

"That's right, Inspector," Henny said. "Now the Kimballs will be losing their house, and for someone like Rosalind Kimball, that is truly a fate worse than death."

CHAPTER 6

—◆—

"Hello, Mrs. Jeffries." The voice came from behind her as she stepped into the lower corridor of St. Thomas' Hospital. She whirled about and smiled in pleasure. "Dr. Bosworth, how nice to see you. I do hope you can spare me a moment."

"Of course. I've been expecting you," he replied. He was a tall man with dark red hair, a bony face, and deep-set hazel eyes. "Let's go to my office. I'll ask the porter to fetch us a pot of tea."

"That would be wonderful, but don't go to any trouble on my account. I know you're very busy."

Bosworth laughed and started down the hallway. "You're in luck today, Mrs. Jeffries. I've already done my rounds and my next consult isn't for an hour. Come along, then, we could both use some refreshment."

She fell into step beside him and they chatted while

they made their way to his small office, stopping briefly so he could ask the porter for the tea.

He opened the door and ushered her inside. She noticed it hadn't changed very much from the last time she'd been here. There was a pile of books on one of the chairs, his desk was covered with stacks of files, and there were half a dozen glass bottles of various sizes and shapes containing colored liquids clustered on the corner. But there was a nice blue rag rug covering the green linoleum on his floor and a nicely done seascape hung on the wall next to his medical cupboard.

He swept the books off the chair and motioned for her to sit down. He went behind the desk, dropped the volumes onto the floor by his chair, and then took his seat.

Dr. Bosworth was one of their special friends. He'd helped on an earlier case and proved himself both reliable and highly intelligent. He was of the opinion that by studying the size and shape of the fatal wound, one could easily ascertain what kind of weapon had been used to do the killing. He had spent part of his medical career studying with a doctor in San Francisco, where, apparently, there was no shortage of bodies or bulletholes. The good doctor was always quick to admit he wasn't the first person to connect wounds and murder weapons, but he was one of the first to make a systematic study of the subject.

Even though his ideas weren't always accepted by other members of the medical profession, he wasn't in the least shy about sharing them and had been gratified when he realized that more and more medical men were taking his concepts seriously. Recently, he'd been thrilled when several other police surgeons had called upon him to consult on their difficult cases and his methods had helped bring the guilty to justice.

He picked up a file and flipped open the cover. "I presume you're here about Arlette Banfield."

She nodded. "Are those the postmortem results?"

"I've not had a chance to go over the report. Dr. Pendleton only sent them to me late yesterday afternoon." He looked at her over the top of the file and grinned. "I think he suspected you'd be along to see me."

"Please convey my thanks." She laughed. She'd met Phineas Pendleton on one of their earlier cases when she'd come here looking for Bosworth. Pendleton had been very helpful then, but she was glad she could call upon her old friend for assistance now.

"I'll do that." Bosworth turned his attention back to the file. "Mrs. Banfield was most definitely poisoned. Someone had laced her drink with what is commonly referred to as prussic acid or cyanide. Once she ingested it, she was doomed. Death happens very quickly, especially with the dose that she received. There were seven grams found in her stomach."

"Where would the murderer have obtained the poison?" she asked. "Surely it's not the sort of thing that one can buy at the local chemist shop."

Bosworth smiled grimly. "I doubt your killer bought it at the chemist's, but the poison is easily obtainable. It has a number of industrial uses and even occurs naturally in the pits of some fruits."

"What kind of fruit?"

"Peaches, for one, and I believe there are several

others as well." He broke off as the porter entered carrying a tray. "Thank you, George, just put it down here on the edge of the desk." He pointed to the empty corner closest to Mrs. Jeffries and went back to reading.

She waited until the porter had closed the door behind him, and then asked, "Would you like me to pour?"

Bosworth nodded absently.

"It's hard to imagine that someone went to all the trouble of bashing open a peach pit to obtain the poison," she commented as she poured the tea into the mugs.

"They probably didn't," he muttered, his attention still on the pages in front of him. "There are far easier methods to obtain it. It has a number of domestic uses; when I was growing up, our gardener used it to kill vermin and, at one time, it was used medically. I can remember one of my great-uncles using prussic acid to treat his varicose veins."

"It's not still being prescribed, is it?"

"No, no." He laughed. "With the development of modern drugs, it's fallen out of favor. Your killer took a big risk using cyanide."

"In what way? Sugar?"

"Two lumps, please. Cyanide emits a very strong odor and the killer risked someone, perhaps even the victim, catching the smell. But then again, the murder took place at a crowded social occasion. There would have been a number of strong scents in the air—food, wine, ladies' perfume. Besides, not everyone has the ability to smell that particular odor."

She handed him his mug. "What other uses does the poison have?"

He thought for a moment. "I'm no expert but I know it's used in manufacturing and in mining . . ." He suddenly grinned. "And I knew a chap at university who used it to kill butterflies."

"What on earth did he have against butterflies?" She was outraged. "Why would anyone want to harm those beautiful creatures?"

"He wasn't trying to harm them, he was trying to study them," Bosworth explained. "He dissolved a few grams at the bottom of his specimen jars and when he popped the creatures inside, they died without damaging their bodies. I know it sounds cruel, but that is how scientific knowledge is gained, and without science we'd still be living in the dark ages."

Mrs. Jeffries thought that sometimes they still were, but she wasn't going to debate the point. "Be that as it may"—she sniffed disapprovingly—"I think killing those lovely insects is dreadfully mean. I hope obtaining the report didn't cause you any problems." She took a drink from her own mug. "I know that the murder wasn't in your district and I don't want to cause you any trouble."

"You didn't. Pendleton knew I'd want to see it," he muttered. He continued reading as he spoke. "Besides, I'm a police surgeon myself and everyone knows I'm interested in the more scientific aspects of murder." He flipped to the next page. "I've noticed that some of my colleagues are now employing my methods to some degree; they're measuring wounds and, on his last case, Pendleton even drew a diagram to ascertain the correct size and shape of the fatal blow the victim had suffered.

So asking for copies of reports outside my district is quite normal procedure for me . . ." His voice trailed off.

Mrs. Jeffries was wise enough to keep silent. She sipped her tea in the quiet room. Finally, he looked up at her.

He looked up and met her gaze. "The postmortem did reveal something else."

"What would that be?"

"Arlette Banfield was pregnant. She was a good three months along."

"I'm sorry, Inspector, but I don't know Mrs. Kimball's address." Mrs. Peyton sighed heavily and crossed the foyer toward the double doors of the drawing room. "And with the funeral tomorrow, we're very busy so I've no time to track it down for you. I'll get Mrs. Banfield; she'll know where the woman lives."

The two policemen were back at the Banfield house. They had planned on interviewing all the others who were sitting at the table with Arlette Banfield, but after what Henrietta Fetchman had revealed, Witherspoon had thought it best to speak to Rosalind Kimball without delay. Unfortunately, they'd discovered that not only had the lady left the Banfield house but she'd neglected to give her address to the police.

"Thank you," Witherspoon said as the housekeeper disappeared into the drawing room. He turned to Barnes. "I'm not looking forward to this."

Barnes nodded in agreement and they both glanced at the closed doors as they heard voices being raised. A moment later, Geraldine Banfield, dressed from head to toe in black, stepped out and charged toward them.

"What is the meaning of this, Inspector? Can't you give us a moment's peace? Our household is in mourning." She halted in front of them and crossed her arms over her chest.

"I'm sorry to intrude, Mrs. Banfield, but it's an urgent matter and I'll not take very much of your time," he replied. "Can you please give us Mrs. Kimball's address? Apparently, she's gone and she didn't leave her address with the constable outside the gate."

"Mrs. Kimball went home, Inspector. The decorators were finished painting the inside of her house so she left."

"She was staying as your houseguest because her home was being painted?" Witherspoon asked.

"Yes, the fumes bothered her greatly, so I invited her to stay here. Mrs. Bickleton was already invited to stay, so I included Mrs. Kimball as well."

"Was Mr. Kimball not invited?" Barnes asked softly.

"No, the fumes didn't bother him. Why are you asking all these questions?" Her eyes narrowed suspiciously. "What do you want with Mrs. Kimball? She was nowhere near Arlette when it happened. She was sitting with me and two other ladies."

"Nonetheless, we need to speak with her," Witherspoon replied politely.

"That's ridiculous. Mrs. Kimball is from one of the finest families in England. She's nothing to do with this matter, and I'm not going to disturb her with an unnecessary and intrusive visit from you." With a rustle of her skirts, she turned on her heel.

Barnes was having none of that. "Was there a reason Mrs. Kimball left so suddenly?"

She stopped but didn't turn to look at them.

"I would think that when the wife of one's host has been murdered, the least one could do is cooperate with the police," he continued. "But then again, maybe Mrs. Kimball's lack of cooperation has something to do with the fact that she very recently threatened the victim."

She whirled back to face them, her mouth open in surprise and her eyes as wide as saucers. "How on earth did you find out—"

"What do you mean, she threatened my wife?" Lewis Banfield's voice cut through the air like a knife.

"Lewis, please, you don't understand," Geraldine began.

He sliced his hand through the air impatiently. "I don't understand," he repeated. He'd come out of the drawing room and he now closed the door very softly. "I heard every word, Geraldine, and I've got one question for you and one question only: why is it that, at every turn, you're doing your best to stop the police from finding out who killed my wife?"

"Oh, Lewis, how can you say such a thing?" she cried. Her eyes filled with tears and she grabbed his arm. "I'm only thinking of the family."

"Rosalind Kimball isn't a member of our family," he snapped.

"Of course she isn't, but she's nothing to do with Arlette's murder . . ."

"How do you know?" he yelled. "If she threatened Arlette, maybe she was the one to slip her the poison."

"She wouldn't do such a horrid thing." Geraldine sobbed. "Oh dear, I know I've handled this badly, but I'm an old woman, Lewis. I was just trying to protect one of my friends. She did something very silly and lost her temper. But she was so upset about Arlette's interfering in your business—"

"Arlette didn't interfere," he said forcefully. "She told me the truth, which is more than you ever did, Aunt Geraldine. You've known about Gregory Kimball's disgusting habits for years and you never said a word."

"I know, I know," Geraldine cried. "I should have said something, but it isn't the sort of subject gentlewomen can speak about."

"Gentlewomen? Have you gone mad? I was getting ready to lend that drug-addicted reprobate thousands of pounds and you were concerned with your own sensibilities about discussing such an ugly matter? Ye gods, Aunt Geraldine, if you couldn't bring yourself to speak of it, you could have written me a note. Thank goodness Arlette wasn't as foolish as you."

"I know I should have been more forthcoming, but she's my friend and she was desperate."

Witherspoon glanced at Barnes, who gave a barely perceptible shrug indicating that he didn't know whether or not to put a stop to this exchange. The inspector decided to say nothing. Perhaps they could learn something useful from the emotional histrionics of a family in grief. He felt a tad guilty, but not guilty enough to stop listening.

But apparently Lewis had had enough. He looked at the two policemen. "I'm so sorry, this must be awful for you. But then again, in your line of work, I imagine you're used to such displays."

"There's no need to apologize," Witherspoon said.

"We do understand. You've lost a loved one in the most horrible manner possible and, at the same time, you've family members who feel it is their duty to protect your privacy."

"That's exactly right, Inspector," Geraldine said quickly. "I want to protect both Lewis' privacy and Arlette's memory. It's a matter of family honor."

"Then I suggest you give us Rosalind Kimball's address," Barnes added dryly. "We need to speak with her."

"It's number twelve Chelton Lane in Mayfair," Geraldine replied. "And all I was doing was trying to protect a silly old woman who'd done something very, very foolish."

"Something foolish like threatening my wife." Lewis smiled sadly. "And you didn't seem to think that was worth telling the police."

Tears flooded her eyes again. "It wasn't like that at all." She pulled a black handkerchief out of her pocket and swiped at her cheeks. "I'm so sorry, Lewis. Please forgive me; you know I'd never do anything to harm either you or Arlette. I'm so sorry that she's gone now. But after it happened and we knew she'd been murdered, Rosalind was terrified the police would think the worst. I've known her since we were girls and I know she's not capable of doing violence. I had to help her. It was the only honorable thing to do."

"When did she leave here?" Barnes interjected.

"She went home yesterday." She turned to face them again. "Please understand, Constable. She was desperately frightened. She knew that you'd find out she'd threatened Arlette and she was terrified you'd arrest her. I kept telling her not to worry, that even the police understood when someone was just being overly dramatic and making wild statements they certainly didn't mean."

"But she did mean it; she must have," Lewis said dully, "because now my sweet Arlette is dead."

"But Rosalind didn't kill her," Geraldine protested. "Arlette was probably murdered by one of those high-strung artists that were here that night. You know what they're like, Lewis, they take offense at the least little thing and see insults where none are intended."

"Was there any particular artistic person who had a reason to be upset with Mrs. Banfield?" Witherspoon looked at Geraldine as he spoke, but it was Lewis who answered.

"Julian Hammond, for one," he murmured thoughtfully. "He's a sculptor. Arlette posed for him before we were married. I was surprised to see him at the ball. He and Arlette had had some sort of disagreement."

"But Arlette asked me to put him on the guest list." Geraldine tucked her handkerchief into her sleeve.

"Why was Mr. Hammond upset with your wife?" Barnes asked.

Lewis shook his head. "I don't know the details, but I know they had words. Arlette told me he was angry with her because of some sort of business arrangement she'd made with a statue he'd done of her."

"Then why did she invite him to the ball?" Barnes shifted his weight a little. He wished someone had asked them to sit down.

He hesitated briefly. "She didn't say specifically, but

I think she wanted to make up with him. Hammond's a dear friend to the Montroses and I think being estranged from him upset her greatly. I know she was delighted to see him come down the receiving line."

"What's Mr. Hammond's address?" Witherspoon asked.

Lewis frowned. "I'm not sure, but it must be written down somewhere; he was sent an invitation."

"It's on the list that Arlette gave me," Geraldine offered. She glanced at the inspector. "If you'll wait just a moment, I'll get it for you."

"Would you care for another cup of tea?" Mrs. Goodge asked the elderly woman sitting across from her at the kitchen table.

Charlotte Temple, former cook to Lady Emma Stafford, shoved her cup toward the teapot and nodded vigorously. She was a tall, thin woman wearing spectacles over her watery blue eyes. She had a sharp blade of a nose and thin, downcast lips. She was dressed in a brown-and-green-checked suit coat over a dark, hunter green day dress. "That's very kind of you, Mrs. Goodge, very kind indeed, and I'll have another one of your delicious scones if I may."

"I'm so glad you came to see me." Mrs. Goodge poured the tea and put another scone on the saucer. "I wasn't sure if you still lived in London. It's been so many years since we worked together I wasn't certain you'd even remember me."

"Of course I'd remember you," the old woman said sharply. "I'm not senile yet, despite what my nephew's wife says. Truth to tell, Mrs. Goodge, it was Annie who insisted I acknowledge your note and accept your invitation. I wasn't going to; we may have worked together, but our stations were far apart. I was the head cook and you were a scullery."

Mrs. Goodge gasped. She couldn't believe her ears; she'd remembered Charlotte Temple as a stickler for the rules when they'd worked in Lord Warbutton's household years ago, but she'd never dreamed the old fool had clung to her hidebound snobbery since she'd retired. Good gracious, who on earth did the woman think she was, the ruddy Queen?

Mrs. Goodge wasn't having any of this. There were other ways to find out information about their case. She pushed her cup to one side, shoved her chair back, and rose to her feet. "I'm sorry you feel that way. I only sent you the invitation to morning tea because I ran into Bessie Jones the other day at the chemist's. She mentioned you lived with family and that you didn't get out much. I pitied you, but obviously I've wasted my time."

The old woman's mouth formed a surprised O before she recovered herself and glared at Mrs. Goodge. "I'll not have the likes of you pityin' me."

"I'll pity anyone I bloomin' well please," she cried. "So you can get off your high horse, Charlotte Temple. You're no better than the rest of us that have to work for a living, but at least I won't end up having to take charity from family."

Fred, who'd been sleeping on the rug in front of the cooker, reared up and fixed his attention on the two women.

"Charity, is that what that stupid Bessie told you?" She snorted in derision. "Don't believe a word she says. I pay for my keep."

"Yes, I'm sure you do, and from what I understand that's the only way they'd take you in," Mrs. Goodge yelled. She was so furious, she was simply saying the nastiest things that popped into her head. She had spent years overcoming her tendency to let her tongue run away with her when she lost her temper and she thought she'd succeeded in overcoming that character flaw. Apparently, she was wrong.

"At least I had enough money saved up to stop working when I got old," Charlotte charged. "And I might pay my own way, but that's better than having to step down in the world to keep a roof over my head."

"What do you mean by that?" Mrs. Goodge put her hands on her hips. Fred got to his feet, his attention focused on the visitor.

Charlotte Temple smiled maliciously. "You got sacked from the position you had before this one, a proper position in a proper house, I might add, not a policeman's home!"

Mrs. Goodge drew a long, harsh breath. A low growl came from the dog and his hackles rose along the ridge of his back. She forced herself to calm down. Fred was fiercely protective and if the tension in the kitchen got any thicker, he might attack. "Sit down, boy," she said soothingly. "It's alright, you lie back down now. It's fine."

Fred cocked his head to one side and stared at her for a few seconds. Then he wagged his tail and flopped back down on the rug. But he didn't go to sleep; he watched Charlotte Temple.

She shifted uncomfortably. "I'd do something about that dog if I were you. He ought not be allowed into the kitchen. Lady Stafford would never have allowed an animal in the kitchen. It's indecent."

"I think you'd better go," Mrs. Goodge said calmly. "I shouldn't have invited you here. Bessie was right about you."

"What did she say about me?" Charlotte demanded. She made no move to get up.

"What does it matter?" Mrs. Goodge protested. "You're too good for the likes of me, so please, just put on your hat and gloves and go."

She didn't respond; she simply stared across the kitchen toward the window.

"Mrs. Temple, didn't you hear me? I said you'd better go."

Charlotte Temple started and then turned her head and gazed at Mrs. Goodge. She frowned in confusion. "What were we talking about?"

Stunned, the cook gaped at her.

"Oh dear, did I say something wrong?" Charlotte's eyes filled with tears. "I did, didn't I?"

Mrs. Goodge found her tongue. "Well, yes, you said some very mean things and I lost my composure and replied in a way that certainly didn't do me any credit, either."

"Now I remember." She sniffed and swiped at her cheeks with a wrinkled, blue-veined hand. "I'm so sorry, I didn't mean to be so rude. Sometimes I don't know why

I say what I say. I'm no better than you are, Mrs. Goodge.
I got sacked from the Stafford house myself and I wish
to God I had another job, even one with a policeman. But
I'm too old to be of much use to anyone and no one wants
me. I can't go home this early. Annie will make a fuss.
She said she wanted the house to herself for a few hours,
and John—that's my nephew—he always takes her part."

Mrs. Goodge was deeply ashamed of her own out-
burst. Charlotte Temple was a pathetic old woman who
sorely needed a friend. For a brief moment, she saw
her own life as it might have been if she'd not come to
Upper Edmonton Gardens. She might have had to live
in a place where she really wasn't wanted; she might
have had to dance to the tune of another person who
didn't much like her; and, most horrible of all, she might
have died clinging to the same silly snobberies as poor
Charlotte. She pitied her most of all for that, for not
having taken a good look at the world around her and
made up her own mind about what was right, proper,
and decent. "Then please stay and have more tea. We'll
talk and we'll both watch our tongues. Being told I'm
less than you because forty years ago we had different
positions in the same household isn't very nice. Work is
work, Mrs. Temple, and we do what we need to do to
survive, but that doesn't mean we need to pass judgment
on others to make ourselves feel better."

"I know, I know." Charlotte smiled broadly. "I didn't
really mean a word that I said, Mrs. Goodge. Sometimes
I let my tongue run away with me because I'm so miserable in my own life, do you know what I mean? But
I promise I'll not be rude again. Truth to tell, I was so

happy when I got your note. No one has invited me out in ages."

Mrs. Goodge sat back down. She suspected that along with being old, unwanted, and lonely, the woman was also going a bit senile. "I'm glad we've cleared this up. Now, tell me what you've been doing all these years. Why don't you start with your last household, Lady Stafford's, wasn't it? Wasn't she one of the guests at that party where that poor woman was poisoned?"

Wiggins spotted Inspector Witherspoon and Constable Barnes as they came out the front door of the Banfield house. He whirled about and quickly walked the other way, toward the high street and the shops. Blast, he was having the devil's worst luck today. It was even worse than yesterday. He'd not found anyone willing to have a chat and now he was hungry and thirsty. Maybe he'd stop in at a café for a cup of tea. He felt in his trousers pocket for coins, pulled out a fistful, and saw that he had enough. He shoved them back inside and went toward the corner, taking care to keep pace with a slow-moving cooper's van in case the inspector or a constable who might recognize him glanced toward this side of the square.

"Excuse me, you dropped something," a female voice said from behind him. He winced, hoping the inspector was out of earshot. Turning, he kept his head lowered as the van moved past him. But he was in luck and the only person close by was the young lady who'd just spoken to him.

She pointed to a paper lying on the pavement. "That fell out of your pocket," she told him.

"Thanks ever so much." He retraced his steps and picked it up. It was a piece of plain notepaper folded in half. He always carried notepaper; you never knew when it would come in handy. "That was very nice of you."

She shrugged and gave him a shy smile. She was stick thin, pale skinned, and very young. She wore a gray skirt and a white blouse that had seen better days; the material was frayed at the sleeves and along the wide collar. Her hair was brown and tucked up under a straw hat. "Anyone would 'ave done the same."

He glanced up and down the street. There was no sign of the inspector and at least this girl appeared willing to speak to him. "My name is Jasper Hill." He extended his hand. "And I'd be pleased to thank you for your kindness by buying you a cup of tea. There's a very respectable café around the corner."

"Oh, I shouldn't." She shook his hand. "I'm Emma Carr. I'm just on my way to the shops."

"Surely your mistress wouldn't begrudge you a quick bit of refreshment," he persisted. "This paper I dropped 'as an address on it and if I lost it, I'd be in trouble. You've saved me job and I'd be ever so grateful if you'd let me show ya my appreciation properly."

Emma giggled. "How did you know I was in service? Oh, never mind, it's the skirt, isn't it?"

"The housemaids at my household wear skirts of the same color," he lied. It hadn't been her clothing, but her manner and speech. This was a rich neighborhood and the only way she'd be here was if she was working close by. "And there's nothin' wrong with bein' in service, it's an honest living."

"That's true enough. Alright, then, you can buy me a cup of tea," she agreed. "My mistress won't be home for ages and when she's out, Cook sneaks off and has a nap, so no one will miss me."

Wiggins tucked the paper into his shirt pocket and gave her his elbow. A few moments later, he escorted her into the café and led her to a table by the window. "Would you like a bun as well?" he asked. Many households were stingy when it came to feeding the servants, so when he had the chance, he always liked to offer a bit of food.

"That would be lovely." She smiled broadly and he couldn't help but notice that despite her thinness, she was quite pretty. "And I'll have two sugars in my tea, please."

He went to the counter and ordered. While he waited, he glanced around the café. It was small, with only a short serving counter and few tables, not the sort of place the gentry would frequent. But even posh neighborhoods needed places to serve their local working people.

"Here you are." The serving woman put two steaming cups of tea and a plate of pastries on the counter in front of him. He paid, then picked up the cups and took them to the table. He made a second trip for the plate of buns.

Her eyes widened when she saw the plate of treats.

"Help yourself," he offered. He was glad he'd ordered extra.

"Thank you." She picked up a pastry, took a bite, and swallowed. "This is very nice of you. Do you work around 'ere?"

"No, my household is in Kensington. I'm only in this neighborhood because my guv sent me to do an errand."

He reached for a bun. "And thanks to you, I've not lost the address. Do you work close by?"

"Yes, I'm the tweeny at a household on Wallington Square."

Wiggins feigned surprise. "Wallington Square, why, that's the place where I need to go."

"You were just there." She laughed and stuffed another bite into her mouth.

"Was I?" He knew that, of course, but he wanted to keep her talking and he'd learned that pretending ignorance often made people eager to show off how much they knew. "Cor blimey, that makes me feel a right idiot. I'll bet I was right by number eleven."

"Oh, my goodness, you were looking for the Banfield house?" She leaned forward eagerly. "They've just had the most awful murder there . . ."

"I know, that's why my guv sent me 'ere. I've a proper letter of condolence to give them," he explained. "But I couldn't find the ruddy house. Do you know anything about them? I know I shouldn't be so curious, but when there's been a murder, it's 'ard not to be interested. I 'eard it was the young mistress of the household that were done in, that she was poisoned."

"It was. Pity, really, that it was young Mrs. Banfield that were killed. She's the one the servants liked the best." She took a quick sip of tea.

"That's what I overheard my guv sayin' to his missus this morning." Wiggins nodded in agreement. "Mind you, sometimes my guv says things he don't know, if you know what I mean. Sometimes he likes to make 'imself sound important when all 'e's done is read the morning papers."

"I know what you mean. My mistress is a bit like that as well." She put her cup down and giggled. "She was goin' on and on at breakfast about the Banfields like they was friends. But Mr. Banfield barely nods to her when he passes her on the street, and old Mrs. Banfield won't even do that much—she pretends not to see her."

"So your mistress wasn't at the ball? She didn't see the murder?"

"She weren't invited, but when her lady friends come over for tea, she talked about it like she'd been there." She made a face. "But the truth is, I know more about them than she does. I have my afternoon out with their tweeny and she tells me all sorts of interestin' things."

He pretended to be impressed. "Cor blimey, you've a friend in the Banfield household? I'll bet you know a lot."

"Well, I wouldn't say I know everything, but Fanny—she's my friend—she does talk about the family. I know servants aren't supposed to do that—you know, tellin' tales about their households—but it's only natural to chat about it, isn't it? My household isn't very interesting. There's just the master and mistress and they wouldn't raise their voices if the ruddy house was on fire." She giggled. "Thank goodness I met Fanny, otherwise I'd have to take my afternoon out on my own and that's never very nice."

Wiggins drew back. Most housemaids in London went home to visit their families on their afternoon off. "You don't go see your family?"

"My parents are both gone and my sister went to Australia when she got married last year. But she promised she'd send for me once she and Liam got settled in. That's why I don't mind being in service. I'll be off to Australia soon and you've got to work hard if you want to make a go of it there. But I'm not scared of a bit of hard work."

"I hope she sends for you soon," he replied. "But anyway, what did your friend tell you about the Banfields?" He cautioned himself not to expect too much. Emma might be as prone to exaggeration as her mistress.

"Well, Fanny says that none of the servants like the older Mrs. Banfield. She's a right old tartar."

"That's what my guv said to his missus," he agreed.

"She's always checking to make sure that poor Fanny is doin' her work properly." Emma leaned across the table, her expression serious. "You know what I mean, running her fingers along the banisters and checking the very tops of the tallboys on the landings. I feel ever so sorry for Fanny." She popped the last bite of the bun into her mouth.

"But lots of households is real strict," he pushed.

"Yes, but Mrs. Banfield isn't just strict, she's downright mean. Two weeks ago when I met Fanny for our afternoon out, she told me her back was hurtin' like the very devil. Mrs. Banfield had sent her up to the attic to bring down one of her old trunks. When Fanny realized how heavy the ruddy thing was, she nipped downstairs to find a footman to help her with it, but Mrs. Banfield was standing in the hallway and told her to do it herself! Can you believe it? Poor Fanny is only a little slip of a thing and she had to drag that blooming trunk down three flights to Mrs. Banfield's room. Then an hour later she had to drag it back up to the attic." She shook her head in disgust. "Treatin' people like that is wrong, especially as all the old woman wanted was some silly book full of newspaper cuttings. Fanny saw it lying on her desk when she went in to dust."

"Why didn't she just have Fanny get her the book?" he mused. He was disappointed but determined not to let it show. Emma seemed a nice girl and it wasn't her fault that she didn't know anything about the Banfield household that might be useful. "Seems to me that would have been easier than draggin' a trunk to and fro."

She giggled again. "That's what Fanny thought."

The police station on Harrow Road was housed in a narrow redbrick building next to a pub. "This shouldn't take too long," Witherspoon said as he went up the short, wide steps to the front door. "We'll still have time to get to Mayfair and have a word with Mrs. Kimball." They'd stopped to pick up the reports and have a word with the local constables.

"I wish I'd been able to have a word with the Banfield butler," Barnes complained as he held open the door for the inspector. "But every time I tried to speak to him, he'd been sent off on an errand or had disappeared up to the attic."

Witherspoon stopped just inside the doorway. "Did you try to see him today?"

Barnes nodded. "Yes. When you pulled Mr. Banfield aside to get the address for Mrs. Banfield's parents, I nipped down to the kitchen and told Mrs. Peyton I'd like to have a word with the man. But he'd already left on an errand."

"Oh yes." Witherspoon sighed. "After that altercation with his aunt, it took Mr. Banfield quite a while to calm down and then it took him ages to lay hands on the

Montroses' street address. I wondered where you'd got to. Where had they sent the man?"

"To the Banfield summer house to pick up china and linens for the funeral." Barnes pursed his lips in disapproval. "Honest to goodness, you'd think these people would realize this is a murder investigation and stay still long enough for me to take their ruddy statements."

"Gracious, they sent the butler to do that? Why not a footman?" Witherspoon started across the gray linoleum floor toward the counter.

The constable followed. "Who knows? They're an odd bunch, if you ask me. But Mrs. Peyton said that Michaels is due back later this afternoon, so perhaps after we speak with Mrs. Kimball, I can nip back and take his statement."

Witherspoon's brows drew together in a frown. "Do you think he's been deliberately avoiding us?"

"No, I think the poor man's just been run ragged trying to get all the arrangements for the funeral reception done. According to the housekeeper, the Banfields are very particular when it comes to burying their dead. They actually have a set of funeral dishes they use for all the family funeral receptions. They've used them for the last hundred and fifty years and there is a special set of linens as well. All their tablecloths must be edged in black and none of the household will be allowed to smile until Arlette Banfield has been buried."

"Gracious, now I can understand why Mr. Banfield made such a fuss about draping his house in mourning cloth. He not only lost his wife, he's now got to go through all this rigmarole to get the poor lady laid to rest," Witherspoon murmured, his expression sympathetic.

The portly, balding police sergeant leaning on the counter straightened to attention. "Inspector Witherspoon, good day, sir." He nodded politely to Barnes.

"Good day, Sergeant," Witherspoon said. "I understand the reports on the violinist and the area search are ready."

"Yes, sir, they are ready for you." He reached under the counter and pulled out a brown file folder. He handed it to Witherspoon. "The violinist is a chap named Howard Thomson. He was very cooperative and answered all our questions. He claimed knocking over the music stands was just an accident."

Witherspoon laid the folder down and flipped it open. He pushed his spectacles up so he could read the report. After a moment, he said, "Did Mr. Thomson have any connection with the Banfield family prior to being hired to play at the ball?" He knew that coincidences did happen, but the timing of this one was very suspect. When Thomson knocked over those music stands, he created a diversion that might have given the killer the opportunity he or she needed.

"Not really, sir. Thomson admitted to meeting Lewis Banfield at the end of last year's ball when Mr. Banfield stopped to congratulate the musicians. But other than that, he claims he didn't know any of them personally."

"How did he get the job?" Barnes asked.

The sergeant blinked in surprise and glanced at the constable. "Through a theatrical agency in the Strand." He tore his gaze away from the constable and spoke to Witherspoon. "All the musicians were booked as a group. We checked with the agency and they confirmed Thomson's statement."

Barnes tried not to smile. He knew exactly what the sergeant was thinking. The fellow was shocked that the constable, as well as the inspector, was asking questions. "That's what Mrs. Peyton said as well."

The sergeant gave him a sharp look. "But we didn't just take the man's word. Thomson said that he is employed to play at the Gaiety Theatre on Saturday evenings, so I sent a couple of lads over to see what they could find out about him. Seems he's a bit of a showman and his taking that bow and larkin' about for the ball guests was very much in character."

"Excellent work, Sergeant." Witherspoon beamed in approval and then glanced at the report again. "I see that the search of the neighborhood hasn't turned up the missing champagne bottle."

"Sorry, Inspector, the lads did the best they could, but there were dozens and dozens of people there that night and when you add in the neighbors and the onlookers, there was so much confusion, no one could recall seein' it."

"We're aware of that, Sergeant. I'm sure your men made a very thorough job of it."

"Thank you, sir." He pointed to the paper in Witherspoon's hand. "As you can see from the report, none of the neighbors saw or heard anything useful. Mind you, I don't rightly see how they could have, seeing as it was such a madhouse. Though there was one other death in the neighborhood. Mr. Millhouse, who lives next door to the Banfields, claims that earlier this week, someone poisoned his cat. But his wife told the constable taking the report to pay him no mind; she said the cat was sixteen years old and that it died of old age." He grinned broadly.

"The constable did say Mr. Millhouse took great exception to his wife's words."

Witherspoon laughed, folded the report, and tucked it into his inside jacket pocket. "Your men have done an excellent job. Please let everyone involved know how much we appreciate their efforts and that all of you will be mentioned in our final report."

Barnes watched the sergeant's eyes widen in surprise. The man wasn't used to hearing words of gratitude from his betters. The constable smiled knowingly and the sergeant grinned back at him as he finally understood why everyone who'd ever worked with Gerald Witherspoon held the man in such high regard.

"Why, thank you, sir," he said to the inspector. "The men will appreciate hearing that. Is there anything else you'd like us to do?"

"Just keep an eye on the place and watch for anyone suspicious hanging about the area. As a matter of fact, if you can spare the manpower, I'd appreciate it if you could keep two men posted in Wallington Square."

CHAPTER 7

Mrs. Jeffries tiptoed past the kitchen and quietly slipped up the back stairs. Mrs. Goodge was talking to one of her sources and she didn't want to disturb them. As she went past the drawing room, she heard Phyllis moving about, so she continued on up to her own room. Opening her door, she stepped inside, went to the window, and drew the green-striped muslin curtain to one side.

She leaned against the window frame and stared out at the street without really seeing anything. Her mind was on the case. One part of her was starting to panic. To date, they'd learned a number of facts, but nothing was coming together in her mind. Absolutely nothing.

Despite their refusal of titles and royal honors, the Banfields were rich, important, and probably as arrogant as the most high-born of aristocrats. Yet oddly enough, according to what the inspector had told her, it wasn't the Banfield family who'd objected strongly to the marriage, it was Arlette's family. But that told her nothing. If the Montroses were so opposed to the marriage that they were willing to go to any length to stop it, they'd have murdered Lewis Banfield, not their own daughter.

She straightened her spine. It was too early to worry about finding patterns or theories that fit the few facts they had; she needed to know more. Taking a deep breath, she closed her eyes for a moment. She wasn't going to get all het up at this stage of the investigation. For goodness' sake, it had only been two days since the woman was murdered. What did she expect? Clairvoyant answers from the beyond, with the name of the killer in limelights? No, just because she'd been wrong and made a mistake in approaching Phyllis, that didn't mean her perceptual or analytical skills were dead and useless.

They'd solve this case. She had faith in herself and the others. They'd find out more and more bits and pieces and when the time was right, her mind would act of its own accord. When she had enough information, her own inner voice would come up with the answer.

She smiled as the thought came into her mind. She'd used the "inner voice" ploy a number of times on the inspector. She'd worked hard to convince him the hints and nudges she'd planted in his mind were his own idea. But the truth was, all human beings did indeed have an inner voice. Perhaps it was the mind making connections and seeing the patterns in a number of divergent facts or perhaps it was an intuitive leap into the dark that sometimes turned out to be correct, but whatever the cause of the phenomenon, she was now convinced the talent was universal. All one had to do was quiet one's mind and let it drift off where it would.

She took off her white cotton gloves and tossed them across the room to her bed before turning her attention back to the window. A hansom pulled up in front of the house and she held her breath, hoping it wasn't the inspector home this early. But it was only Mrs. Copley from next door coming back from her shopping.

Mrs. Jeffries was glad she'd gone to see Dr. Bosworth. At least now they knew what kind of poison had killed the victim. But that didn't help very much. Arlette Banfield had been murdered in full view of over two hundred people and, what was worse, any of them could have killed her.

The poison acted quickly and, from what she'd discovered from the doctor, was easy to obtain if one set one's mind to acquiring the lethal stuff. But what else had they learned? The victim was a free-spirited woman who clashed with the restrictions of the class she'd married into, but otherwise didn't appear to have any mortal enemies. But she must have had at least one. Someone had murdered her.

The slamming of a door snapped her out of her reverie. She glanced at the clock over her dresser and realized it was almost time for their afternoon meeting.

Mrs. Jeffries left her room and went down the front stairs. As she reached the bottom, Phyllis came out of the drawing room, a duster in her hand. "Mrs. Jeffries, may I have a word with you?"

"Right now?" She could hear the sound of crockery and the murmur of voices from the kitchen. "Can it wait?"

"It can. I see you're busy. I just wanted to explain

things a bit more—you know, why I was afraid to agree to help you and the others."

"You don't owe us an explanation." The housekeeper continued on down the hall to the back stairs.

"Yes, alright, then, I'll just finish up the drawing room."

"Go up to your room and have a rest, Phyllis," Mrs. Jeffries called as she started down the stairs. She felt guilty. She didn't want the girl to think she was angry at her for refusing to join their little band of sleuths. But she simply didn't have time to chat with her now. "You can finish the drawing room tomorrow."

Luty was coming up the back hall as she reached the bottom of the staircase. She stopped and waited for her.

"Is everyone else here?" Luty frowned irritably. "Dang, I knew I was goin' to be late. But I got stuck in the worst traffic jam on the Westminster Bridge."

"It certainly sounds as if we're the last to arrive," she replied as they went into the kitchen.

Mrs. Goodge, who was pouring tea, looked up. "Oh, good, you're here. We're anxious to get started."

"From the general air of excitement"—Mrs. Jeffries took her seat at the table—"it appears most of you have something to share. Who would like to go first?"

"I'll go," Smythe volunteered. "I went to Wallington Square and had a word with the drivers at the hansom stand on the Edgware Road. The Banfield household gives them lots of business, so every one of 'em knew who I was askin' about. One of the drivers told me that the Banfields generally send a footman over when they need a cab, but in the two weeks before the murder, the ladies of the household had taken to coming over themselves."

"Now, that is peculiar," Mrs. Goodge observed. "Even in these modern times, ladies don't generally do that sort of thing, not when they have footmen and housemaids to fetch for them."

"That's what I thought," Smythe agreed, "and truth to tell, the cabbies were a bit surprised as well."

"Which household ladies are we talking about specifically?" Hatchet helped himself to a slice of seedcake.

"As the drivers put it, young Mrs. Banfield, the elder Mrs. Banfield, and both the houseguests." He grinned. "They weren't so startled to see Arlette get her own cab—apparently she does that all the time—but they were right shocked when the houseguests each come along and then Geraldine Banfield did it twice in a two-week period."

"Did the drivers recall where they took the ladies?" Mrs. Jeffries asked.

"Arlette Banfield went to her regular places: an art gallery on New Bond Street or to an address off Russell Square."

"Her parents live in that area," Mrs. Jeffries volunteered.

"Geraldine Banfield got her own hansom twice and both times she went to Paddington Station."

"What about the houseguests?" Luty asked. "Where did they go?"

He shook his head with a frown. "The drivers couldn't tell which lady was which; they only knew they'd picked both of them up at previous times from Wallington Square. But one of them went to the entrance to Hyde Park and they picked up another woman, a younger one, and went on to an office building off Haymarket," he replied. "The second time, which was the day of the murder, one of them went to

Battersea and went into a shop. But like I said, the drivers who took them didn't know which lady was which."

"Good gracious, why would anyone want to be taken to Battersea?" Mrs. Goodge exclaimed. "What kind of shop could there be in that neighborhood? It's filled with nasty-smelling factories and gasworks."

"Maybe that's precisely why she went," Mrs. Jeffries mused. She was thinking of all the places one could obtain cyanide. As the good doctor had stressed, there were any number of legitimate industrial uses for the stuff. "Dr. Bosworth confirmed that Arlette was killed by cyanide poisoning—and what better place to obtain it than a factory of some sort or another?"

"But it's not like they sell it on the streets," Luty pointed out. "That stuff is deadly and most places keep it under lock and key. I know for a fact it's used in silver mining, but no one that I know was ever careless enough to just leave it lyin' about for any Tom, Dick, or Harry to pick up."

Mrs. Jeffries hadn't thought of that. "True, but if one wanted the poison, one could bribe someone who had access to it, couldn't one?"

"I think we ought to find out exactly which woman it was that was taken to Battersea." Betsy looked at her husband. "Do you think the driver would recognize her?"

Smythe looked doubtful. "I don't think so; he said the lady was wearin' a bonnet with a blue veil and a matching blue jacket. That's 'ow he knew she were from the Banfield house. He'd picked her up there only the day before."

"That's simple enough to find out, then," she replied. "We'll have to discover which of those two ladies has a blue jacket and a bonnet with a matching veil."

"I can do that," Wiggins offered. He thought that might be the sort of thing that Emma Carr would know. "I'll 'ave a quick word with the servants in the area and find out what's what."

"Good," Mrs. Jeffries said. "I'll go next, then, if no one objects." She told them about her visit to Dr. Bosworth and what he'd said about the poison. But before she could tell them about the other pertinent fact she'd learned, they began speaking.

Hatchet interrupted first, his eyes narrowed in thought. "Now that we know for certain it was cyanide, that does broaden the field a bit, and apparently there's any number of ways to get one's hands on the lethal stuff. As has been rightly pointed out, it has many industrial uses. I'll wager there are dozens of factories in Battersea or in London where one can obtain it."

"But like the doctor said, a factory isn't the only place one can find it," Mrs. Goodge pointed out before Mrs. Jeffries could tell them she wasn't finished. "When I was first in service," the cook continued, "there was a rumor that the lady of the manor in the next village had murdered her husband by splitting open peach pits and pounding out the insides before adding the mash to his pudding. Mind you, she was never arrested and nothing was ever proved. But she was seen on the morning he died, climbing a peach tree."

"Cor blimey, peach pits is 'ard," Wiggins said. "'Ow did she crack 'em open?"

"I don't know." The cook grinned. "And you're right, of course: getting a pit open wouldn't be easy."

"Perhaps she was really determined," Ruth suggested with a laugh.

Mrs. Jeffries glanced at the clock. She'd wait to the end to tell them the rest. "We'd better move along, it's getting late."

"That's all I've got," Smythe said.

"I'll go next," Luty offered. Without mentioning the name of her source, she told them what she'd discovered about the Banfields from her visit to John Widdowes. "So it looks like the family wasn't as rich as everyone thought, at least not back when Garrett Banfield was running the business."

"It certainly sounds as though if it hadn't been for Lewis Banfield's business acumen, the family might have been faced with a dire financial situation," Ruth murmured.

"Well, my source didn't exactly say that, but he implied that Lewis had come along just in time," Luty agreed. "Actually, he did let it slip that one of the lenders was gittin' ready to foreclose on the Banfield country estate. Garrett Banfield had mortgaged the place to invest in a tea plantation in the Far East. But the feller had the worst luck. First the crop was wiped out two years in a row with bad typhoons and then the tea leaves got tainted with some plant disease. The plantation ended up being abandoned and all the investors lost everything."

Hatchet nodded. "Investing in the Far East is never the sure thing that people think it is. Fortunes are often made, but they're just as easily lost." He'd spent a number of years traveling the world and knew firsthand what life in the tropics entailed.

"So if old Mr. Banfield hadn't died, there's a good chance the Banfields would have ended up broke?" Betsy clarified. An idea had popped into her head, but as she asked the question, it popped right back out again and she couldn't recall the details.

Luty winced. "My source didn't come right out and say that, but he sure hinted things was goin' in that direction. But then old Garrett had a heart attack and Lewis took over. That's all I found out today." She grinned at her butler. "How'd you do?"

"Not as well as you, madam, but I had a fruitful encounter of my own," he declared. He was bluffing; he'd gone to see his friends the Manleys, but they were out of town and not due back until tomorrow, so he'd tracked down another source. But he hadn't learned much.

"What did you find out?" Mrs. Jeffries interjected. Luty and Hatchet were very competitive with one another and she wanted to get this meeting moving along.

"Not much more than we already know," he admitted with a shrug. "Namely, that it was Arlette Banfield's family that objected to the marriage. But I did hear that her father, Crispin Montrose, was so upset over the match he almost didn't go to the wedding. But he changed his mind at the last minute and showed up at the ceremony. The Montrose family is well thought of in London's art community. Before she married, Arlette did a lot of modeling for painters and sculptors. My source told me that the piece she posed for before her wedding was done in two mediums, a small one in brass and a large one in stone. Both are supposedly exquisite, and the sculptor, an artist named Julian Hammond, gave her the brass statue as a wedding present."

"I wonder why her family was so against her marrying Lewis Banfield," Ruth muttered. "I know what

Elizabeth Montrose told the inspector, that she had nothing but contempt for the class of people the Banfields represented, but honestly, it does seem a bit of an overreaction. Do you think there might be another reason she didn't want them to marry?"

Mrs. Jeffries cocked her head to one side. "You might have something there. The Montroses do seem to have been unduly upset. Perhaps we ought to investigate this further." She looked at Ruth. "Do you think you could find out about this for us?"

Ruth thought for a moment and then nodded. "I've a number of acquaintances who know everything that goes on in London society. I'm sure one of them will be able to shed a bit more light on the Montroses' objection to the wedding. Considering that I found out nothing useful today, it's the very least I can do."

"Find out if the two families have any history with one another," Betsy suggested. "Sometimes old sins cast long shadows." She looked at Hatchet. "Are you done?"

"I am," he replied. "I'm seeing a good source tomorrow and I hope I'll have something more to report at our afternoon meeting."

"I'll go next, then," Betsy said. "I went back and had another go at the local merchants, but I didn't find out anything new. Sorry, I tried my best, but most of the clerks had very little to say about the Banfields."

"You've done as well as the rest of us," Smythe said dryly.

"I heard a few things," Wiggins volunteered. "It's nothin' particularly about the murder, but it does give us an idea of what kind of 'ousehold the Banfields really 'ave." He told them about his encounter with Emma Carr.

When he'd finished, he shrugged and said, "Like I told ya, it weren't much. But I feel lucky to 'ave found anyone to talk to from that neighborhood. I've larked about the area for two days and she was the only servant I could find."

"Can I go now?" the cook asked. "I need to get the roast out of the oven and let it rest properly before the inspector gets home." She paused briefly and, when no one objected, she continued. "I had a source in today that knew a bit about the Banfields from many years ago. She used to work for Lady Stafford, who was one of the women that was sittin' with Geraldine Banfield at the ball."

"Used to work?" Wiggins repeated. "You mean she don't work there now?"

Mrs. Goodge wasn't offended by the question. "I'm afraid not, and she didn't really have all that much to say. She just rambled on about how grand the Stafford household was when she worked there. When I finally managed to get her to concentrate on anything Lady Stafford might have said about the Banfields, the only thing she remembered was one time when Lady Stafford and Mrs. Banfield had had too much to drink she overheard them reminiscin' about how they'd once borrowed the housemaids' cloaks and snuck into the courtroom during the assizes at Aylesbury."

"That's an odd thing to do," Ruth said.

The cook shrugged and pushed back her chair. She really did need to check the roast. "Apparently there was some Quaker on trial for murderin' his mistress, and back in those days such things weren't even spoken about in the presence of well-bred young ladies." She moved toward the cooker, grabbing a tea towel on her way. "But they'd heard about it and read about it in the broadsides, so they slipped off when no one was lookin' and managed to get inside." She opened the oven door and, using the tea towel to protect her fingers, pulled out the roasting pan. "This looks about right."

"Is that all?" Mrs. Jeffries asked.

"Yes." The cook put the roasting pan on a large metal trivet. She grabbed a sheet of brown paper she'd cut earlier and placed it on top of the meat. Then she draped the whole thing with a clean tea towel. "Sorry, I know it isn't very much, but so far, my sources have really let me down."

"It's early days yet," Mrs. Jeffries commented. "And we often go through a period of time when it seems as if we're not doing very well." She glanced at Ruth. "You really didn't learn anything today?"

Ruth forced a smile onto her face. Since the murder, she'd endured two boring social events and learned nothing, but she wasn't giving up. "No one at the luncheon knew anything. It was very annoying. But I've a dinner party this evening and tomorrow I'm going to the funeral and the reception afterwards at the Banfield house. I have high hopes I'll hear something useful at one of those places."

"I'm sure you will. If we keep asking questions, someone eventually tells us a pertinent piece of information. Actually, I wasn't quite finished with my report from Dr. Bosworth. He told me another fact that may or may not end up being significant." Mrs. Jeffries looked over her shoulder, making sure that Phyllis hadn't slipped down the staircase. She didn't want the girl to overhear what she was about to say. The maid was easily shocked.

"According to the postmortem report, Arlette Banfield was going to have a child. She was three months along."

"Oh no, the poor woman, how awful," Betsy cried. "It's bad enough to be murdered in such a horrible way, but to know your child was dying as well."

Smythe looked at Betsy. There was a disapproving frown on her pretty face, but she didn't look unduly distressed. Relieved, he relaxed.

"None of the people we've talked to have mentioned she was in the family way," Wiggins murmured. "Maybe she didn't know she was goin' to be a mother."

The women all looked at him. After a few moments, Mrs. Jeffries said, "I imagine she had some idea she was with child." She wasn't sure how to continue. Everyone at the table knew the facts of life, but Wiggins was a single lad and she wasn't sure he really understood the details that pertained to women.

She was saved from further comment by Smythe, who said, "More importantly, I wonder if Lewis Banfield knew he was to be a father."

"Why wouldn't she have told him?" Betsy said. "They'd been married for enough time to stop tongues wagging."

"True, but as Wiggins has just pointed out, no one has mentioned her condition to either the inspector or to us. Seems to me that there was a reason she wasn't sharin' the 'appy news with everyone."

"You do look a bit tired, sir," Mrs. Jeffries said to Witherspoon as she handed him a glass of sherry. She sat down opposite him and put her own drink down on the side table. The debate about Arlette Banfield's reasons for not mentioning her delicate condition to anyone had been cut short by the unexpected arrival of the inspector. He'd come home early. When they heard the hansom pull up out front, they'd barely had time to get everyone safely out the back door before he came in the front.

Witherspoon smiled thinly. "It wasn't so much fatigue that brought me home as it was this wretched headache."

"Shall I get you a powder, sir?" she asked. "I bought some Cockle's headache powder for the household and I hear it works very well." She studied him for a moment, hoping he wasn't taking ill. Witherspoon wasn't a complainer. If he came home this early, he must be in severe pain.

"I'll have it later," he replied. "Right now I'd like to relax for a few moments."

"Good idea, sir," she agreed. "Was your day particularly difficult?"

"It was the usual dashing about trying to gain information and that sort of thing. As a matter of fact, we found out quite a bit today. I'm just not sure that it's going to help me catch the person who murdered Mrs. Banfield. The day started off well enough. Sir Ralph Fetchman and his wife were very cooperative." He took a sip from his glass and told her about the visit to the Fetchman house. "Naturally, after we heard about the altercation at the art gallery, we decided to go see Rosalind Kimball. But she'd already left the Banfield household and had neglected to give her address to the constables in the square. But then again, the encounter ended up being quite enlightening. Lewis Banfield and his aunt had words again." He told her about everything that had happened. "Unfortunately, by then, my head had begun to hurt and I remembered we needed to nip into the local station."

"Whatever for?"

"They did the interviews with the local people and they were the ones conducting the search of the area," he replied. He went on to describe the visit, smiling as he told her about the alleged poisoning of the Millhouse cat. When he'd finished, he sighed. "I say, my headache seems to be easing somewhat, but it's still there."

"Headaches are so unpleasant. I take it you'll be interviewing Mrs. Kimball tomorrow?"

"Indeed we will, but the funeral is tomorrow morning, so we probably won't be able to speak to her until late in the afternoon. Perhaps we'll see or hear something useful at the funeral." It had become customary for police officers to discreetly attend the services for their victims.

"What a strange day you've had, sir," she said softly. Her mind was racing, she had so much she wanted to convey to him, but right now wasn't the best time. When one's head hurt, one wasn't usually receptive to hints. But there was something she wanted to know. "Did you have an opportunity to look at the postmortem report, sir?"

He yawned and took another drink. "Not as yet, but I expect it'll not tell us much more than we already know."

"Then you'll be going into the station tomorrow morning?" She'd make sure to mention Arlette's pregnancy to Constable Barnes. He'd ensure that Witherspoon had a look at the postmortem report. She had a feeling it was very important.

"We usually do." He yawned again, drained his glass,

set it on the side table, and got up. "I'll take that headache powder now. Have Phyllis bring it up to my room,
please. I've time for a short nap before dinner."

The next morning, Mrs. Jeffries had a quick word with
Barnes when he came to fetch the inspector. "Now, that
is interesting," he said. "We've not heard so much as a
whisper about her being with child."

"Perhaps she'd not told anyone," Mrs. Goodge suggested as Samson, her mean-tempered, fat cat, leapt
up onto her lap. She shoved back from the table as he
curled his great bulk into a ball and flicked his tail in
displeasure. "Some women don't like speaking of such
personal matters to anyone, not even their husbands."

Barnes shook his head and rose to his feet. "That may
be true enough, but from what we know of Arlette Banfield, I don't think she'd be unduly shy about such a thing."

"I agree." Mrs. Jeffries got up as well. "It would be out
of character for her to keep it a secret. Unless, of course,
she had reason to keep the information to herself."

They heard Witherspoon coming down the main staircase. "I'd better go on up," she said as he went toward the
hallway. Mrs. Jeffries picked up the breakfast tray the
cook had prepared earlier and followed the constable
upstairs to the dining room.

The cook sighed and stroked Samson. "I wonder, did
Arlette Banfield keep quiet about her condition because
she didn't want her husband to know she was expecting?"

Samson's tail flicked again. "Is that a 'yes'?" She
laughed. "Oh well, she'd not be the first married woman
to try such a trick. But then again, she'd have had to

know the baby wasn't his in the first place, wouldn't she? I'm just being silly, aren't I? We've no reason to believe she was anything but faithful to her husband. Still, it is odd that she'd not mentioned being in the family way to anyone, isn't it? Perhaps I'll bring it up again at our morning meeting."

But she changed her mind when the others arrived. It just seemed a bit unfair to the dead woman. As she'd told her cat, they had no evidence that Arlette Banfield was anything but a loyal and loving wife.

Hatchet had no idea what the others might be up to this morning but he knew exactly who he wanted to see. He stepped down from the hansom, paid the driver, and then pulled out his pocket watch. It had just gone half past nine, an unusual hour for a visit to an elegant Mayfair mansion, but it was a visit that he hoped would be welcome. He went up the walkway and banged the door knocker.

A few moments later, the door opened and the butler stared out at him. "May I help you?"

Hatchet met his gaze. He was a butler himself and he could outsnob this fellow in a heartbeat. "I'd like to see Mr. or Mrs. Manley."

"At this hour?" He sniffed disapprovingly. "I hardly think Mr. or Mrs. Manley is receiving."

Hatchet smiled and cocked his head to one side. "Why don't you go and tell them that Hatchet is here and he'd like a moment of their time."

He hesitated a fraction of a second before stepping back and motioning Hatchet inside. "Wait here," he instructed.

"Thank you," Hatchet replied graciously. He waited in the foyer. Bright sunshine came in through the high transom windows and splashed onto the cream and rose tile floors. A round mahogany table on an intricately carved pedestal stood in front of the broad curving staircase that swept up to the upper floors. A blue and green Chinese urn the height of a man stood in the corner across from a grandfather clock with a face inlaid with gold leaf and mother-of-pearl.

He turned at the sound of footsteps and broke into a wide grin at the sight of the lady of the house, Myra Haddington Manley, coming up the corridor. "Hatchet, how lovely to see you. We're just having coffee in the morning room—rather, I'm having coffee; Reginald is painting. You know what he's like, he's always trying to catch just the right light. But once he knows you're here, he'll put down his brush."

Myra Manley was a tall, middle-aged woman with brown hair streaked with gray, slightly buck teeth, and a superb complexion. As always, she was beautifully turned out in a teal-colored day dress with a white bodice and long sleeves. A double strand of pearls was around her neck and matching pearl earrings hung from her lobes.

He swept into an elegant bow. "Do forgive my barging in like this, and morning coffee sounds wonderful."

"You're only forgiven if you're here for the reason I think you're here." She laughed, took his arm, and led him down the hallway.

Myra Manley was one of the wealthiest women in England. She'd met and fallen in love with Reginald Manley, a handsome, not very successful artist, when they were both well into middle age. Reginald had spent years being subsidized by rich women, but once he'd said his wedding vows, he'd become the most loyal and affectionate of husbands. Reginald might not have been in love with his wife when they married, but Hatchet had no doubt that he was genuinely in love now and would probably stay that way for the rest of his life. Myra was equally besotted with her artist husband.

A young housemaid was putting more cups on the table when they entered the bright, sunny morning room. Myra gestured for Hatchet to sit and dismissed the maid with a wave and a smile. "I've sent the butler to tell Reginald you're here. He'd never forgive me if I kept you all to myself."

Hatchet laughed and took his seat. "You know why I've come?"

"Of course." She took her own chair. "We were out of town when the Banfield murder happened. We returned last night. I was very upset. I told Reginald that if we'd been here, you'd have already been around and we'd have known what was going on."

"And you'd have been correct. I came by yesterday afternoon. I was bitterly disappointed when the maid told me you were in the country. How did you know that the inspector would get the case?" he asked curiously.

The Manleys had given him information in several other of Witherspoon's cases. They were honest, discreet, and dedicated to the cause of justice. Myra Manley, for all her wealth, was a good woman who believed passionately that everyone, especially the rich, had an obligation to make the world a better place. Reginald felt the same.

She raised an eyebrow. "Because he always gets these cases. God knows what the Home Office would do if your inspector went on holiday to the continent and someone important was murdered."

"Hatchet, old fellow, I knew you'd come to see us." Reginald Manley strolled into the room. He dropped a kiss on his wife's cheek and took the empty seat next to her.

This time Hatchet raised his eyebrows. "I don't just come to see you when there's been a murder," he insisted. "I was here for tea last month and no one had died."

Manley laughed. "True enough, old friend, and you're always welcome. But now that you're here and there has been a murder, I've got all sorts of interesting things to tell you about the Montroses. Arlette Banfield was one of them, you know. Though how she ended up married to a philistine like Lewis Banfield is a real mystery. He wouldn't know a decent piece of art if his life depended on it."

"I imagine people have said the same thing about you and me," Myra said as she picked up the coffeepot and began filling their cups. "You're an excellent painter, but no one in my family has an artistic bone in their body."

"Nonsense, you're one of the most creative women I've ever met and you genuinely love art."

She laughed. "Well, one certainly couldn't accuse the Banfields of being art lovers."

"The Montroses considered the Banfields to be little more than rich barbarians," Reginald explained to Hatchet. "And they weren't quiet about their feelings, either. Elizabeth Montrose and her husband made it known to the entire London art community they didn't want this match. It's not often you find a family of modest means objecting to their daughter marrying into one of the richest clans in the country."

Hatchet sighed inwardly. He'd been hoping to find out something other than this particular nugget. They'd already learned that the Montroses were opposed to the marriage. "Yes, we'd heard those rumors. Was their objection merely because the Banfields weren't artistic? That hardly seems a reason to object so vocally and publicly."

"That's the excuse they gave," Myra answered. "But I've always wondered if there was some other reason that Mr. and Mrs. Montrose were opposed to the match. So when I heard about the murder, I made some inquiries to see if there were any old connections between the two families that weren't common knowledge." She grinned at Hatchet as she spoke. "Don't worry, I was very, very discreet."

"I wasn't in the least concerned," Hatchet replied. "Did you find out if there was a connection?"

"There might be," she replied slowly. "I'm only hesitating because the source of this information is a very old woman. It's my aunt Theodora. We were visiting her when we heard about the murder. But I'm not certain she was fully aware of what she was saying."

"I don't understand."

"What she means is that Aunt Theodora is going senile." Reginald reached across and patted his wife's shoulder. "Sometimes she's perfectly fine and then, a moment later, she seems to slip away. Sometimes it's just for a minute or two, but lately it takes her longer and longer to come back to us. It's very distressing for Myra. She and her aunt are very close."

"She raised me." Myra smiled sadly. "And I love her dearly. But that's neither here nor there. What you need to know is what she told me. She'd read about the murder in the papers, of course, so when I brought the subject up in conversation and asked if she knew anything about the Banfield family, she replied she most certainly did. She told me that Garrett Banfield had once been in love with a girl named Anna Montrose." She handed Hatchet his coffee. "I was stunned and I asked her if she was certain about the name of the girl. Montrose isn't a very common name and I wanted to be sure she hadn't just read the name in the newspaper. Aunt Theo claimed she knew perfectly well who she meant because Garrett Banfield, Lewis Banfield's uncle, and Aunt Theo's husband, my late uncle William, had gone to Cambridge together. They were apparently very good friends." She gave the second cup to her husband.

"Thank you, dearest." Reginal took a sip of coffee and then looked at Hatchet. "Anna Montrose was Crispin Montrose's older sister."

Witherspoon and Barnes didn't see or hear anything at the funeral service. But they noticed that Rosalind Kimball wasn't among the mourners, so as soon as the service was over they went straight to Mayfair.

From the outside, the Kimball house didn't look all that different from its neighbors, but as the two policemen made their way up the short walkway to the front door, they both saw the shabbiness not visible from the street.

"The place could use a coat of paint, sir," Barnes observed. "But you don't notice it until you get close because in the spots where it's peeled, the undercoat is the same color."

"And parts of the façade are crumbling as well," Witherspoon replied. "In another few years the coating will be completely gone."

As they reached the front door, the constable looked at the chipped stonework on the corners of the door stoop and then glanced up at the brass lamps on each side. Both lights had turned a sickly shade of green. "I think I can understand why Rosalind Kimball got so upset at Mrs. Banfield for stopping her husband from making a loan on the property. He was probably her last hope. This house is in a miserable condition." He pointed at dark patches on the fanlight window. "That's water damage and it looks bad, sir."

"Supposedly, Mrs. Kimball was staying with the Banfields because there was painting being done here." Witherspoon banged the knocker against the wood. "So perhaps they were trying to make some repairs."

"Let's see if we smell fresh paint," Barnes said softly as they heard feet shuffling on the other side of the door. "Otherwise, we'll have to conclude that Mrs. Kimball may have had other reasons for staying at the Banfield house."

The door opened and a short, balding butler stared at them. "Yes?"

"We'd like to see Mrs. Kimball." Witherspoon smiled politely.

"She's not receiving," the butler replied. He started to shut the door.

Barnes jammed his foot in the opening. "This isn't a social call. As you can plainly see, we're the police. Now, I suggest you go tell your mistress either she can speak with us here or we'll have to ask her to come down to the station."

His mouth gaped open, his expression stunned. "You'd better come inside," he sputtered when he'd recovered. He opened the door wider, waved them into the foyer, and almost ran down the short hallway to a set of double doors.

The inspector gazed at his surroundings. The furniture consisted of a small reception table draped with a pink, fringed cloth and holding a potted fern with scraggly, drooping fronds. The floor was covered in a green-and-gray-patterned carpet that was frayed, and there were square blank spots on the faded gray walls of the winding staircase where paintings had been removed.

"I expect they've sold the pictures," Barnes whispered as he followed the inspector's gaze. "And I don't see anything that looks like it's been recently painted. This room hasn't had a coat in many a year."

The butler suddenly reappeared. "Mrs. Kimball will see you in the drawing room. It's this way."

"I understand you've had some painting done here," the inspector said as they followed him back to the double doors.

The butler paused briefly. "I really couldn't say, sir." He turned the knob and shoved into the room. "The police to see you, madam," he announced.

The two policemen stepped past the butler, who quickly shut the door. Rosalind Kimball sat on a settee in the middle of the room. It was as dismal as the entryway. The walls were cream colored and dotted with the outlines of missing paintings, pink curtains hung limply at the windows, and the tabletops and cabinets were bare or covered only in cloth runners. There were none of the expensive knickknacks one would expect to see in a Mayfair mansion. Nor did the inspector smell paint.

"Good day, Mrs. Kimball," he began politely. "We're sorry to disturb you, but you left the Banfield house without being interviewed."

"I wasn't aware I needed to make any kind of a statement to the police," she retorted. "I know nothing about who could have killed that woman."

"You also neglected to leave us your address," Barnes added. "And we very specifically requested that everyone leaving the house provide us with that information."

"Just ask your questions, please," she replied. "I've a busy day ahead of me."

Barnes reached into his pocket and pulled out his notebook. She wasn't going to ask them to sit down, but he'd taken notes standing up on many other occasions. He could do it here as well.

"I understand you and Mrs. Bickleton overheard an argument between the Banfields at luncheon on the day of the murder," Witherspoon began. "Is that correct?"

She shrugged. "Margaret Bickleton's the eavesdropper, not me."

"But she specifically said you were there too," Barnes pressed. "She claimed you couldn't hear them very well because you're slightly deaf and she kept having to shush you because you kept asking her what they were saying." He paraphrased Mrs. Bickleton's words.

"That's a lie, I could hear perfectly well. I wasn't the

one eavesdropping; it was Margaret who had her ear plastered to the door while the two of them argued," she snapped. "She was delighted to hear them going at it like cats and dogs. Delighted, I tell you."

"Did Mrs. Bickleton have a reason for wanting discord between the Banfields?" Witherspoon asked. He already knew the answer but he was curious as to what she would say.

"Of course." Rosalind smiled slowly. "She hated Arlette. She claimed that Lewis had been on the verge of asking her daughter Helen to marry him when Arlette appeared on the scene and snatched him away. That's nonsense, of course. It was obvious to everyone that his interest in Helen Bickleton was merely polite."

"Why do you say that, ma'am?" Witherspoon shifted his weight slightly but kept his gaze on her face, hoping to tell if she was deliberately trying to cast suspicion on Margaret Bickleton. But despite his best efforts, he simply wasn't very good at reading some expressions. Rosalind Kimball merely looked annoyed.

"Oh, for goodness' sake, man, he was barely polite to the chit." She sighed. "Margaret is great friends with Geraldine, and the two of them had already decided that Helen would be a good match for Lewis. The Bickletons have no aristocratic lineage, but they are rich. But so are the Banfields, and Lewis isn't the sort to meekly do what he's told."

"So he was polite to the girl and nothing more," Witherspoon clarified.

She nodded. "That is correct. Back then, Geraldine ran the household and oversaw all the social events.

Helen was always seated next to Lewis at formal teas and dinner parties."

"We understand that Mrs. Bickleton wasn't the only person with a grudge against Arlette Banfield," Witherspoon said. "Our information is that you had words with her very shortly before she was murdered. Is that correct?"

"That's ridiculous!"

"As a matter of fact," he continued, "we have a witness that says you threatened her."

CHAPTER 8

—◆—

Wiggins knocked softly on the door to the servants' entrance of 3 Wallington Square. He wore his best jacket and matching trousers, his navy blue tie, and a pristine white shirt. After spending half the night thinking about how to have a word with Emma Carr, he'd come up with what he considered a very ingenious plan. He'd also timed his visit very carefully so that he could avoid any encounters with the master or mistress of the house. He'd hung about the square for a bit when he arrived and seen them both leave.

Emma opened the door. She was surprised, but then her expression changed to alarm. "We're not allowed male followers," she hissed, looking frantically over her shoulder. "You've got to go; if Cook sees you, she'll tell the mistress and I'll lose my job."

"I must talk to you," he whispered back. "It's urgent; someone's life might be at stake."

Startled, she drew back. "What are you on about?" She started to close the door. "Are you trying to get me sacked?"

He shook his head. "No, I'm telling the truth. I'm a private inquiry agent and you've got information that will help us catch a killer."

She stopped and stared at him, her expression doubtful. But then her expression changed and softened as she stared at the way he was dressed.

Wiggins was glad he'd worn his best clothes. "Please, I need your help."

"I don't want to lose my position," she insisted.

"Carr, who's out there? Who are you talking to?" a woman's voice said from inside the house.

"Tell the cook that a young man has come to the back door and he's lost," Wiggins explained quickly. "Tell her he's the son of a friend of the Banfield family, that he's lost the address and you're going to take him around to the Banfield house. Tell her to come and have a look at me if she doesn't believe you."

"Carr, didn't you hear me?" the voice cried again.

"It's a young gentleman that is lost," Emma yelled back. "He's wanting to go to the Banfield house for the funeral reception. Would you like to come speak to him or should I take him round there?"

The voice was silent for a moment. "Go along, then, but mind you hurry back."

"Yes, ma'am." She grinned at Wiggins and stepped out into the mews. "Come along, then, young sir," she said loudly. "The Banfield house isn't far."

"Thanks ever so much," Wiggins said softly as they

started for the far end of the mews. "I really needed to speak with you."

"Wait till we're at the road," she whispered. "Cook knows everyone along here and I don't want someone from another house telling tales on me. We can nip around the corner. No one can see us there, but you've got to hurry. I have to get back quickly."

He nodded and didn't speak again till they turned onto the short street leading to the square. "I'm so sorry to have bothered you." He whirled about so he could face her. "But it really was important."

"Are you really a private inquiry agent?" she asked.

"I am, and when we had tea yesterday you gave me some valuable information," he replied. "We've been hired to investigate Mrs. Banfield's murder."

"Isn't that what the police should be doing?" She crossed her arms over her chest and stared at him suspiciously.

"I can ask questions and go places that they can't," he said. "And my employers will be passing along any information we get to them." Emma wasn't quite as naive as he'd thought. She looked as if she didn't believe a word he said. But now that he'd started down this path, he couldn't stop. "Please, Arlette Banfield was a very nice woman and she didn't deserve to die."

"I know she was a decent person. Like I told you, my friend Fanny is the tweeny at that house," she said, her expression softened a bit. "I don't see how I can help any, but I'll try. Ask me your questions, but be quick about it. Cook'll have my head if I don't get back soon."

"Do you think you can ask Fanny which of the two houseguests that were staying with the Banfields last week has a blue jacket and a bonnet with a matching veil?"

"I don't need to ask Fanny." She uncrossed her arms. "I know who it was. It was a Mrs. Bickleton."

"Cor blimey, you're a clever one. 'Ow do you know that?"

"Because Mrs. Bickleton was getting in a hansom last week when we had our day out together and she was wearing a bright blue jacket with a matching hat and veil. Fanny and I had to duck into a doorway so she wouldn't see us," Emma explained.

"Why didn't you want her to see you?" he asked. But he suspected he already knew the answer.

Emma giggled. "Because there was a young man with us. He's sweet on Fanny. The minute we come around the corner and Fanny spotted her climbing into the hansom, she made Paul walk on and pushed me into a shop doorway. Fanny said to me, 'If that Mrs. Bickleton sees me with a boy, she'll tell Mrs. Banfield the elder and I'll be in trouble.' At the time, I thought it was funny. Why do you care about her jacket and veil?" She stared at him curiously.

Wiggins wasn't sure what to say. He liked Emma and didn't want to lie to her any more than he had to, but he couldn't tell her the truth. "Well, um, someone gave us some information and we had to try and find out if our informant was tellin' us the truth." He grinned sheepishly. "I'm not tryin' to avoid your question, but I'm really only an assistant private inquiry agent and I only do what I'm told."

"I know what you mean." She smiled sadly. "I spend my life doin' what I'm told as well."

* * *

Ruth squeezed herself into a tiny space between a potted fern and an oversized curio cabinet in a corner of the Banfield drawing room. She'd picked this spot because it was just off the hall and she hoped to get a bit of fresh air.

She peeked out and looked down the corridor. She could see that the dividers between the second reception room and the dining room had been opened, exactly as they had been the night of the ball. The servants were setting out food on a long buffet table.

Ruth leaned against the wall and sighed. Funeral receptions were never pleasant and this one was no exception. The windows were tightly shut, people were speaking in low, somber tones, and it was obvious that the family had divided into two camps.

Crispin and Elizabeth Montrose were on this end of the huge drawing room while Lewis Banfield and his aunt had taken over the other end. People moved between the two groups paying their respects and speaking to the mourners. It had been like that at the funeral as well. Arlette's parents had sat on one side of the church while Lewis and his aunt had sat on the other. The pews behind each side were filled with their friends and family; flamboyant artistic types wearing far less mourning colors sat behind the Montroses while those sitting behind the Banfields were uniformly in black. Ruth had dithered for a moment and then sat down several pews behind her friend Elizabeth.

She surveyed the room, looking for a likely source of information. Lady Emma Stafford and Margaret Bickleton were sitting on a love seat next to Geraldine Banfield. Next to them and closest to Lewis was a frail-looking young lady with brown hair and a long, bony face. Ruth suspected that must be Helen. As she watched them, she saw the girl lean over and speak to him, but he made an impatient gesture with his hand and she drew back. Margaret Bickleton, who'd also seen the exchange, frowned at her daughter.

Ruth didn't think she'd learn much from that quarter. She scanned the faces in the room, looking for a likely candidate, but most people were clustered together in small groups, speaking softly and waiting for the food to be served.

She had to get some air. The room was so stuffy she didn't think she could draw another breath. A puff of air washed over her as she stepped into the hallway and she realized the side door was open. She went in that direction and as she reached the doorway, she heard voices.

"I'm sorry about it, Mr. Bigglesworth, I don't know what to tell you," a woman's voice said. "But today is hardly the time or the place to pursue the matter."

Ruth peeked around the corner of the door. She saw the Banfield housekeeper with a burly man dressed in an ill-fitting suit.

"I know it's not a good time, Mrs. Peyton," he insisted. "The young missus was always nice to me and I mean no disrespect by bringing this up at her funeral. But that's a ruddy great hole we've got down there and someone's got to give me leave to speak to the builders and at least get a cost estimate for the repairs."

Mrs. Peyton closed her eyes and sighed. "But Mrs. Banfield has already done that. Surely you don't need to bother Mr. Banfield on today of all days."

"But she didn't do it," he replied. "She come to the house but she didn't examine the hole in the attic. She just asked me for the keys to the outbuildings and then sent me off to fetch the trap and pony so I could take her back to the station. I sent Mr. Banfield a telegram and asked him if I should speak to the builders directly, as she'd left me no instructions, but he never answered me. I'm quite capable of taking care of the matter, Mrs. Peyton, but I can't keep putting up tarps every time it rains. The wet is getting into the walls."

"Are you in need of assistance, madam?"

Ruth turned and came face-to-face with the butler. "Oh no, I just needed a breath of air. It's very warm in there and I thought I'd step outside for a moment but the area in front of the door is occupied and I didn't wish to interrupt."

The butler's expression didn't change. He looked over her shoulder. "That's Mrs. Peyton, our housekeeper, and Mr. Bigglesworth, the gardener from the country house. I don't think they'd have minded being interrupted. You're a guest."

By this time, the housekeeper and the gardener were both staring at her. Ruth could feel a flush climb her cheeks. She knew good and well that all of them knew who she was, that she was the woman who'd insisted on calling the police when Arlette died. They probably thought she was deliberately snooping. Well, in one sense she was, but she wasn't trying to overhear what these two said on purpose. "Servants are entitled to courtesy the same as everyone else, and I didn't want to barge in when they were having a private conversation." She inclined her head and continued on toward the open door.

Ruth stepped outside into the narrow passage between the houses. The walkway was paved, so she strolled toward the back of the house, breathing deeply and sucking in as much fresh air as possible before she had to go back inside. As she approached the corner, she heard voices, so she eased her steps, hoping that no one had heard her. She didn't want to be accused of eavesdropping twice within ten minutes. But whoever was talking hadn't heard her or, if they had, they didn't care that someone was coming, because they kept on with the conversation.

"I don't know what to do; I don't want to run tellin' tales to Mrs. Banfield, but I think I ought to say something." The voice belonged to a young girl.

"Keep out of it," a male voice admonished. "She'll not thank you for it. No one wants to know one of their friends has been snooping through their things. Besides, you don't owe the old cow anything. She's never been very nice to you; she wouldn't even let me help you with that ruddy great trunk of hers."

"I don't like her, either, but I might not have been the only one that spotted Mrs. Bickleton goin' up to the attic—"

"And you shouldn't 'ave followed her up there," he interrupted. "That's why you'd best keep your mouth shut about it. If anyone saw you comin' out of the attic, they could just as likely run tellin' tales that you was the one putting your nose where it didn't belong. If it comes down to it, it'll be your word against one of her friends, and which side do you think she's likely to take? Besides, you told me that all the Bickleton woman was doin' was taking a look at that old book of newspaper cuttings. You said you saw her leavin' the attic and she didn't have anything with her, so she weren't stealin. She was just bein' nosy."

"But why was she so interested? That's what I want to know," the girl insisted. "You know there's been murder done in this house."

"But you brought that ruddy trunk down two weeks before Mrs. Banfield the younger were killed. It's got naught to do with anything."

"Was it that long before the ball? How do you remember everything like that?" she asked. "Oh, bother, we'd better get back inside, here comes Lydia."

"I remember because it were the same day that Mrs. Banfield the younger and her mother had that awful argument . . ." Their voices faded away as they went into the house.

Ruth stood there for a moment and then turned and went back to the house.

"That's a lie." Rosalind leapt to her feet. "I didn't threaten her."

"What exactly did you say?" Witherspoon asked. "Our witness was very certain of what she heard."

"I can't remember my exact words, but I most certainly didn't threaten to kill the woman," she cried. She began to pace back and forth in front of the settee. "I'll admit I was furious with Mrs. Banfield—her interference had caused me a great deal of aggravation and grief—but people of our class don't solve their problems by violence." She stopped in front of the inspector and stared him straight in the eye. "We use solicitors."

Witherspoon held her gaze, and she was the first to

look away. She continued pacing. "It's absurd even to ask me such a question," she muttered.

"I don't think it's absurd, Mrs. Kimball. Isn't the bank going to foreclose?" Barnes said softly. "Isn't that the reason you went to Lewis Banfield in the first place? Because you were desperate and terrified of losing the one thing you had left, your home?" He was guessing; he'd no idea if the Kimballs had an outstanding loan or not.

"We won't lose it now. She's dead and Geraldine will convince Lewis to lend us the money." She stopped and clamped her mouth shut. Her hands clenched into fists and she closed her eyes briefly. "That didn't come out the way it should have. I'm very sorry that Arlette Banfield was murdered but I had nothing to do with it."

"Yet now that she's gone, you're sure that your friend can get the victim's husband to make you a private loan?" The inspector stared at her skeptically. He had a feeling that Rosalind Kimball was in for a surprise.

"But of course. Our families have been friends for years."

"Why didn't you go to Mrs. Banfield's funeral service?" the constable asked.

"I'm not a hypocrite, Constable," she replied. "As you know, the late Mrs. Banfield and I weren't friends."

"But you're going to ask her husband for a loan," Witherspoon reminded her. "And by all accounts, he loved his wife dearly. Do you think he'll forgive a slight like that?" He'd no idea what he was trying to find out by this line of questioning, but she'd already revealed animosity toward the victim and he wanted to see how deep her hatred went.

For a moment, she looked uncertain, then she straightened her spine. "He'll understand and his aunt will intervene on my behalf."

"You stayed as a houseguest in Mrs. Banfield's home; I should think it would only be polite to have gone to her service," Barnes pointed out. He didn't believe for one minute that she'd stayed away from the funeral of her own volition. She was looking to Lewis Banfield to save her home. She wouldn't risk offending him.

She glared at the constable. "Whether I went or not is none of your concern," she snapped.

"I'm afraid that's not quite true, Mrs. Kimball," the inspector said. "You threaten the victim only days before she's murdered, then you continue to stay in her home, accepting her hospitality—"

"It wasn't her house," she interrupted. "It belongs to the Banfield family and she was just an interloper. But if you must know, I didn't go to the funeral because Elizabeth Montrose told me I'd better not. She was here yesterday afternoon and she told me if I dared show my face at the church, she'd make a scene that would haunt me for the rest of my days." She broke off and sank to the settee. She shrank into herself, crossing her arms over her chest and holding her elbows with her hands as her shoulders slumped forward. "It was awful, Inspector," she continued, her voice ragged with pain. "Truly awful. No one has ever spoken to me like that before."

Witherspoon felt a surge of pity for her. "Yes, I'm sure it must have been," he said quietly.

"She made it perfectly clear she knew what had happened that day at Gillette's and she also made it clear that

Arlette had told her about . . . about . . . my husband's habits." Her voice caught and she took a long, deep breath. "And that now that her beloved daughter was dead, she didn't care what anyone in London or for that matter all of England thought or said about propriety, she'd tell everyone about Gregory, about what he's done to our family and our good name."

"Perhaps it was only Mrs. Montrose's grief speaking," the inspector suggested. "Surely she knows that you're not responsible . . ."

She interrupted again. "What happened to me didn't matter to her. All she could see was her own pain." She sighed and turned to look at the two policemen. "So I decided not to go to Arlette's funeral. I didn't dare. All I have left is a bit of dignity and I couldn't risk Elizabeth Montrose taking that away from me." She smiled bitterly. "And you're right, you know. I've been fooling myself. Lewis won't forgive the slight. Despite what I may or may not have thought of Arlette, he loved her more than life itself. He'll never forgive anyone who hurt her."

The constable wasn't as kindhearted as Witherspoon. He had a few more questions he needed answered. "Before the ball started, people milled about and chatted while the wine was being served. Did you notice anyone other than the servants going to or coming from the area near the butler's pantry?" he asked.

"I didn't notice."

"Did you go near that area yourself?" he pressed.

Her head snapped around. "I don't think so, Constable, but I can't recall every step I took that night."

"We don't expect you to, ma'am," he replied. "Did you know which glass was Mrs. Banfield's?"

She shrugged. "Not really, I only knew that she drank champagne."

"Really, Mrs. Kimball, we have it on good authority that you knew perfectly well that Mrs. Banfield used the glass her mother had made her."

"Oh yes, that's right." She smiled coldly. "I'd forgotten."

He returned her smile with an equally chilly one of his own. "You seem a very intelligent woman, Mrs. Kimball. I bet if you try hard, you'll be able to recall whether or not you went near the butler's pantry or the screened area before the ball started."

"I may have wandered over in that direction, but I didn't go anywhere near her champagne flute. But you might have a chat with Margaret Bickleton about that glass. I saw her handling it. It was right before she went to join the Banfields in the receiving line. Oh, and when you're talking to her, you might ask her what she hoped to accomplish by sending Lewis a message to come home for lunch that day. That was what caused the horrid row you asked me about between him and Arlette." She got up. "But that's probably why she did it."

Smythe sat down across from Blimpey. "I 'ope you've got something useful for me. I've not 'ad much luck findin' anything out on my own today."

"Have I ever failed ya?" Blimpey laughed. "That's why ya pay me, to get ya the goods. Do ya have time for a pint?" He started to raise his arm to get the barman's attention, but Smythe quickly pulled it back down.

"I don't dare," Smythe replied. "I've already 'ad three pints today and it's barely lunchtime. But the only way you can get anyone to talk to you in a pub is to buy a drink or two."

Blimpey looked amused. "You look to me like the sort who can hold his liquor."

"I can if I don't drink too much of it. Truth of the matter is, the stuff gives me a bit of a headache. But what 'ave you got for me?"

"Not as much as you'd like and I'd wanted," he admitted. "But that's neither here nor there. I did find out that the Banfields are richer than sin but came close to losing it all a few years back when old Garrett Banfield started investin' wildly in the Far East."

"We'd 'eard that as well—and that if Lewis Banfield hadn't invested in a gold mine in southern Africa, the family would be broke."

"I figured you had." Blimpey grinned. "But I'll bet you don't know that Lewis borrowed the money to invest in the mine that saved their bacon from the Bickleton family."

Smythe sat up straighter. "We didn't know that bit." Apparently Luty's source didn't, either.

"It was a private loan between friends, so to speak," Blimpey said. "But it came with a few strings attached. Hiram Bickleton made the deal with the understanding that young Lewis wouldn't just pay the money back, but that he'd marry Helen Bickleton, Hiram's daughter."

"Blast a Spaniard. Are you sure about that? We've not heard nary a bit of gossip along those lines."

"It was done on the hush-hush." Blimpey leaned

closer. "Hiram didn't want his daughter to think he was buyin' her a husband. But he didn't figure on dyin' right after he made Lewis the loan, either, and that's what happened. He dropped dead of a heart attack two weeks after they cut the deal."

"But we heard that the Banfields pride themselves on their behavin' with honor. Ignorin' a promise just because the man died doesn't seem right or honorable."

"But that's exactly what he did. Banfield paid the loan back, but he never asked for the young lady's hand in marriage." Blimpey shrugged. "Mind you, we don't know if anyone outside my informant knew about the situation; the marriage agreement wasn't common knowledge."

"What about Margaret Bickleton? Surely she knew."

"Maybe, maybe not. The only thing they put in writing was the financial details. But that's not all I've got for ya. I also found out that Lewis Banfield wasn't the only one in the family who was good at business. A few weeks before she was murdered, Arlette had made a deal to have reproductions of some statue that she'd posed for mass-produced. An engraving company in Battersea had offered her a lot of money for the rights to copy the thing, cast it, and reproduce it. Now, supposedly the artist made a fuss, but as she was the legal owner of the statue, there weren't anything he could do about it."

"How bad a fuss?" Smythe asked.

"Not as much as you'd think." Blimpey grinned. "Apparently, she reminded him that he'd given her the statue as a wedding gift and it was hers to do with as she pleased. Do you know, the the odd thing was it weren't her husband who objected to the fact that a seminude likeness of his wife was going to be available for anyone with the ready to buy, it was her parents. They didn't raise a ruckus because of what she was or wasn't wearin' when she posed for the statue; they objected because it was going to be made at a factory, sold by the hundreds, and was going to make Arlette a lot of money! She was a clever one, she was; her deal with the engraving factory is a good one. She was going to make a percentage commission on every unit that was sold."

The hansom pulled up at the end of the mews. Barnes got down, paid the driver, and walked the short distance to the rear of the Banfield house. From here, he couldn't tell if the funeral reception had ended or not, but he was bound and determined to talk with the butler. The inspector had stopped at the station to go over the reports the locals had done for them. He'd agreed with the constable that, funeral or not, they had to finish their interviews.

The properties along the mews were fenced in with high wooden gates, so he reached up and over, feeling for the latch and hoping it didn't require a key. His fingers found a length of string, he gave it a tug, and the gate opened. He stepped inside and started up the walkway to the servants' door. He noticed that the barrier between this house and the next was a fence and trellis combination with solid wood on the bottom half and scraggly ivy vines entwined about the wood on the top. At certain angles, he could see through the vines to the small terrace of the house next door.

He reached the servants' door and saw it standing

wide open so he stepped inside. He almost collided with a young maid.

"Oy . . . you scared me," she cried, almost dropping the empty platter she carried. "I didn't know the police were still hangin' about the place."

"I'm sorry, miss." He smiled apologetically. "I came to this entrance because I didn't wish to disturb the family during the funeral reception. When I saw the door open, I decided to just come in. I didn't think anyone would hear me if I knocked." He nodded at the dish in her hand. "I thought everyone would be very busy."

"We are, sir." She grinned. "And you're right, you could have stood out here banging for donkey's years and none of us would 'ave heard you. It's a madhouse here, with everyone runnin' to and fro. But that's not why you're here, is it. Would you like to speak to the master?"

Barnes recognized the girl. She was a thin young redhead with a scattering of freckles across her nose. "You're Fanny Wilson, aren't you? We had a brief chat when I was here before."

"That's right." She glanced toward the back stairs. "Pardon me, Constable, I've got to get this platter to the kitchen. They need more roast beef upstairs." She edged down the hall, clearly torn between not wanting to be rude and not wanting to get into trouble with her mistress.

"That's fine. I'll accompany you to the kitchen, if you don't mind."

"Mrs. Peyton is down there. Perhaps she can help you," Fanny replied. "We've been runnin' ourselves silly, and everyone is afraid that we're goin' to run out of food. They've had far more people show up than was expected or invited, but Mrs. Banfield the elder can't say a word because they were all invited by the Montroses."

They'd reached the stairs and the constable stepped back to let her go down first. "That must be hard on the staff," he murmured. He wanted to keep her talking. Experience had taught him that one could learn a lot from listening to servants gossip.

"Oh, it is, Constable. You've no idea. But, then, these whole past few weeks have been a right old misery." She'd reached the bottom of the stairs and she turned to face him. "First we had the fuss over Mrs. Bickleton claiming someone had stolen her clothes—"

Barnes interrupted. "What do you mean? Stolen what?"

Fanny pursed her lips. "It was silly, really. The woman had forgotten where she'd put her coat and hat, so she come screaming into the kitchen demanding to know which one of us had taken them. Mrs. Peyton calmed her down and took her upstairs, where they had a hunt. They found her stupid jacket and veil in the wardrobe in her room."

"When was this?"

Fanny thought for a moment. "It was a day or two before the ball—I remember because I heard Mrs. Peyton complaining to Mr. Michaels that having the houseguests here while we were getting ready for the ball was three times the trouble!"

"Wilson, are you going to stand there all day with that platter or are you going to take it to the kitchen?"

They both turned to look. The butler stood by the entrance to the kitchen staring at them with a disapproving frown.

"I'm sorry, sir." Fanny cringed and started toward the kitchen.

"Don't blame Miss Wilson." Barnes stepped in front of her. "I asked her to bring me down here so I could speak with you." He'd always loathed the way some households addressed their servants by just barking out their surnames. "You seem to have gone out of your way to avoid being interviewed, so I insisted she take me directly to you," he lied.

Michaels drew back slightly in surprise. He was a tall, thin man with curly gray hair and hazel eyes. "I've not been avoiding anyone," he snapped defensively.

Barnes raised his eyebrows. "Really?" He looked at Fanny. "Thank you very much for your assistance, Miss Wilson. I'll tell Mr. Banfield how readily you cooperated with us. I know he very much wants to ensure his wife's murderer is caught and hanged."

The girl gave him a quick, grateful smile and hurried off to the kitchen.

Michaels came toward him. "If you wish to interview me, I've a few moments to spare now. We can go into the servants' dining hall. It's this way."

The constable followed him around the staircase and into a room furnished with a long oak table and a bench on each side. Cane-backed chairs for the cook and the butler were on the ends. Shelves holding crockery, linens, and cutlery lined one wall. The other was painted a pale, ugly green.

Michaels pulled out a chair, sat down, and nodded at the spot on the bench next to him. "You can sit there."

"Thank you." Barnes took a seat. The bench was

uncomfortably narrow and hard as the proverbial rock. He wondered how anyone could eat a decent meal in this miserable room. He took out his notebook and pencil. "Mr. Michaels, on the night of the ball, what time did you go down to the butler's pantry?"

"I don't know the exact time; I didn't look at the clock," he replied coldly.

Barnes sighed inwardly. He'd obviously ruffled the man's feathers but he was in no mood to play about. "Mr. Michaels, you're a very important witness in this investigation and I'd appreciate it if you'd be a bit more cooperative."

"I am cooperating," he replied, but he had the grace to look embarrassed. "I went to the pantry when the family lined up to start receiving guests. That was about seven o'clock. The buffet supper was scheduled for eight o'clock."

"That's quite a long period of time." Barnes looked up from his notebook. "Was that the usual custom?"

He nodded. "The family always spent a good half hour receiving guests, so by the time they came into the ballroom there was only half an hour before supper was served. They liked to give people time to mingle and chat before the meal and the dancing."

"When did you begin serving the alcohol?"

"As soon as the first guests came into the ballroom," he replied. "The bottles were already opened so the wine could breathe. When the guests started trickling in, the waiters each took a bottle of white and red and began pouring."

"The glasses were already on the tables?"

"That's correct. That was much easier than giving

them all trays to lug about." He snorted. "Some of the waiters were from an agency and, frankly, it was obvious they'd never served anything in their entire lives."

"When the girl brought up Mrs. Banfield's champagne, was it opened immediately?"

Michaels thought for a moment. "One bottle was, but the other was never opened at all. When it came up from the wet larder, I stuck my head out and saw that the elder ladies had taken seats."

"You mean the elder Mrs. Banfield and her friends," he clarified.

"Correct. Once Mrs. Banfield was seated, I knew the formal receiving was done and that the master and mistress would be in shortly. As most of the guests had been served by then, I wanted to ensure that they were served immediately."

"We understand that Mrs. Banfield had her own champagne flute. Where was it kept?"

He frowned in confusion. "In the butler's pantry—that's where most of the glassware is kept. We did keep the champagne flutes in the storage room, as they're not used very often for large functions like the summer ball; after all, even the rich don't like serving champagne to over two hundred guests. But after one of the maids chipped Mr. Banfield's glass, I moved the set to a separate shelf in my pantry. As the late Mrs. Banfield's mother had made the flutes, I wanted to take charge of them so nothing like that would happen again."

"Mr. Banfield's glass had a chip on it?" Barnes asked sharply.

"Yes, as I said, one of the maids got careless when

she was taking it to be washed and cracked a tiny bit off the base." He sniffed. "The defect is hardly noticeable, but Mr. Banfield was very upset about it. Not that it mattered on the night of the ball. Mr. Banfield told us he'd be drinking wine that night and not champagne, so I didn't bother getting his glass out."

"He told you beforehand what he'd be drinking?"

Michaels nodded. "He often did that. As I've said, just because they are wealthy, they don't like wasting money any more than anyone else. As Mrs. Banfield was the only one to be served champagne, I only ordered two bottles be brought up from the larder. Even then, the second bottle would only have been opened if one of the guests had specifically requested champagne instead of wine. The late Mrs. Banfield rarely drank more than two or three glasses during the course of an evening."

"So everyone in the household knew that only Mrs. Banfield would be having champagne?"

"I suppose so," he replied slowly. "It wasn't a secret. Mr. Banfield told me at luncheon that day that he'd be drinking wine at the ball. The ladies were present when he gave me the instructions, as was a serving maid."

"Back to the champagne flute." Barnes smiled slightly. "Where specifically in the butler's pantry was the flute when the wine was being served?"

"It was on a silver tray on the serving table at the far end of the buffet. I didn't want it getting knocked about, so I put it as far away from the activity as possible."

Barnes thought back to how the room had been set up on the night of the ball. The butler's pantry opened up on the far left of where the screens had been placed, but the food had started coming up and into the room from the right. "But what about when the food was served, wouldn't there have been a lot of activity then?"

"The food wasn't coming up until a quarter to eight. By then, I'd already retrieved the flute and taken Mrs. Banfield her drink."

"Other than the staff, did anyone else go in or out of the buffet area where the glass was sitting?"

He shifted uncomfortably. "I'm not certain, Constable. You've got to remember, we were frightfully busy that night and I had my hands full opening the wine and supervising the waiters. I'm not at all sure about what I saw. From the angle where I stood, it was impossible to tell whether she'd just come out of the back hall or if she'd been in the buffet area."

Barnes nodded agreeably. "I'll keep that in mind. Just tell me who you saw and I'll do the rest."

"It was Mrs. Bickleton." He sighed. "I'd peeked around the screen to see if everyone was being served, and just then I saw Mrs. Bickleton and it appeared as if she'd just stepped out of the buffet area. But I can't be sure."

"And Mrs. Banfield's glass was in the buffet area?"

"That's correct."

"Was she the only person you noticed go anywhere near where the glass was?"

"Yes. But she could just as easily have stepped out of the corridor after coming down the back stairs."

Ruth started down the front walkway and had almost reached the gate when she heard footsteps behind her. Turning, she saw Lady Emma Stafford coming toward her. She was unaccompanied by a maid or a companion and she stumbled down the walk, her sight encumbered by the thick black veil covering her face. Ruth knew it was Lady Stafford because she'd seen the woman flip the veil back so she could eat.

Lady Stafford rapidly closed the distance between them. She was almost at the gate when she suddenly tripped and lurched forward. "Blast and damnation," she cried as her arms flew out and flapped wildly in an attempt to regain her balance.

Ruth managed to grab her shoulders before she hit the ground. She pulled hard against gravity, finally steadying the woman. "Are you unharmed, Lady Stafford?"

Panting, she flicked her veil away from her face and tried to catch her breath. "Gracious, thank you, Lady Cannonberry. Had you not been here, I would have had a very nasty fall." She looked down at the ground, searching for what had caused her mishap. "I don't see anything here, but I know I tripped over something."

"Whatever it was, I'm glad you didn't hurt yourself, ma'am," Ruth said politely. "Please, take my arm and let me escort you. Has the footman gone to fetch your carriage?"

Lady Emma responded with a loud snort. "Humph . . . no, my wretched nephew sold the carriage two months ago. He claims that keeping a carriage and four in London is utter madness. So I'm reduced to taking hansom cabs. I loathe the contraptions—they're ugly, uncomfortable, and slow—but if I want to have any social life at all, I've no choice." She fixed her gaze on Ruth and narrowed her eyes. "Do you have a carriage?"

Ruth was tempted to lie and say she, too, was going to take a hansom, but as the footman had been sent to get her carriage, she was afraid it would come rumbling around the corner just as she got Lady Stafford to the street. "Yes, I do, and I'd be pleased to offer you a ride to your home."

"I wasn't hinting," Lady Emma protested. "But nonetheless, I'll gladly accept your kind offer. It's jolly decent of you; I know you don't like me."

Ruth opened the wrought-iron gate and stepped back to let her companion go through first. "I don't dislike you, Lady Stafford," she began. "I simply don't know you very well and I suspect we have very different points of view about many things in life and society. Look, there's my carriage now. Where do you live? I'll need to give my coachman your address."

"Don't you have a footman to do that?"

"No, the coachman is sufficient," she replied as the carriage pulled up. The Banfield footman leapt off the back of the coach before it even came to a complete halt. He opened the door and pulled down the carriage steps.

"I live at number seven Chevron Way in Marylebone," Lady Emma told her as she put her foot on the bottom rung. The carriage lurched slightly as she heaved her bulk inside.

Ruth gave the coachman the address and then pulled a sixpence piece out of her pocket and handed it to the footman. "Thank you for your help, young sir," she said.

"No, ma'am, thank you," he gushed as he tucked the money into his pocket.

Ruth got inside and took the spot across from Lady Stafford, then she banged on the ceiling and they were off.

"You'll only spoil him, you know," Lady Emma said crossly. "Now he'll expect a gratuity from everyone and he was just doing his job."

"No, he's employed by the Banfields as their footman, not mine."

"He's employed to do what he's told," she snapped, her face wrinkling into a fierce frown. "And it's people like you who are going to ruin the world for the rest of us."

Ruth burst out laughing. She couldn't stop herself. This red-faced old harridan who hadn't done a day's work in her entire life really thought that the world as she knew it would crumble over a sixpence.

Lady Emma glared at her and Ruth managed to get herself under control. "I'm sorry, that was very wrong of me. Of course you're entitled to your opinion about society, Lady Stafford."

"And you think you're entitled to yours, is that it?" she shot back. But some of the anger had left her face.

"Yes, I think that if we don't change and become a more humane and equitable society, we'll sow the seeds of our own destruction. The world is changing. People don't like being treated as if they only exist to serve the upper class, and they're beginning to rebel against it."

The older woman said nothing for a moment; she simply stared at Ruth, only now her expression was speculative. "You're very sure you're right, aren't you?"

"I am right." Ruth lifted her chin.

"Don't be so certain," she replied dryly. "You'll change your mind when you get to be my age. But let's not quarrel; it's very good of you to take me home, and I am decidedly grateful. Actually, I expected the Banfields to provide me a coach home, but this time they didn't. I expect they were preoccupied with burying their dead."

"How long have you known the Banfield family?" Ruth asked.

"All of our lives. The Banfields and Staffords have connections going back at least a hundred years. We have great-great-grandparents in common. We're all proud of our ancestry, of course, but Geraldine speaks about hers as if the Banfields came over with the Conqueror, and of course they didn't."

"Was Mrs. Banfield a Banfield before she married?" Ruth asked curiously.

"She was indeed. She and her husband, Garrett, were second cousins. That isn't done much these days, but it was quite common fifty years ago."

Phyllis stuck her head into the kitchen as the housekeeper was setting the table for their afternoon meeting. "Mrs. Jeffries, do you have a few moments? I'd like to say something."

"Of course, Phyllis, we've plenty of time before the others get back." The housekeeper put the tray of cups down and slipped into her seat. She nodded at the spot next to her.

"Thank you." Phyllis pulled out the chair and flopped down. She said nothing for a long moment, but simply sat there, breathing heavily.

Mrs. Jeffries waited patiently.

Phyllis' mouth was open as she struggled to catch her breath and her chest heaved up and down.

"You seem very upset." Mrs. Jeffries reached over

and patted her arm. "It's alright, Phyllis, no one is angry at you. If you go on like this, you'll make yourself ill."

"I wish I'd said yes," Phyllis blurted out. "Oh dear, that didn't come out like I wanted it to, but Betsy said if I explained things properly, you'd understand. Betsy is ever so nice, she could see how worried I was about the situation . . ." Her voice trailed off and she looked down at her hands, which were clasped tightly in her lap.

"Phyllis, if this is about your preference to stay out of the inspector's cases, you don't owe me or anyone else an explanation."

"But I do," she cried. "It wasn't that I didn't want to help, I was just afraid."

"You don't need to worry about losing your position—"

"But it weren't just that," Phyllis interrupted. "It was because I can't do any of those things the rest of you do." Her eyes filled with tears and her face turned red. "I'm not easy with people. I couldn't get a clerk in a shop to talk if my life depended on it and I'm not good at striking up conversations with housemaids or footmen and I'd get hopelessly lost if I tried to follow anyone. So when you asked if I wanted to help and you told me what all of you did, I knew I couldn't do any of those things. I knew I was just a useless girl who'd probably just get in your way." She broke off and pulled a handkerchief out of her sleeve; she was full-on crying now.

Thinking it would do her good to get it out of her system, Mrs. Jeffries let her weep for a few moments. "Phyllis, you're not useless, and whoever made you feel that you are should be horsewhipped."

"Yes, I am. I'm a scared little rabbit." She sniffed

and swiped at her cheeks. "I try to be strong and clever like the rest of you, but I don't know how. I've listened behind the door when you've had some of your meetings and I want to be a part of it, I really do. You're doing something so important, and I want to help. But I can't do anything except polish furniture and scrub floors. That's all I'll ever be good for."

Mrs. Jeffries blinked hard as tears filled her own eyes. She felt like a worm. She ought to have tried harder with the girl, ought to have understood that the fear she'd seen on her face was probably the result of terrible experiences in her past. "That's not true. You're a very intelligent young woman and we'd be glad of your help."

"But there's nothing I can do," she wailed. "Nothing."

"Again, that's not true." Mrs. Jeffries reached over and patted her arm. "Everyone has something they can contribute. It may take us a bit of time to determine precisely where your talents lie, but I know you can help."

"Do you really think so?" she asked, her expression hopeful.

"But of course," Mrs. Jeffries lied. She couldn't think of one thing the girl could do. "And starting this afternoon, we'll expect you at our meetings."

CHAPTER 9

—⊸—

Ruth stepped inside the back door of Upper Edmonton Gardens and raced up the hall to the kitchen. She skidded to a halt at the unexpected sight of Phyllis sitting at the table. Recovering quickly, she smiled at the girl as she slipped off the ugly black mourning hat and gloves. "I'm so sorry to be late," she apologized as she tucked the gloves into the bonnet and then hung them on the coat tree. "But I took Lady Stafford home after the funeral reception and the traffic coming back was dreadful. But I think I may have learned some interesting facts."

"We've only just sat down." Mrs. Jeffries poured her a cup of tea as she took her chair. "As you can see, Phyllis has decided to join us today. When today's meeting is finished, I'll bring her up to date, so to speak, on the progress of our case."

"You don't have to do that. I've been listening most

times at the door," Phyllis blurted out. When she realized what she'd just said, she blushed a fiery red. "Oh no, I don't mean that in a bad way . . . it's just I so wanted to help and—and—"

"Don't fret, child," Luty interrupted with a laugh. "I've listened at doors many a time. We all have. It's one of the best ways of finding out things."

"We understand what you meant, Phyllis," Mrs. Jeffries said. "Now, who would like to go first?"

"Let me," Betsy offered. "I'll not take long. I spoke to one of the maids from another house on Wallington Square, and the girl knew who the Banfields were, but the only thing she could tell me was that a few days before the ball, she'd seen a lady come out of the back of the Banfield house and she was carrying a jug and small tin."

"Was it a servant?" Ruth took a sip of tea.

"No, the woman was well dressed. But she was heavily veiled, so the girl wasn't able to see her face."

"What color was the veil?" Wiggins asked. "If it was the blue one, I know who she was," he declared.

"It was the blue one." She grinned triumphantly. "I made a point of asking the color. But that's about all I heard today. The maid didn't know anything else."

"Wiggins, you go next," Mrs. Jeffries suggested. She helped herself to a slice of brown bread.

Without mentioning that he'd pretended to be an assistant private inquiry agent, he told them about his meeting with Emma Carr. "I also asked her what day it was that she and Fanny had seen Mrs. Bickleton and it was last Friday."

"Margaret Bickleton is the lady in blue," Mrs. Jeffries

mused. "And she's the one who went to Battersea, not that that in and of itself means anything. But it is curious. I wonder what she was doing in the mews." An idea flew into her head and then just as quickly vanished.

"I wish we knew." Betsy sighed. "But it was probably something perfectly innocent."

"I'll go next, then," Mrs. Goodge offered. "My sources were short on the ground today, but I did find out that Rosalind Kimball could easily get her hands on the kind of poison used to kill poor Mrs. Banfield."

"Cor blimey, that doesn't sound as if your sources were short of anything," Wiggins exclaimed. "'Ow'd you find that out?"

She laughed. "One of my former colleagues came by today. He used to be a footman but now he owns a tobacco shop. Bernie Poole has come up quite a bit in the world. But he happened to run into Ida Leahcock, and she gave him my address, so he stopped in to say hello, but that's not what you're interested in hearin'. Bernie didn't stay very long, but we had a cup of tea and naturally I started dropping names left and right, hopin' he'd know one of them. Well, he did. Turns out his brother works as a butler for the Harpers and they live next door to the Kimballs in Mayfair. But more importantly, it seems the Kimball house is in such a miserable state that they're overrun with vermin and, rats bein' what they are, they invaded the Harper mansion. Well, the Harpers weren't havin' it. They sent Bernie's brother next door with a big brown bottle of poison and you'll never guess what this poison was made of: prussic acid. Bernie's brother makes it up himself."

"Did you find out when this happened?" Mrs. Jeffries

asked. She glanced at Phyllis and noted that the girl was staring at the cook with an expression of interest, not fear.

Mrs. Goodge beamed proudly. "Bernie couldn't remember the exact date, but he knew it was sometime last spring."

"And we know that Rosalind Kimball hated Arlette Banfield," Hatchet added. "But, then, from what we're learning, there were a number of people who were displeased with Mrs. Banfield the younger."

"Who would like to go next?" Mrs. Jeffries asked.

"My turn," Smythe volunteered. He told them what he'd learned from Blimpey Groggins. "So it seems as if Lewis Banfield isn't quite as 'onorable as he lets on."

"They never are," Mrs. Goodge interjected dryly. "Especially when it comes to affairs of the heart. Poor girl, she must have been humiliated when Banfield didn't keep up his end of the bargain."

"Helen Bickleton might not 'ave known about it," Smythe said quickly. "My source told me the marriage agreement wasn't in writing and was deliberately kept quiet. Hiram Bickleton didn't want his daughter thinking he'd bought her a husband. Still, it does put Lewis Banfield in a whole different light, doesn't it?"

"This ain't fair—all of you found out all sorts of things and I spent the whole day dashin' from place to place without learning one danged thing worth mentioning." Luty turned and stared at Hatchet. "I'll bet you found out all sorts of interesting bits and pieces."

"One doesn't like to boast, madam, but I did have a very successful day." He smiled smugly and then told them about his visit to the Manleys. He took his time in the telling, making certain he didn't forget any of the details. There was a general murmur of excitement when he finished by telling them the connection he'd found between the Banfield and the Montrose families. "So you see, all our instincts were correct."

Everyone began to talk at once. "I knew there had to be something more to the Montroses not wanting their daughter to marry into that bunch," Luty declared.

"Cor blimey, I wonder if Arlette Banfield knew her husband's uncle was once in love with her father's sister," Wiggins added.

"It doesn't seem like much of a connection," Smythe muttered. He wondered why Groggins hadn't uncovered this particular fact.

"And even if old Mr. Banfield was supposedly in love with Arlette's aunt, it doesn't seem to be a motive for murder," Mrs. Goodge added.

Mrs. Jeffries said nothing. Her mind was working furiously as one theory after another was considered and then discarded. She had no idea how this last news would fit into the overall picture; if anything, she was more confused than ever.

"I'm sorry to interrupt." Ruth raised her voice over the din to be heard. "But may I go now? I've a dinner party this evening and I must get home to change before I go."

Mrs. Jeffries smiled apologetically. "Please go on. We're the ones who ought to be apologizing to you. What happened today?"

"The funeral was very much as you'd expect, except that all the friends of the Montroses sat on one side of the church while the Banfields sat on the other," she replied. "It was the same at the reception, too. Crispin and

Elizabeth Montrose took over one end of the room while the Banfields held court at the other end. I learned nothing directly from any of them but I did overhear two other conversations that might be of interest." She told them about Mrs. Peyton and the gardener. "Then two minutes later, I stepped outside to get some fresh air and I overheard another extraordinary conversation." She recounted the exchange between the two servants. "But I couldn't see who was doing the talking; I could only hear them. After they left, I went back inside to express my condolences to both families but I heard nothing useful and I was one of the last people to leave. Lady Stafford was leaving at the same time, and I offered her a lift in my carriage. She had quite a bit to say." She smiled as she repeated the chat she'd had with the old woman. "She told me that Geraldine Banfield was a blood relative of the family, not just related by marriage. Isn't that extraordinary—no wonder the woman is so keen on family honor and duty."

They broke up soon after that and Mrs. Jeffries took Phyllis upstairs to help her in the dining room. As they laid the table, the housekeeper gave her a full report on everything they'd learned thus far.

"But you don't need to go over it for my benefit," Phyllis protested. She put a crisp white serviette by the inspector's silverware. "I've been listening to most of your meetings. I've missed one or two, but I think I've heard enough to catch on. I don't want you thinking I'm slow."

"I'd never think anything of the sort." Mrs. Jeffries opened the cupboard and took down a water goblet. "Frankly, I'm going over all this as much for my benefit as for yours. We've learned so much today that it could easily get very confusing. I find one of the best ways to keep the facts straight in one's mind is to say them out loud. Now, what do you make of what we heard today?" She wasn't trying to put the maid on the spot, but she did want to know how good her memory might be.

Phyllis bit her lip and looked down at the floor, then she took a deep breath and said, "Well, to begin with, Betsy told us that a veiled Mrs. Bickleton was seen out in the mews a few days before the murder," she began. She went on to recall everything they'd discussed at the meeting.

As Mrs. Jeffries listened, the oddest idea began to form in her mind, and this time she wasn't going to let the wretched thing get away. As Phyllis recited more and more facts, the idea changed and took on a different, but just as important, shape in her mind.

When the girl finished, Mrs. Jeffries smiled but said nothing.

Puzzled, Phyllis stared at her. "What are you lookin' at me like that for?"

"You don't understand, do you?" The housekeeper laughed in delight. "I've no idea why you think you're thick or slow, Phyllis. You've remembered every single detail and, furthermore, hearing you has helped me. I don't quite understand everything yet, but I'm well on my way."

Witherspoon was late getting home that evening. "I got called to the Yard," he explained as he handed his bowler to Mrs. Jeffries. "I'd gone to the local station to go over the interview reports that their inspector had done on our behalf when I got the message that the chief inspector wanted to see me." He sighed as he slipped off his jacket. "So it took even longer than usual to get to the Yard, and I'm sure you can imagine what the CI wanted."

Mrs. Jeffries took his suit jacket and hung it next to the hat. "He wants this case solved right away, doesn't he."

"He didn't come right out and say that," the inspector said glumly. "But Chief Inspector Barrows told me he was getting messages from the Home Office two and three times a day asking for progress reports and wanting to know if an arrest was imminent." He sighed heavily. "I've never considered myself particularly astute when it comes to politics, but even I managed to take his point. He wants an arrest as soon as possible. But honestly, Mrs. Jeffries, I can't just go around arresting someone because the Home Office is putting pressure on the CI. It simply wouldn't be right."

"Of course not, sir, and I'm sure Chief Inspector Barrows is very much aware that you'll only arrest someone when you're sure that person is guilty. Now come along, sir, a nice glass of sherry will do you just fine."

Witherspoon followed her down the hall and into the drawing room. He sat down, and she went to get the glasses and the bottle of sherry she had put on the cabinet earlier and poured both of them a drink. "Other than your trip to the Yard, how was the rest of your day?" She handed him his Harvey's and sat down opposite him.

He took a long sip of his sherry before he answered. "We had a good start to the day in that we were able to interview Rosalind Kimball immediately after the funeral service."

"She didn't go to the reception?"

"She didn't go the funeral," he replied. "So we went to Mayfair as soon as the cortege left for the cemetery. I must say, she might have a posh address, but the house is in a terrible state. But it was a successful interview in that she revealed a bit more than she intended." He told her all the details of their visit. She listened closely, occasionally breaking in and asking a question or making a comment. When he'd finished, he drained his glass and said, "But then the day seemed to get away from us. Constable Barnes went to the Banfield house to speak with the butler, and I went back to the local station to go over the reports on the interviews with the other people sitting at the Banfield table."

She stared at him in surprise. "You didn't interview them?" That wasn't like the inspector.

He shook his head. "Unfortunately, we simply ran out of time, so yesterday I asked the local inspector if he could do it for us. He interviewed both the Fortnoys and the Kingsleys and to his credit he did an excellent job."

"I'm sure he did, sir," she muttered. Blast, this wasn't good, this investigation was moving far too fast. She'd not deliberately ignored the people who'd been sitting at the Banfield table, but thus far, their snooping about hadn't revealed any real connection between the victim and the other two couples. But she'd meant to dig a bit deeper. Still, it was very frustrating. There seemed to be so many avenues that weren't being explored.

"Both the Kingsleys and the Fortnoys are business acquaintances of Lewis Banfield, and neither couple seemed to have any connection with the victim. But, of course, I shall confirm that with Mr. Banfield when I see him tomorrow."

"You're going to interview him again?" She noticed his glass was empty and she started to get up. "Would you like another sherry?"

"Only if you'll have another one with me." He handed her his glass. "And I most certainly do intend to speak to Mr. Banfield tomorrow. I'm afraid I've been a bit derelict in my duty and I mean to rectify the situation immediately. Honestly, Mrs. Jeffries, sometimes a very important bit of information seems to fall right out of my head."

"We all forget things occasionally and you've never been derelict in your duty, sir." She poured them both another sherry. She went back to her seat, pausing long enough to hand him his drink.

"That's kind of you to say, but the postmortem report revealed an interesting fact about the deceased and, for the life of me, I either neglect to bring it up when I'm asking questions or I simply forget it altogether."

She was pretty sure she knew what it was and, truth be told, she'd wondered why he'd kept silent on the matter. "What was it?"

"Arlette Banfield was expecting a baby." He looked down at the drink in his hand. "And I know it might be important, but it keeps slipping my mind. I think it's because our Betsy is in the family way and, well, I feel so badly for Mr. Banfield and the Montroses. Mind you, I haven't actually seen either of them since I read the postmortem report, but still, I've got to face Crispin Montrose and Lewis Banfield tomorrow. I know the subject must be dealt with; it could have a bearing on the murder. But I'm not looking forward to it."

"I'm sure you'll be very tactful and very delicate," she assured him. She was secretly relieved that he was finally dealing with the matter.

"I'll do my best. I've got to ask Banfield if I can

search his house for a second time. Gracious, that's not going to be pleasant, either."

"Why are you going to search again? Has someone come forward with additional information?"

"No, but Inspector Grainger—he's the local man—had the same thought I did, that it was a warm summer night and the guests weren't wearing heavy outer garments. He reinterviewed all the Banfield servants and a number of the local people who were on the square that night, and none of them recall seeing anyone leave with any sort of curious bulges about their person and, let's face it, Mrs. Jeffries, trying to hide something as large as a champagne bottle would be very difficult, very difficult indeed."

Mrs. Jeffries yawned as she came downstairs the next morning and went into the kitchen. Samson hopped down from his stool by the pine sideboard and began weaving back and forth around her ankles. She looked down at the cat. "You don't fool me, you silly old cat, you're not being affectionate, you just want your morning dish of cream."

"But of course he's being affectionate," the cook exclaimed. She came into the kitchen from the wet larder holding a small, flat dish in her hand. "I don't understand why the household always thinks he's up to something." Samson, upon seeing her, immediately flew across the floor and began butting his big head against the cook's shins. She put his dish in front of him. "Here you are, lovey, it's just the way you like it."

"He bites everyone but you."

Mrs. Goodge laughed. "What are you doing up this early? Is it the case?"

"I think so," she admitted. "I've got some ideas but we're going to need some very specific information and I'm not sure how to proceed."

"Just tell us what you need done and let us take care of doing it," the cook advised.

Barnes looked around the beautifully proportioned drawing room and nodded appreciatively. He knew nothing about the art of decorating, but the difference between the Montrose home and most others was remarkable. He glanced at the inspector and saw him gaping open-mouthed at a painting over the fireplace. It was a beautiful dark-haired woman in red medieval dress sitting on a broken tree branch in the middle of a forest. She held up a garland of white flowers toward the sky. "I say, I believe this is Elizabeth Montrose," he murmured.

Barnes thought that was a good guess, considering they were in the Montrose house. "It certainly looks like her, sir." He continued studying the room. A long carved bench with cushions upholstered in green and gold paisley served as a settee. Opposite that was another settee, only this one had wide arms and was set in a long frame. The wood looked to the constable like it was mahogany. The cushions were the same pattern as those on the bench. There weren't any curio cabinets or elaborate tallboys, but there were several low mahogany tables with simple, clean lines placed near the sitting areas. Wooden bookcases filled with books, sculptures, glassware, paintings, and colorful exotic objects of various sizes and shapes covered the wall opposite the windows. A fat black cat was asleep in a woven basket by the hearth, and there were newspapers and magazines scattered about on the tabletops. Barnes had an inkling of why the Montroses hadn't wanted their daughter to marry into the Banfield clan. This house was warm, welcoming, and as different from the Banfield house as night from day.

"She's a very handsome woman." Witherspoon dragged his gaze away from the painting. "I'm not looking forward to this interview."

"I know, sir; if Mr. Montrose didn't know about the baby, it's going to break his heart when he finds out he's lost both a daughter and a grandchild."

"Then we've got to ask Lewis Banfield if he knew." Witherspoon frowned. "Sometimes I thoroughly dislike my responsibilities. But duty is duty, so when we're finished here we'll do what needs to be done. We must stop in at the station beforehand, though; I'll want to have the lads ready for the search."

"Providing he'll give us permission to search," the constable muttered. He'd spoken with Mrs. Jeffries earlier and she'd passed along the information the household had learned. But now he was in a quandary. It was likely that Crispin Montrose would be very upset when he found out his murdered child was herself in the family way. If the fellow got hysterical, it would be very hard to get him to open up about his family's past connection to Garrett Banfield. Having the inspector's household out and about gathering information was very useful, but it did sometimes cause the devil's own mess.

They both turned as the door opened and a tall, slender, dark-haired man wearing a maroon dressing gown over a white shirt and black trousers stepped into the room. His hair was brown, his face pale, and there were dark circles around his eyes. "Good day, gentlemen, I'm Crispin Montrose. I understand you wish to speak with me."

"I'm sorry to disturb you at such a time, Mr. Montrose." Witherspoon crossed the room, his hand extended. "I'm Inspector Gerald Witherspoon and this is Constable Barnes. Please accept both our condolences for your loss."

Montrose smiled slightly and the two men shook. "Thank you, Inspector." He nodded politely to Barnes and pointed to the bench settee. "Please sit down and make yourselves comfortable. You can ask me whatever you like. I want nothing more than to see my daughter's killer hang."

The two policemen took a seat where he'd indicated, and Barnes pulled out his notebook.

"What do you wish to know?" Montrose used his leg to push a leather ottoman out from behind the other couch and sat down.

"When was the last time you saw your daughter?" Witherspoon asked.

"The day she died. She came by just after breakfast that morning. She wanted to ask us again if we could go to the ball. But we couldn't, and I'll regret that till the day I die. Unfortunately, we had a prior engagement. We'd promised to go to a gallery showing for one of our friends."

"Was Mrs. Banfield upset or worried about anything when she came by to see you?"

He shook his head slowly. "No, she and my wife had had a very nasty disagreement, and I think the real reason she stopped in was to make sure that all was well between the two of them. But mothers and daughters being what they are, they ended up having another squabble before she left. It's upset Elizabeth greatly. I'm not sure my wife is going to recover from this."

The inspector gazed at him sympathetically. He had the distinct feeling the man was going to fall apart when he told him. "Do you know if your daughter was frightened or concerned that someone was trying to harm her?"

"Arlette wasn't scared of anyone; it wasn't in her nature to be a coward. But she was annoyed." Montrose's expression hardened. "She said that Geraldine Banfield had deliberately invited two women to stay at the house that she knew didn't like her. She also said she knew that Geraldine Banfield wasn't particularly fond of either woman, either."

"Did she think Mrs. Banfield the elder extended the invitations out of spite?" Barnes asked.

"Absolutely." Montrose nodded. "Margaret Bickleton hated my daughter and Rosalind Kimball certainly was no friend. But when she brought the subject up to Lewis, he claimed that his aunt frequently had people to stay and that she should just avoid them."

"So Mr. Banfield sided with his aunt and not his wife." The constable knew he was pressing and he didn't like it, but it was the only way to get the interview where he hoped it would go.

Montrose raised an eyebrow. "Arlette didn't put it quite that way, but yes, that was more or less the truth of it. But knowing the Banfields as I do, I wasn't surprised."

This was the opening he'd been hoping for, so Barnes dived in before the inspector could ask another question. "Are your families connected in any way, Mr. Montrose?"

Crispin Montrose stayed silent for a few moments.

Finally, he said, "Yes, we are. I've had some familiarity with them since I was a child."

Witherspoon gaped at him. "We've interviewed both the Banfields—"

Montrose interrupted. "Neither Lewis nor Geraldine was aware that many years ago I was acquainted with Geraldine's late husband, Garrett Banfield. I must say, when Arlette came home from that dinner party where she and Lewis met and began talking about him as though he were a god descended from Olympus itself, I was beside myself. I didn't want my daughter anywhere near him or his relations."

Witherspoon had recovered from the surprise. "I assume this was because of your previous acquaintance with Garrett Banfield," he stated calmly.

"You assume correctly," Montrose replied. He shifted, causing his dressing gown to gape open, so he pulled it closed. "I had a sister named Anna. We were the only two children in my family that lived past the age of five. She was fifteen years older and we lived in Chalfont St. Giles in Buckinghamshire. I've no idea how the two of them met, but Garrett Banfield fell in love with my sister."

"Did she return his affections?" Witherspoon asked.

"No." Montrose broke into a wide smile. "She was engaged to a young blacksmith and loved him deeply. But Banfield wouldn't leave her alone. He simply couldn't believe that a village girl preferred another man to him. When she rejected him, he began a series of harassments that extended to our family and her fiancé. The only reason it ended was because his cousin arrived and a few days later it was announced they were engaged."

"His cousin was Geraldine Banfield," Barnes clarified. He did that more for Witherspoon's sake than his own.

"Did Geraldine Banfield know of his feelings for your sister?" The inspector rested his arm on the wide wooden side rail.

"We were harassed by the bastard, but they were such a powerful family I don't think my father told anyone. It wouldn't have done any good. From what I learned in later years, Banfield kept his feelings about Anna to himself, and Geraldine certainly never let on that there was any connection between our families. All I really remember is how relieved Anna was when he got engaged and got the hell out of her life."

Witherspoon nodded. "Mr. Montrose, I've some information to share and it may be quite painful."

He lifted his chin and met the inspector's gaze. "My child is dead and my wife and I are out of our minds with grief. How can anything be more painful than that?"

"Mr. Montrose, did your daughter tell you she was expecting a baby?"

During the train ride from Paddington, Hatchet had thought about the best way to approach the gardener and had come up with a very good plan. He'd even practiced what he would say as he'd walked the half mile from the station to the Banfield country house.

At their morning meeting, Mrs. Jeffries had given some of them a specific list of information to acquire and, difficult as his assignment might be, he was determined to do his best. He stood for a moment, staring through the big iron gates at the house while he gathered his nerve. The Queen Anne–style house sat fifty yards up a drive filled with white stones. It was a three-story redbrick home with a conservatory on one side and a row of separate outbuildings on the other.

He pushed open the gate and started up the drive, wincing at the loud crunch of his steps against the loose pebbles. The place looked absolutely deserted. There was no cooking smoke from the chimneys and even from this distance he could see all the curtains were drawn tight. He hoped that the gardener hadn't decided to go into the village for a quick pint; he didn't want to miss the next train back to London.

"Can I help you, sir?" A man's voice broke into his thoughts.

Hatchet turned and came face-to-face with a burly man holding a scythe. "Are you Mr. Bigglesworth?"

"I am, and who might you be?"

"My name is Josiah Bennington and I am here to seek your help." Hatchet smiled broadly and reached into his coat pocket. He pulled out his flat black leather purse. "Is there somewhere close by where we can talk business? I've a proposition that might interest you."

"What kind of proposition?" Bigglesworth eyed him suspiciously. "I'm an honest man, so—"

"I know," Hatchet interrupted. "That's why I've come to see you. I don't want your formula, I just want to buy some of it."

Bigglesworth stared at him in confusion. "Buy some of what? I don't know who you think I am, but I don't 'ave anything for sale."

"Really, that's most disappointing." He put his purse back in his pocket. "That's very disappointing. We heard your formula was simply the very best. Oh well, I suppose my mistress will simply have to use some of that dreadful commercially produced material one can find at the chemist's or the ironmonger's."

Bigglesworth's face fell when he saw the purse disappear. "Er, uh, what exactly was ya lookin' for?"

"Poison," Hatchet replied. "My mistress's house is getting overrun with vermin and we've tried everything, but nothing has worked. One of Madam's acquaintances mentioned she'd acquired some excellent vermin poison that wouldn't smell up the house like a gasworks factory, because it was a homemade formula, and that you were the one who'd invented it. But perhaps she was mistaken. I'm so sorry to have troubled you." He nodded politely and turned to go back the way he'd come.

"Not so fast, sir," Bigglesworth said. "Come on up to my cottage. I think maybe we can do a bit of business."

"Did Emma really send you 'ere? And are you really an assistant private inquiry agent?" Fanny stared at Wiggins speculatively.

"She did and I am," he replied. "I know you've not had a chance to speak with her—"

"Yes, I have," Fanny interrupted. "With all the comin' and goin' between the funeral reception and the condolence calls, we're always running out of something or other. Cook sent me out this morning to the butcher's to pick up another ham and I saw Emma. We walked to the high street together and she told me about you, about how you was trying to find out who murdered Mrs. Banfield the younger."

Wiggins sent up a silent, heartfelt prayer of thanks. Mrs. Jeffries had given him a very specific task and making contact with Fanny was the first step. He'd hung about the mews, watching the back of the Banfield house and hoping she'd come outside. "Did you like her?"

"I liked her ever so much." Fanny's lip trembled. "Now that she's gone, I'm going to be looking for another position. It's goin' to be miserable here now"—she jerked her head toward the house—"now that she's gone. Mrs. Banfield the elder is a right old tartar. But I don't have much time; they're expecting me back. Mrs. Peyton only sent me to the shop for this." She held up a tin of tea. "They run out of that as well."

They were standing in the mews behind the house next door to the Banfield home. Wiggins wasn't sure how best to phrase his question. "Uh, Emma mentioned that you had to drag an old trunk of Mrs. Banfield's down from the attic, is that right?"

"That's right, the old cow wouldn't let me call the footman for a bit of help, and Danny's a good lad, he'd have been glad to do it for me. Then an hour later, she made me drag it back up to the attic."

"Emma said you told her that the only thing Mrs. Banfield had taken out of the trunk was a book of newspaper clippings. Did you see what they were about?" He hoped it had been Fanny that Ruth had overheard yesterday.

"'Course I did." She giggled. "And so did Mrs. Bickleton. That's what give me the idea to have a look, you see. I'd gone up to start cleaning the box rooms on the third floor when I heard footsteps goin' up the little staircase. I peeked out and saw Mrs. Bickleton goin' into the attic as bold as you please."

"Mrs. Bickleton was already staying at the house then?"

"No, that's what made me so curious. She'd only come to have morning coffee with Mrs. Banfield. But then Mrs. Banfield the younger and her mother, Mrs. Montrose, got into a horrible row and Mrs. Banfield the elder sent Mrs. Bickleton out the door. But here she was two hours later sneakin' up to the attic. So I crept up the stairs and I had a peek myself: she'd opened the trunk and was goin' through the book that Mrs. Banfield had taken out earlier and then put back in."

Wiggins frowned in confusion. "I don't understand. 'Ow did she get back in the house if Mrs. Banfield the elder had sent her packing?"

"Danny told me he overheard Mrs. Peyton sayin' she'd come back because she wanted to search for an earring she'd lost. She told the housekeeper she didn't want the servants looking because it was valuable. But that was a lie. She was just using that as an excuse to go upstairs and have a snoop."

He still didn't quite understand. "But if she'd just come for morning coffee, how did she know about the trunk?"

"She'd just arrived when Mrs. Banfield the elder called me downstairs and told me she was through with it and that I should get it from her room and take it back upstairs. As I was leaving to do her bidding, I overheard Mrs. Bickleton asking her about it. Like I said, she's a right nosy old thing." She gave a quick, worried glance toward the house. "Look, I've got to get back . . ."

"Just one more question, miss." Wiggins still wasn't sure about the sequence of events but he'd worry about that later. "What were the clippings about?"

"I hate to sound cold and heartless, sir," Barnes said. They were in the foyer of the Banfield house, so he kept his voice low so no one could overhear. "But can we obtain Mr. Banfield's permission to search the house before you ask him if he knew about his late wife's pregnancy? If he reacts the way Mr. Montrose did, we'll have a right old mess on our hands."

Witherspoon visibly winced. Upon hearing about the loss of his grandchild, Crispin Montrose had let out a scream of grief and then collapsed. He'd flailed his fists against the carpet and sobbed. Luckily, his wife ran into the room and stopped the fellow from seriously harming himself, as he was by this time banging his head against the floor as well. Elizabeth Montrose had taken the news better than her husband, but her grief had been written all over her face. "I think that is a very good idea," he murmured.

Lewis Banfield came out of the drawing room. "Good day, gentlemen. Mrs. Peyton says you need to speak with me again."

"That is correct, sir, we've a few more questions to ask about the sequence of events on the night of the ball."

"Of course, Inspector. Let's go into the drawing room." He turned back toward the hallway.

"Before that, sir, we have another request," Witherspoon said.

He stopped and looked over his shoulder. "What would that be?"

"We'd like your permission to search your house again."

"Is that really necessary?"

"We think it is, sir," the inspector replied. "The original search was conducted when the house was filled with people and we're concerned that some evidence might have been overlooked. I assure you, Mr. Banfield, our men will be very careful to disturb your household as little as possible and we'll put everything we touch back into its proper place."

Banfield hesitated.

"You did say you wanted your wife's killer caught, sir," Barnes reminded him.

"I meant that," he snapped. "Of course you can search. Are your men outside?"

"We asked them to wait in the mews."

"I'll go and bring them in," Barnes offered as he started for the servants' stairs.

"I'll come with you," Banfield retorted. "I'll need to let Mrs. Peyton know. Make yourself comfortable in the drawing room, Inspector. I don't know what you expect to find at this late date, but I'll do as you request."

Witherspoon watched them disappear down the hallway. He wasn't sure there was anything for them to find, but his inner voice was telling him that a search was absolutely necessary.

But within twenty minutes, his inner voice would be proved right as well. They were in the drawing room when one of the constables opened the door. "Excuse me for interrupting, sir, but we've found something upstairs that you need to see. We've left it right where we found it, sir. We know your methods."

Witherspoon and Barnes both stood up and hurried toward the door.

Lewis Banfield, who'd just learned of his late wife's pregnancy, wiped a handkerchief across his cheeks, leapt up, and fell into step behind them. "I'll accompany you."

Moving quickly, the constable led them up the stairs to the first floor and down a long, wide corridor. "It's in here, sir." He pushed open a door near the end and stepped inside.

The two policemen entered the bedroom. Another constable was on his knees next to the massive four-poster bed. When he saw them, he rose and pointed. "It's just under the bed, sir. I can't imagine how it could have been missed during the first search."

Barnes got there first. He flicked up the bottom of the gold damask spread and bent down. By the time the others reached him, he'd pulled out an open wooden box. The constable stared at it for a moment and then lifted it so the inspector could see the contents.

Witherspoon heard a gasp come from Lewis Banfield. He looked over his shoulder. "Is this the champagne bottle from the ball?"

"Oh, my God, it's the brand we always buy." He went to reach for it, but Witherspoon jerked the box out of his reach. "Careful, sir, if this contained poison, it could still be dangerous." He laid the box on the bed and pulled out his white handkerchief. He didn't know enough about cyanide to risk touching it without protection, for he knew some types of poisons could be absorbed through the skin.

The bottle was nestled in a thick layer of straw and was corked. Wrapping the kerchief around his fingers, he picked it up at the base and lifted it out, revealing another item.

A small brown bottle with a cork stopper.

"What on earth is that?" Banfield exclaimed.

"I imagine it's some form of cyanide," Barnes said dryly. He looked at Witherspoon. "Should I fish it out or should we leave it for the police surgeon?"

"Let's leave it." Witherspoon held up the champagne bottle. "This isn't empty. Once it's analyzed, we should know if this was the means by which Mrs. Banfield was poisoned or if the poison was only in her glass."

Carefully, he put the bottle back, picked up the box, and handed it to the constable standing behind Barnes. "Get this to the station and entered into evidence. As soon as it's logged, get it to the police surgeon and make sure he understands we want the contents of both bottles analyzed as soon as possible. If there's a problem, get a message to either myself or Constable Barnes. We're going to need the report by tomorrow morning." He looked at the constable who'd come to the drawing room to fetch them. "Were you here the night of the murder?"

"Yes, sir, I was."

"Did you take part in the house search?"

The constable shifted uneasily. "I did, but I wasn't up here, sir. I searched the kitchen and the ballroom."

"I'm not looking to accuse anyone of dereliction or

shoddy police work, I'm merely trying to ascertain if this room was searched."

"It wasn't," Lewis Banfield answered. "By the time the constables had finished downstairs it was so late, the rooms up here were already occupied by our guests, all of whom had retired for the night."

"This is a guest room?" Witherspoon asked. "Who stayed in it?"

Lewis ran a hand through his hair. "Margaret Bickleton."

Mrs. Jeffries paced the kitchen as she waited for the others to return for their afternoon meeting. They should be there any moment. She wasn't sure she was right about this case, but if the others had been successful in learning even half of what she'd asked, she thought she knew who had murdered Arlette Banfield.

But she wasn't sure. The motive was there and so was the malice, but on the other hand, she wasn't certain all the facts fit her theory.

"Are you fretting?" The cook put a platter of buns on the table next to the teapot. "They'll be here soon enough and you'll know whether you're right or not."

"But if I'm not correct, then I've not got a clue as to who murdered the poor woman and we'll be right back at the beginning. You know the inspector is under pressure . . ."

Mrs. Goodge gave an impatient wave of her hand. "He's always under pressure to solve his ruddy cases, and if you're wrong about this one, then you'll have to have another think about it. We'll still have all the bits and pieces we've got now—no, I tell a lie, we'll have even more. I've got a feeling in my bones that the others were very successful today."

Mrs. Jeffries laughed. "You do make me feel better; you're right, of course. I must say, your information was the one piece that made it all fit together. Fancy you remembering that case. It was years ago."

"And it caused a right old sensation," the cook replied. "Oh, good, someone's back."

Wiggins came bounding into the room, and within five minutes the others followed. Phyllis appeared as soon as they were seated and took her place at the end of the table.

Betsy went first. "I did what you asked, Mrs. Jeffries, and I had a bit of luck. I found the boy that took the message from the Banfield house to Lewis Banfield's office. He described the woman and, from his description, it was Rosalind Kimball who gave him the note."

Mrs. Jeffries' spirits began to sink. That wasn't what she expected to hear at all. "How did he describe her?"

"Short, skinny, and with a lump growing out of her back." Betsy could tell that the housekeeper was disappointed.

"Unkind as it may be, that's definitely Rosalind Kimball," Ruth affirmed. "Margaret is tall and ramrod straight."

"Can I go next?" Wiggins helped himself to a bun. When no one objected, he repeated everything he'd learned from Fanny. "So, Margaret Bickleton was up in that attic, and Fanny saw her lookin' at them old clippings." He turned to Mrs. Jeffries. "What's that all about? What do some newspaper cuttins about an old murder trial at Aylesbury have to do with this case?"

Mrs. Jeffries laughed. She was enormously cheered. This was good news and fit right into her theory. Perhaps Betsy's information didn't mean anything. "I think those clippings inspired our killer."

"I'll go next, then," Luty declared. "I had a run of luck, too. The maid at the Millhouse home told me that an hour or two before the cat Hector was found dead, she'd gone out to pound the rugs and seen the woman in blue. She was leaning against the Banfield gate and had a jug in her hand. It was one of them metal ones with a top on it."

"That sounds like the type I use for cream," Mrs. Goodge added.

"And then an hour later, poor old Hector was dead. The maid swears that Mr. Millhouse is sure the poor thing was poisoned."

"Madam, you've done exceedingly well." Hatchet gazed at her in admiration. "Frankly, I didn't think you'd be able to do it."

Luty shrugged modestly. She'd die before she admitted that her "run of luck" involved hurling pebbles at the Millhouse kitchen window and then bribing the maid to talk. "It was nothing."

"I'm very impressed." Mrs. Jeffries swallowed her disappointment about Betsy's information and put a cheerful smile on her face. "I gave you all very difficult assignments and you seem to have come through with flying colors."

"I'm afraid my informant wasn't nearly as forthcoming," Ruth said quickly. "She had no idea if there was vermin poison at the Bickleton household. But I'm having dinner tonight with Caroline Clenninger. She knows absolutely everything that goes on in London, so hopefully I'll have more information by tomorrow morning."

"Not to worry, Ruth," Hatchet said. "That's why Mrs. Jeffries sent me to the Banfield country house, and my source confirmed there is indeed vermin poison there and that it is a homemade recipe containing prussic acid."

"Excellent, Hatchet," Mrs. Jeffries exclaimed. "And had Margaret Bickleton been there recently?"

Hatchet's smile disappeared. "Actually, Mrs. Jeffries, she hasn't been there since last summer."

CHAPTER 10

———

Mrs. Jeffries forced herself to listen as Hatchet finished his recitation of meeting with the gardener at the Banfield country house. She'd only sent him there because Ruth had mentioned him yesterday when she'd repeated what she'd overheard at the funeral reception.

"And he was quite annoyed that Geraldine Banfield ignored the real problem the household was facing," Hatchet said. "Instead, all she did was to ask him for the keys to the outbuildings and then she sent him off to harness the pony and trap to take her back to the station."

"Exactly when was this again?" Smythe asked.

"Almost two weeks before the murder." He reached for a slice of buttered brown bread. "And then the poor fellow waited and waited for either Mrs. Banfield the elder or Mr. Banfield to get back to him with instructions for the builders but they didn't. Finally, on the nineteenth, which was the day of the ball, he sent Mr. Banfield a telegram asking for instructions. The tarps weren't doing a very good job of keeping the wet out, and he was afraid the rain was getting into the walls."

"Did he get an answer?" Ruth asked.

"No." Hatchet frowned. "He didn't. That's why he approached Mrs. Peyton at the funeral reception. But he said she was adamant the household hadn't received a telegram on the day of the ball."

"But they did." Smythe said. "You lot weren't the only ones that had a bit of luck." He grinned at the house-keeper. "I wasn't able to find out about everyone who'd come or gone to the house but I come close."

His assignment had been the most difficult. He'd been told to learn as much as possible about who came and went from the Banfield home on the days leading up to the murder. It hadn't been easy, but passing a bit of coin about among the hansom drivers and the street boys had given him the information he needed. "One of the street lads saw the telegraph boy coming to the house with a message that morning. He said that before the lad was halfway up the walk, an older woman come out. He gave her the telegram."

"But then why wasn't the message given to Mr. Ban-field?" Hatchet mused.

"Maybe it was," Luty suggested. "Considerin' that his wife was murdered, maybe he just forgot it. A leaky roof might not have seemed important."

"Fanny didn't mention anyone getting a telegram," Wiggins said. "And she knew I was interested in every-thing that happened that day."

"If Mrs. Banfield or one of her houseguests intercepted the telegram outside, perhaps Fanny didn't know
about it," Ruth said. "Did your source give you a description of the person who took the telegram?"

Smythe nodded. "The lad said she was tall and on
the portly side. I reckon it had to be Geraldine Banfield.
Mrs. Bickleton is tall but thin, Mrs. Kimball is small,
and Lady Stafford wasn't there that mornin'."

Mrs. Jeffries paced again, only this time it was in the hallway by the front door. She walked because she was trying
to make sense out of it all and couldn't. On the one hand,
she was certain she knew who the killer must be, but on the
other, the facts she'd learned today simply didn't fit with
the scenario that she'd developed in her head. She found
herself at the door again. It was getting late and she wished
the inspector would come home. Perhaps he had learned
something that would help her make sense of it all.

She cracked the door open and peeked outside. But
there was no sign of a hansom. She kept going over and
over everything she knew. She took a deep breath and
tried to put the information in a logical sequence; Ruth
told them that Arlette Banfield had confided that they
were going to ask Geraldine Banfield to move to the
country house, which could be a motive of course. But
Ruth had had the definite impression Arlette and Lewis
had come to that decision the very day of the ball because
Geraldine had insisted all the glassware be washed again.
She'd interfered with the household one time too often.
So that motive wouldn't work; Geraldine wouldn't have
known she was going to be asked to leave.

And what about Lewis Banfield? Did he have a reason for wanting his wife dead? By all accounts, he'd appeared very much in love with her. Yet Mrs. Jeffries knew that appearances were almost always deceiving.

Now that she was dead, Lewis was going to inherit a substantial amount of art worth a great deal of money. But according to what Luty and Hatchet had learned, he had restored the family finances to such a level that he didn't need more money. So financial gain wouldn't have been his motive. Besides greed or hatred, there was usually only one other reason a man would want to get rid of a wife: another woman. But there was no evidence whatsoever that Banfield had any romantic attachments.

She stopped and leaned against the newel post, her arms crossed in front of her as she went down the list of suspects in her mind. Rosalind Kimball loathed Arlette and had actually threatened her. She had access to poison; she'd been given cyanide to kill the vermin in her house. But how could she have put the lethal dose in the champagne bottle? For that matter, how could any of the suspects have done that? Constable Barnes had reported that the bottles had come up from the wet larder and were only opened in the butler's pantry.

She straightened up. "My gracious, the poison probably wasn't in the champagne bottle, it must have been in the glass itself. A glass that was sitting in the pantry and which anyone could have tampered with at any time that day," she muttered aloud. But was that possible? According to what they knew, there were two champagne glasses in the set and they were exactly alike, so how would the killer have known which one Arlette would be using?

Because they weren't exactly alike. She started pacing again. She was no expert on champagne glasses, but these hadn't been made in a factory, they'd been blown by a master craftsperson, Elizabeth Montrose. Surely there must be small differences between the two items. Would the killer have known which glass was which? Surely, but would that matter?

She put the problem out of her mind and continued down her list of suspects. The other couples at the Banfield table seemed to have nothing to do with Arlette, so they were out of the running, so to speak.

Julian Hammond, the artist, was there that night, but other than the fact that he'd been upset because she'd made a business arrangement to have one of his works massproduced, he had no real motive. Furthermore, no one had reported seeing him either near the pantry where the champagne and glass were kept or near the Banfield table, so he wouldn't have had an opportunity to poison her.

Lady Stafford didn't like Arlette but she had no reason to want her dead.

Mrs. Jeffries had saved her number one suspect for last. Margaret Bickleton had a motive: she hated Arlette for stealing her daughter's fiancé. Everything pointed to her. She winced slightly as she recalled what Hatchet had told them. The Bickleton woman hadn't acquired the poison from the Banfield country house as Mrs. Jeffries had assumed, but they knew she'd taken a hansom to Battersea where there were dozens of factories where one could obtain cyanide. That was a bit of an exaggeration, she told herself, but nonetheless, there were a number of establishments where a resourceful person could have laid hands on the lethal stuff.

She sighed and wandered into the drawing room. She wasn't sure what to do next. She'd sent everyone out today with specific instructions for acquiring information that proved Mrs. Bickleton was the killer and they'd done her proud. But some of the pieces they'd brought back didn't fit with the theory she'd concocted. So she wasn't certain she ought to push the inspector in that direction. She went to the window and pulled back the curtain. The street was empty save for a housemaid washing the steps of the house across the road.

But it had to be Mrs. Bickleton, she thought. It had to be. She went into the foyer and resumed her pacing. Why else would the woman have gone to all the trouble of sneaking into the Banfield attic and reading Geraldine Banfield's clippings about that old murder in Salt Hill? It was a rather famous case. John Talwell, the killer, had used prussic acid in a bottle of stout to murder a most inconvenient mistress. Despite dressing like a Quaker and protesting that men of his ilk couldn't do such a terrible thing, Talwell was caught, convicted, and hung for the crime. As she recalled the details, she heard a hansom pull up outside and hurried to the door.

Peeking outside, she saw the inspector alighting from the cab. She was at the ready when he stepped through the front door. "Good evening, Mrs. Jeffries."

"How was your day, sir?" she asked as he handed her his hat.

He thought for a long moment, as though he were

taking her question very seriously. "It started quite badly and then ended quite well."

"Really, sir? I can't wait to hear all about it. Are you having a sherry this evening?"

"Indeed I am," he replied.

A few moments later they were both settled in their favorite spots with their drinks. "Now, sir, do tell me about your day."

He took a quick sip before he spoke. "We started out at the Montrose home," he began. "I had to interview Crispin Montrose. Honestly, Mrs. Jeffries, I certainly wasn't looking forward to it at all. Not only is he grief stricken over losing his child, but as part of our interview we needed to find out if he knew Mrs. Banfield was in the family way."

She stared at him over the rim of her glass. "And did he?"

Witherspoon shook his head. "No, and he reacted as badly as I feared. If Mrs. Montrose hadn't come downstairs and intervened, I think he would have hurt himself."

"Oh dear, sir, that must have been very upsetting."

"It was, but we did learn a few interesting things before the poor fellow lost control of his emotions." He told her about the remainder of the Montrose interview.

"Arlette Banfield actually told her father she thought Geraldine Banfield had deliberately invited two women she didn't like to stay as houseguests for the sole purpose of annoying her?" she clarified. Again, there was a niggle in the back of her mind, as if something important was right in front of her but she couldn't see it.

"That's what he reported." Witherspoon took another sip. "But he was really more concerned about his wife. He didn't think she'd ever get over having had another, sillier argument with Mrs. Banfield because she couldn't go to the ball. But I will admit our day did get a bit better. After leaving the Montroses', we went back to the Banfield home and we found something very useful, very useful indeed." Taking his time, he told her everything that had happened, starting with Lewis Banfield's tearful reaction to learning about his wife's pregnancy to their finding the champagne bottle and possibly the poison under the bed in the guest room.

Mrs. Jeffries' spirits soared. She knew it, she knew it, she was right. "And Lewis Banfield was sure that was the room that Mrs. Bickleton occupied?"

"She's still there, Mrs. Jeffries. She and Mrs. Banfield had gone out for a walk shortly after we arrived and hadn't returned by the time we left. If we're lucky, Mrs. Bickleton will have no idea we've found the box and the bottles."

"What if she looks under the bed?"

"If she saw the box was gone, she'd probably try to leave."

"You mean escape," Mrs. Jeffries corrected. "I mean, if she's the murderer."

"Precisely. But we've taken measures to prevent her from disappearing," he said. "We've got constables posted in the square and the mews. They're watching all the doors."

"But of course, sir. I should have known that. Do you think you'll have the results of the analysis by tomorrow?"

"I think so. I stopped in at the local station and had a quick word with Inspector Grainger. He assured me that the contents of the box had been entered into evidence and everything was on its way to the police surgeon and the chemist. He was a bit embarrassed, I think."

"Why?"

"Well, his lads were the ones tasked with searching the house and, as I said, by the time they reached the bedrooms, people had retired for the night."

"Ah, I think I see the problem, sir." She nodded in agreement. "And they didn't insist on having a proper search. They allowed themselves to be intimidated."

"I'm afraid so," he replied. "But I can hardly fault the men. In our society, the upper class does have substantial influence and I imagine it was one of the superior officers who made the decision not to disturb the Banfield guests." He thought back to the night of the murder, to the young constables who'd been so worried that he would think they hadn't done a proper job. One of the lads had supposedly been chased out of a bedroom by an old lady with an umbrella, and he imagined it had been that incident that had prompted an officer to call off the house search. "But what's done is done. At least we found what we hope is the murder weapon."

"If it is the poison, I wonder why she didn't dispose of it," she murmured. "Surely she must have realized the box and its contents would be found."

Witherspoon stroked his chin. "Constable Barnes and I discussed that very thing on our way to the station. We concluded that she didn't think we'd be back to search the house and planned on disposing of it later."

"But even if Mrs. Bickleton didn't expect the police to search again, surely she must have realized the box was likely to be found. The maids come in to clean every day."

"Do they always look under the bed?"

She opened her mouth and then clamped it shut just as quickly. Truth to tell, she suspected that most maids didn't look under a bed very often. She certainly didn't when she cleaned. "Not really, not unless they're going to shove a broom or a mop underneath and give it a clean, and of course that kind of cleaning would be done after a houseguest left. That's when they'd strip the linens and give the room a good scrub."

"Our thoughts exactly," he said. "Servants are generally worked so hard they don't do anything they're not required and that's not a criticism on my part. I'd not like to get down on my knees to peek under a bed unless I had to, either. But tomorrow we shall know if we really did find the murder weapon in the box."

"And if you did, sir?"

"Then we're going to arrest Margaret Bickleton."

Mrs. Jeffries should have slept like a baby but she didn't. She was up and out in the communal garden before the sun came up. She'd made herself a mug of tea and brought a towel with her. Moving slowly in the darkness, she made her way to the wooden bench under the oak tree. She wiped the dew away and sat down. Sipping her tea, she stared into the distance and let her mind wander. If the analysis of either bottle proved to be any form of cyanide, then the killer had to be Margaret Bickleton.

Then why had she tossed and turned all night as bits of information drifted in and out of her mind? If she were honest, she'd admit to herself that she'd sensed something incorrect about her theory from the beginning.

Something was wrong, but she couldn't put her finger on what it might be. Yesterday she'd gone over everything in what she hoped had been a concise and logical manner. That hadn't done the least bit of good.

The feeling was still with her. Stronger even than it had been before. She took another sip from her mug as the night shifted toward dawn. She sat there for a long time. Down the path, a rabbit jumped out from behind a bramble bush. It looked her way and then hopped off. Birds started to sing and the morning breeze sprang up, rustling through the tree branches and the bushes.

Logic and reason don't seem to be working, she told herself, *so let's try another method.* She closed her eyes and relaxed her shoulders. She sat like that for a good few minutes and let the snatches she remembered from the night before wander back in and out of her consciousness. *"All she"—Geraldine Banfield—"did was to ask him for the keys to the outbuildings and then she sent him off to harness the pony and trap to take her back to the station."*

She took a deep breath. *"But the Banfields prided themselves on being honorable and doing their duty to Queen and country. Which is why it was such a surprise when Garrett began to borrow so heavily."* Then another one, this time about Rosalind Kimball. *"Now the Kimballs will be losing their home and for Rosalind, that's a fate worse than death."* The bits and pieces came drifting in as they would, not in any particular order but because there was something her own inner voice wanted her to understand.

She was seen walking out in the mews holding a jug and a small dish. And right behind that, another item that had nothing to do with it. *"She came flying into the kitchen, screaming that someone had stolen her clothes."*

She started as she heard a back door slam. Getting up, she went back to the house. Mrs. Goodge was sitting at the table when she came into the kitchen. "Oh, so there you are." She nodded at the teapot. "I helped myself to a cup. I figured you'd gone out to have a bit of think on your own."

"You were right." She took her seat and reached for the pot. "Not that it did any good."

"What's wrong? You told us last night that the inspector is probably going to make an arrest today."

"I don't know," she admitted. "But something isn't right."

"But I thought you were convinced that Margaret Bickleton is the killer."

"I was—I mean, I am—oh, blast a Spaniard, I don't know what I mean. On the one hand, my reason assures me we're right, but on the other hand, I've a feeling the picture is right in front of me but that I'm looking at it from the wrong angle."

"Stop your fretting, Mrs. Jeffries." The cook glanced at the clock. "Constable Barnes should be here soon. Let's see what he's got to say about the matter. Perhaps he'll know if they've finished their testing and they really did find the murder weapon in her room."

Before they'd retired last night, she'd told Mrs. Goodge and Wiggins everything the inspector had told her. "But that's just it, I can't imagine that she'd be stupid enough to shove such damning evidence under her bed and leave it there."

Mrs. Goodge frowned and cocked her head to the side. "Yes, she would. Inspector Witherspoon was right about that. Margaret Bickleton thought she was safe. She'd kept the police out of her room on the night of the murder and it never occurred to her they'd be back. She thought she had plenty of time to dispose of the evidence."

"I suppose you're right."

Mrs. Goodge got up. "I'm going to get the breakfast started. Why don't you make us a fresh pot of tea?"

The household was well into the morning routine by the time Barnes arrived. "That tea smells good," he said as he slipped into the chair next to Mrs. Jeffries.

Mrs. Goodge handed him a mug. "You're late, Constable. We've been waiting for you."

He nodded his thanks as he took the mug. He didn't waste time with preliminaries. "I went to the station before I came here. The report was there. They found enough prussic acid in that little brown bottle to kill half of England."

"What about the champagne bottle?" Mrs. Jeffries asked.

"It didn't have anything in it but champagne," Barnes replied. "And that's puzzling me. Why would the killer have bothered to hide the ruddy thing if it didn't have anything to do with the murder?"

"Maybe just to muddy the waters a bit," the cook

suggested. "Or maybe the killer was going to pour herself a toast to celebrate what she'd done. In any case, does it really matter? The inspector told Mrs. Jeffries you'd arrest Margaret Bickleton if you found any poison."

"We are." Barnes frowned heavily. "But I've got a funny feeling about it. I don't think we ought to do it."

"Why ever not?" Mrs. Jeffries asked. The constable was a very intelligent policeman and he had excellent instincts.

"I'm not sure," he admitted, his expression glum. "Maybe it's because of the way we found that box under the bed. I can't believe she'd be that stupid. Oh, and when I was at the station, I asked around and found out it weren't Margaret Bickleton that chased one of their lads out of her bedroom with an umbrella; it was Geraldine Banfield. The inspector told you about that, didn't he?"

"He mentioned it earlier," she replied. "Is that what caused the search to be called off that night?"

"Probably, but the officers at that precinct would chew off their right arms before they'd ever admit that was the reason they'd stopped searching the premises. But take my word for it, none of them wanted to cross a Banfield, and when she chased them out, they scurried down to the inspector and began whining about how late it was getting." He broke off and frowned. "Don't mind me; I'm more annoyed with myself than I am with the local boys. I should have insisted we continue searching. Inspector Witherspoon relied on me and I let him down."

"Don't be absurd, Constable," Mrs. Jeffries said. "You made the best decision you could at the time."

He shrugged. "I don't know. Maybe. But that's not

the only thing botherin' me. Finding that poison just seemed a bit too convenient, if you know what I mean. It was only sheer luck that the whole thing didn't blow up in our faces anyway." He took a quick sip from his mug.

"What do you mean?" Mrs. Jeffries asked.

"We were alone with Mr. Banfield when we asked his permission to search the house. The two ladies were in the house, but we didn't know that at the time. Lewis Banfield went down with me to the kitchen so I could go out and bring the constables into the house. He said he had to tell Mrs. Peyton what we were doing so the staff wouldn't get upset, but what I didn't know, because I went on out to the back, was that Mrs. Banfield was in the kitchen giving the housekeeper the weekly menus. She knew what we were going to do and she told Mrs. Bickleton."

"Which means that Mrs. Bickleton would have known her room was going to be searched," Mrs. Jeffries murmured.

"Right, and only a fool would have left that evidence lying about under her own bed like that," he agreed.

Mrs. Jeffries regarded him curiously. "If you went out to the mews, how did you find out Mrs. Banfield was in the kitchen when Lewis Banfield told them about the search?"

"Constable Long told me this morning. He's one of the local lads and we'd posted him at the front door. He overheard Mrs. Banfield and Mrs. Bickleton talking as they left for their walk. Mrs. Bickleton commented that Mrs. Banfield wasn't to upset herself anymore and that leaving the house would be easier on her nerves than watching policemen tear through their things. But

Mrs. Banfield was very angry and didn't bother to lower her voice one whit. Of course the constable eavesdropped; he even followed them up the walkway on the pretense of opening the gate for them. Mrs. Banfield said she'd given Mrs. Peyton strict instructions to go into each room as soon as the police left and make sure everything was put back in its proper place and that she was going to hold them responsible if anything was missing or damaged."

"So both women knew that the house was to be searched?"

"That's what it looks like to me, which makes me think that someone else might have planted that box under Margaret Bickleton's bed. There were lots of people there for the funeral reception and any one of them could have nipped up, taken it out of a hiding spot, and put it in her room."

"But you can't prove it, can you?" Mrs. Jeffries murmured.

The constable shook his head and finished giving them his perspective on the previous day's events. Then he went to get the inspector.

As Mrs. Jeffries handed Witherspoon his bowler, he commented to the constable that he wanted to go to the Yard first. He wanted to tell Chief Inspector Barrows that they'd be making an arrest at the Banfield house. "I agree with you about the box." Witherspoon put on his hat. "But unless a witness comes forward and tells us they saw another person carrying that box into Mrs. Bickleton's bedroom, we've no choice in the matter. The evidence does point directly to her."

"I know, sir." Barnes opened the front door and stepped outside.

"I don't think I'll be late this evening," the inspector called over his shoulder to Mrs. Jeffries as he followed the constable down the front stairs to a waiting hansom.

Mrs. Jeffries nodded a good-bye, closed the door, and went to the kitchen. The others were just sitting down. Everyone was present; even Fred had come to the table and wedged himself between the footman and cook.

Luty looked at Mrs. Jeffries. "Did you get anything useful out of the inspector?" The morning meetings didn't waste time with preliminaries. Unless someone had been out on the previous evening, the only information to be shared was what had been learned from Witherspoon or Barnes.

"Not just him, but the constable had some news as well," she replied. She poured herself a cup of tea. The others had already served themselves. "It appears as if an arrest is imminent," she began. She brought them up to date on the latest developments in the case. "So you see, even though the inspector is a bit suspicious of the way the evidence was so conveniently found, because the house wasn't as properly searched as it should have been, he's no choice but to arrest Margaret Bickleton."

Hatchet regarded her thoughtfully. "You don't think she's guilty, do you."

"No, I've gone over and over it in my head and some of the evidence does point to her, but not all of it. But the only other person who might have done it simply doesn't have a motive."

"It's too bad the inspector is gettin' ready to make an

arrest." Luty sighed dramatically. "Last night at Lady Barrington's dinner party, I heard something mighty interestin'."

"What'd ya 'ear?" Wiggins reached down and petted Fred on the head.

Luty grinned. "It weren't much, but everyone at the table was talkin' about the murder and some of them was braggin' about how they'd been there that night and wasn't it awful. So I started pepperin' the conversation with the names of our suspects and talkin' about poison and where you could find it and what else it was used for. You know, that sort of thing. All of a sudden Lillian Shepley pipes in and says that she saw Geraldine Banfield at the Aylesbury train station a couple of weeks ago. She was goin' to go over to say hello but her train was just pullin' into the station and she didn't have time. She said that as it was leavin', she saw Mrs. Banfield the elder open her handbag and pull something out and hold it up to the light. Lillian couldn't see what it was; the train started movin' too fast. Anyways, I just thought that was interestin'."

Mrs. Jeffries tried to imagine what the woman could have been holding up. It would have had to have been something small enough to fit into a handbag. But what, and did it have any relevance to the case? "When did this happen?"

"I made it a point to corner Lillian and I asked her. She said it was the sixth."

"That's almost two weeks before the ball," Betsy murmured thoughtfully. "Maybe it doesn't have anything to do with the murder; maybe she just had to go to the Banfield country house. It's near Aylesbury, isn't it?"

"It is," Mrs. Goodge answered. "Remember, my old colleague Charlotte Temple told me about overhearin' Lady Stafford goin' on about how when they were girls, she and Geraldine Banfield had slipped out of the house and gone to watch that murder trial at Aylesbury."

Mrs. Jeffries snapped to attention as one of the last pieces of the puzzle fell into place.

"She mentioned Aylesbury to me as well," Ruth added. "Lady Stafford dropped it into the conversation when I was giving her a ride home from the funeral reception. I found out something as well. I mentioned to you that I was going to Caroline Clenninger's for supper. Of course, much like Luty's dinner party, everyone was talking about the murder."

"So what did your friend Caroline have to say?" Mrs. Goodge asked.

"Caroline had nothing to say, but Rebecca Abbot did. Rebecca's brother does business with Lewis Banfield and they see the family socially. About a fortnight ago, Rebecca and Thomas were invited to dine with the Banfields and they were having sherry in the drawing room before dinner. Arlette Banfield had come home late and had gone upstairs to change clothes."

"Was Geraldine Banfield present?" Mrs. Jeffries asked. A different picture was starting to take shape in her mind, one that used the same information they had thus far but came up with a very different image.

Ruth nodded. "And she was visibly annoyed that Arlette was late. But Lewis wasn't in the least upset. He laughed when she stuck her head into the drawing room and apologized to the guests for her tardiness and told her husband that she'd had a very successful day. As soon as she disappeared, Lewis made some comment about how proud he was that his wife was almost as good a businesswoman as he was a businessman and that if he weren't already married to her, he'd hire her to work for him." She paused. "According to Rebecca, that's when the evening got interesting because Geraldine Banfield made some snide comment about how it wasn't fitting for a woman to indulge in such behavior and Lewis shouldn't encourage her wild plans. He laughed again and told his aunt not to be so old-fashioned. He said that Arlette had negotiated a very shrewd deal and that he was delighted she was a modern woman."

"Was this the mass-produced version of her statue that they were talkin' about?" Wiggins asked curiously.

"That's right. But after Lewis made his comment, Geraldine said nothing and, a few moments later, Arlette came down and they went into the dining room. During dinner, the conversation turned to business and Lewis asked Arlette what kind of terms she'd arranged with the manufacturer. At this point, Geraldine Banfield cut into the conversation and said she hoped Arlette's mother could talk some sense into her because she thought the whole idea was dishonorable and disgusting. She leapt up and stormed out of the room."

"Cor blimey, I'll bet that stopped the conversation," Wiggins muttered.

"I'm sure it did," Hatchet agreed.

"What happened then?" Betsy asked eagerly. "Did Arlette hold her ground or did she jump up and go after her?"

"She held her ground," Ruth confirmed. "Rebecca said that both Arlette and Lewis apologized on behalf of Geraldine and they changed the subject. The remainder of the dinner was very pleasant. Arlette and Rebecca went into the drawing room while the men had their port. Rebecca made some comment about seeing Elizabeth Montrose's work at Gillette's and Arlette confided in her that it wasn't just Geraldine that was upset because she was letting the statue be reproduced; her mother was even more furious. But for entirely different reasons." She broke off and took a quick sip from her cup. "She wasn't looking forward to her mother's visit the next day."

"So do you think this dinner party was the night before Arlette had the horrid row with her mother?" Mrs. Jeffries muttered. Even as she asked the question, she was deep in thought, trying to fit all the pieces together into a pattern that worked. Almost, almost, she could see how it must have happened, but what she didn't understand was the *why* of it.

"I think so," Ruth replied. "But Rebecca didn't say it specifically, and, frankly, I didn't think to ask her about dates. All she said was it was *about* a fortnight ago."

Mrs. Goodge gave her an admiring glance. "You heard an earful, didn't you?"

Ruth laughed. "I got very lucky. But I'm not finished."

"Nellie's whiskers! You're tryin' to outdo me—and Hatchet's the only one who is allowed to do that," Luty exclaimed good-naturedly.

"Don't keep us waitin', then, what else did you find out?" Smythe asked eagerly.

"It wasn't much," Ruth said modestly. "Only that Grace

Alperton was at Caroline's dinner party, too, and she mentioned that she'd run into Helen Bickleton in Liberty's on the fifteenth—Grace remembered the date because that's when she gets her quarterly funds from the bank. But I digress. Helen said that Margaret had been thrilled to be invited to stay at the Banfields' as a houseguest. She claimed her mother had been angling for an invitation for weeks and had almost given up hope but right before Helen left the house to go shopping that morning, a messenger had arrived with an invitation. Grace, of course, said she'd never accept an invitation on such short notice."

"That can't be right." Betsy frowned and looked at Mrs. Jeffries. "Margaret Bickleton told the inspector she'd gone for morning coffee with Geraldine Banfield to discuss what clothes she should bring when she came to stay, remember? And that was the day they overheard the argument between Arlette and her mother. That's supposedly the reason Geraldine hurried her out of the house."

"Do we know what day they had a row?" Mrs. Goodge asked in confusion. "I can't keep track of it all."

"It's confusing to me, too," Phyllis said quietly. She gave the cook a shy smile.

Mrs. Jeffries couldn't, either, but she sensed that Betsy was right. She started to ask another question, but Hatchet spoke up. "Didn't you tell us just a few minutes ago that Crispin Montrose said that Arlette thought both the houseguests had been invited out of spite?" he asked her.

Mrs. Jeffries nodded slowly as she recalled Witherspoon's account of the meeting with Arlette's father. For a moment, she stared past them toward the window over the sink. Finally, she said. "Yes, but I don't think spite was the only reason she wanted houseguests." Her voice trailed off as the picture changed and grew, emerging into crystal clarity as the events unfolded in the same sequence, but with an entirely different killer. In her mind's eye, she saw a figure reaching for a blue champagne flute, saw a pair of gloved hands pull out the stopper of a minuscule brown bottle and pour six or seven tiny grains into the bottom of the flute. A flute that the killer knew would only be used by one person.

She knew she was right, but there was so little evidence. "She was very clever," she mumbled. "She's going to get away with it. There's not enough real evidence to convict her of murder. She didn't make the same mistake that John Talwell made. That's why she wanted to reread those newspaper clippings. That's why she wanted the house filled with people who hated Arlette."

"If you don't think Margaret Bickleton is the killer, then we'd better do something quickly," Mrs. Goodge said bluntly. "The inspector is goin' to be arrestin' her this morning."

"But I'm not sure we can do anything about it," Mrs. Jeffries cried. She broke off and forced herself to think. "There has to be a way, there simply has to be a way. If only I could get him to see it the way I see it."

"See what?" Wiggins cried. He looked at the others. Everyone was staring at Mrs. Jeffries, their expressions hopeful and eager. Even Samson, perched on his stool by the pine sideboard, had stopped licking his back paw and turned his big head toward the housekeeper.

"How it was done and, more importantly, who did it," she murmured. She was trying to come up with a method that might work, her mind assessing and discarding various ideas and schemes. But nothing seemed right. She slumped back against her chair. "We'd have to come up with a way to trick her, and I fear she's too clever for that. She'll not slip up unless . . . unless . . . oh, that won't do."

"What won't do?" Luty demanded. "Nell's bells, we'll figure it out. We ain't goin' to let the killer walk and we ain't goin' to sit back and let an innocent woman git arrested, even one as mean and cranky as Margaret Bickleton. Now, tell us what you're thinkin'."

Mrs. Jeffries took a deep breath. "It's very risky and it could easily fail."

"Life is filled with risk and failure, but that shouldn't stop us from doing what is right," Mrs. Goodge declared.

"Yes, of course. But we'd need a sample of Chief Inspector Barrow's handwriting and I'm not sure we've got one . . ."

"Yes, we do." Betsy sprang up. "It's in the inspector's study. Remember, he sent him that nice note last February when the inspector was ill with influenza." She charged for the back stairs. "I know exactly where it's at. I'll get it."

"Bring down his ink pot and pen," she called. "And some blank notepaper."

"I'll bring it all," Betsy yelled as she charged up the stairs.

"Right, now, what else do ya need?" Luty pressed.

"Let me think for a moment." Mrs. Jeffries drummed her fingers against the tabletop as the plan she'd come up with fell into place. "Yes, that should do it. We'll have to make her think the police have a witness," she muttered more to herself than the others. She nodded briskly. "Right, then, this is going to be the difficult part. I'll need to forge the chief inspector's handwriting and that's going to be very difficult."

"Let me do it."

Surprised, everyone turned and stared at Phyllis.

CHAPTER 11

———◆———

Mrs. Jeffries finally found her voice. "You?"

"I'm an excellent forger, Mrs. Jeffries," she explained earnestly. "I've had ever so much practice. My old mistress used to make me forge letters to her husband's bank manager."

They heard Betsy running down the back stairs.

"Slow down," Smythe cried anxiously. He shoved his chair back and started to get up but sat back down when she gentled her pace to a sedate walk. "That woman is goin' to give me even more gray hairs," he muttered.

Betsy smiled sweetly at her husband as she came into the kitchen. She was carrying the long, rectangular basket Mrs. Jeffries kept by the back staircase to hold old copies of the inspector's *Illustrated London News*. After he read them, he left them there for the rest of the household. "I've brought some plain notepaper, envelopes, and the inspector's fountain pen and ink pot." She put her burden on the table in front of the housekeeper. "And the letter from the chief inspector is right on top."

Mrs. Jeffries rose, grabbed the receptacle, and raced for the end of the table. She put the basket down, grabbed the letter, and handed it to Phyllis. Everyone else got up and hurried to crowd around the maid. Phyllis pulled the letter out and opened it.

"What's going on?" Betsy asked as she trailed after her husband.

"Phyllis is a forger," Wiggins replied cheerfully.

"It isn't her fault she's a forger," the cook explained as she moved into the vacant spot next to Mrs. Jeffries. "It was her old mistress making her forge letters to the bank manager."

"Huh?"

"I'll explain later, love." Smythe drew his wife next to him.

"Can you do it?" Mrs. Jeffries asked anxiously.

Phyllis studied the letter for a moment more and then smiled. "Oh yes, this will be very easy to copy. But you'll have to tell me what to write."

"And you'd best be quick about it," Mrs. Goodge warned. She looked at the carriage clock on the sideboard. "Otherwise, the wrong woman will be arrested."

The traffic was awful and it was almost eleven o'clock when the hansom pulled up in front of the Banfield house. "I'm not happy about this, either," Witherspoon said as he stepped down. "But the chief inspector is right: the evidence does point to Margaret Bickleton."

Barnes paid the driver. "I know you're not, sir, and, well, I've explained my position on the matter. We're only arresting her because the poison was found in her room." He nodded to the constables standing by the front gate. They'd sent a message to the local station, and additional men had been posted by the back door as well.

"That's not the only reason," Witherspoon interrupted. "There is plenty of additional evidence. And I'll not have you blaming yourself because the search was terminated before that room was properly explored. I was the one who made that decision, not you, and frankly, Constable, I think I'd make the same decision again in those circumstances."

"I still feel bad, sir." Barnes smiled grimly. "I was hoping that gossip I picked up from the Banfield servants might have some bearing on the case, but I guess it was just that, silly rumors of one sort or another." On the drive over, he'd tried to pass along everything he'd heard from Mrs. Jeffries. He'd pretended it was just talk he'd picked up casually but hadn't included in his reports because the information hadn't been gained in formal interviews. "But at least the chief inspector can get Whitehall off his back." They started for the house. "Do you really think the evidence we've got will hold up in the dock, sir?"

"No." He smiled slightly. "A good barrister should be able to get her off. All we can prove is that she hated the victim, that the murder weapon was found in her room, and that she may have purchased cyanide while on a trip to Battersea."

"I don't think hatred is much of a motive," Barnes muttered as he opened the gate and they went up the walkway. "Half of London would be dead if that's all it took." He gave the inspector a sideways glance. "This isn't like you, sir. You've never before wanted to arrest someone unless you were sure. Why now?"

They'd reached the front door. Witherspoon banged the knocker. "Because there is one part of me that thinks she might be guilty and her motive isn't just hatred. With Arlette out of the way, she probably hoped Lewis Banfield would turn to her daughter for comfort and then marriage."

"Good day." Michael opened the door wide. "If you'll come in, I'll let the master know you're here." He disappeared into the drawing room.

They stepped inside but neither of them spoke as they waited. Lewis Banfield came out of the drawing room and closed the door softly. "You're not wanting to search the house again, are you?" He tried to smile but didn't quite manage it. He knew why they were here.

"I know this is distressing, Mr. Banfield, but the poison that killed Mrs. Banfield came from the bottle we found in Mrs. Bickleton's room," Witherspoon said.

"Was it in the champagne?"

"No, it was in the smaller brown one," he replied. "We've no idea why the killer didn't leave the champagne in the butler's pantry. There was nothing in it but champagne."

Lewis stared at them and then swallowed heavily. "Are you going to arrest someone?"

"We're going to ask Mrs. Bickleton to come to the station and help us with our inquiries," he said. "I do hope she's still in residence here."

"She is. She wanted to leave this morning, but Aunt Geraldine asked her to stay." He smiled grimly. "They're in the morning room." He turned and went down the corridor. He was moving quickly, almost running. "It's this way."

"We know where it is," Witherspoon said as he hurried after him. "You might want to stay here. I doubt this will be very pleasant."

"No." He looked over his shoulder, his expression hard. But he didn't slow his steps; if anything, he picked up his pace. "I want to see her face when you take her away. If she murdered my wife and my child, I want her to suffer."

Constable Barnes tried to stay in front of Banfield, but the other man was too quick. Suddenly, Banfield cut in front of the constable and sprinted the last ten yards. He burst through the door of the morning room and slammed it shut behind him.

Alarmed, the two policemen ran after him. Barnes grabbed for the doorknob just as they heard the click of the lock being thrown. "Open the door!" he yelled.

Blast, thought Witherspoon, *this isn't good.* His last glimpse of Banfield's face made him fear for the two women in that room. "Get help," he said to Barnes.

Barnes rushed back the way they'd just come.

Witherspoon banged on the door. "Mr. Banfield, you must let us in. Let the police handle this matter."

But inside the morning room, Lewis Banfield stood against the locked door and stared at the two women sitting at the table. They were having morning coffee and there was a silver coffeepot and cups in front of them. Geraldine had been reaching for a lump of sugar with a pair of tongs.

At first she was so startled, she froze with the tongs suspended from her fingers in midair. Then she recovered and dropped the implement next to her cup. "Lewis, what on earth is wrong with you? How dare you come bursting in here like an ill-mannered barbarian."

He ignored her and focused his attention on her companion. From behind him, he could hear the inspector pounding on the door and shouting at him. He ignored that, too. "You disgusting old cow, how could you? Did you really think that by murdering my wife I'd ever in a million years turn to that horse-faced hag of a daughter of yours?"

Margaret cried out in hurt and surprise. "I didn't murder Arlette."

"How dare you speak to her like that." Geraldine started to get up, but Lewis' hand came down on her shoulder and pushed her back into her chair.

Witherspoon twisted the knob again and then gave it a good kick with his foot. From inside, he heard a woman's soft cry of distress. "Mr. Banfield, can you hear me?" he shouted. "You must open this door immediately. You've no right to take the law into your own hands. No one in that room has been convicted of anything, so if you do anything to harm either of those women, I'll arrest you."

"She murdered my wife," he cried.

"But I didn't, I didn't," he heard Margaret Bickleton sob.

"Lewis, this is absurd. Get away from that door and let us out," Geraldine Banfield commanded. "You're making a fool of yourself."

"You never accepted her, did you?" he said, his tone accusing. "Did you plan it together—was it both of you who decided she had to die?"

"This has gone far enough, Lewis. I won't tolerate being treated like this," Geraldine said. "Now get your wretched hand off my shoulder or I'll slap your face."

Shut up, you silly woman, Witherspoon thought as he glanced down the corridor hoping to see help on the way. *Stop provoking him.* He heard a slap and then a sob.

"You hated her," Banfield screamed. There was a thud as if a chair had been kicked aside and then another one and another.

"No one hated Arlette!" Geraldine yelled. "And I shall never forgive you for this, never. I demand that you stop it this instant. How dare you put that interloper before your own blood?"

"Mr. Banfield, open this door in the name of the law." Witherspoon banged on the wood again.

"You're not in any position to make demands," Banfield shouted. "This bitch has murdered my wife and you're to blame as well. You don't even like the woman; you simply invited her to spite Arlette."

The inspector tried again. He was afraid this was going to end in tragedy. "Mr. Banfield, open up, open up, open up." He continued to pound on the door. He looked down the hallway and saw Barnes and three constables racing toward him. Thank God.

"For God's sake, Margaret, stop cowering in the corner. Lewis isn't going to hurt you. Lewis, Lewis, what are you doing? Let go of her."

There was a scream and then the sound of breaking crockery. "No, Lewis, no," Geraldine cried as another loud crash filled the hallway.

Fearing that Banfield had gone insane and was hurting the women, the inspector hurled himself at the door, but it held.

"Step away, sir," Barnes yelled as he and the three

constables reached him. Witherspoon scrambled out of the way while the constables lined themselves up in a row in front of the door.

"Now," Barnes ordered and all four of them thrust hard against the door with their shoulders. Wood splintered but the door held. "Again," he instructed, and this time door flew open and they were flung into the room.

Witherspoon raced in behind them. The room was in shambles: three of the four chairs had been overturned, the coffeepot was on the floor, and Margaret Bickleton, her hair hanging around her narrow face, was curled up in the corner. Her hands were raised protectively over her head, and Lewis was standing over her, one of his fists raised in a threatening manner while Geraldine Banfield had hold of his other arm and was trying to pull him back.

"Get him away," Witherspoon commanded. The constables sprang toward him, but Banfield lowered his arm and held up his hand.

"I didn't hurt her," he said as the policemen grabbed him from both sides. They held him firmly between them and marched him away from the women. "I wanted to"— Banfield began to weep—"but I didn't. I'm not a murderer."

"Neither am I," Margaret said, her voice trembling. "And I don't know what is happening. But I want to go home."

"I'm afraid that won't be possible," Witherspoon said. "You'll need to come with us now."

"Why should she come with you?" Geraldine snapped. "What's she supposed to have done? Surely you don't believe the mad ranting of my lunatic nephew?" She glared at Banfield, who was standing by the door between two constables. Another constable stood in front of him, and Barnes was in the corridor, picking up something from the floor.

Witherspoon didn't answer her. He tried to think what to do with Banfield. He needed the men to take Mrs. Bickleton into custody, but he didn't want to leave Banfield on his own. He didn't trust that he'd behave himself.

"Let me stay, Inspector," Banfield pleaded. Tears flooded his eyes. "I promise I'll be civilized. But I want to see justice done for my Arlette. At least give me that much."

"Humph," Geraldine snorted.

Witherspoon nodded and then his gaze shifted to the hallway. Barnes was reading a letter. "Constable Barnes?"

The constable looked up. "Sorry, sir, but there was a messenger boy delivering this just as I reached the lads. I took the liberty of reading it. I think you'd better see it before you do anything else." He handed the letter to the inspector and tucked the envelope into his pocket. Witherspoon opened the folded paper and read it. Puzzled, he read it again and then looked at the constable. "I don't know what to make of this."

"The letter is from the chief inspector, isn't it?" Barnes asked blandly. He had the strongest suspicion that Barrows had no more written that letter than the man in the moon.

"Yes, but this is most unorthodox," Witherspoon muttered. "But then again, most of our cases tend to end in an unorthodox fashion." He noticed that Margaret Bickleton was still huddled in the corner on the floor. He walked across the room and helped her to her feet.

Dazed and confused, she stared at him. "What should I do now?"

"Just stay here for the moment," he said gently. "And please accept my apologies for what you've endured, ma'am."

"I'll take her upstairs." Geraldine started for the door. "Come along, Margaret, you need to rest."

Witherspoon stepped in front of her, blocking her path. "Mrs. Banfield, would you please explain why you went to your country house two weeks ago?"

Surprised, she stared at him for a moment. "That's none of your concern," she replied. "And I don't need to stand here and be spoken to as if I'm a criminal."

"But it is our concern." The inspector looked over her shoulder and spoke to the constables holding Banfield. "Let Mr. Banfield go. I don't think he'll try to do anything foolish."

"I won't," he promised. "You have my word."

Barnes looked surprised, but said nothing.

"I've no idea what you think you're doing, Inspector." Geraldine drew herself up to her full height. "But this has gone too far. First my idiot nephew bursts in here like a madman hurling vile accusations, and now you have the temerity to question me."

"Just tell me why you went to the country house that day," Witherspoon pressed. "It's a simple enough question."

"If you must know, I went to look at the roof. Lewis asked me to assess the damage before we asked Mr. Bigglesworth to speak to the builders. He's merely a gardener, and if I hadn't gone to have a look, they'd try to sell us a new roof."

"Then why do you think it is that Mr. Bigglesworth told Mrs. Peyton that you'd done no such thing, that you'd come to the house and demanded the keys to the outbuildings? But you certainly never looked at the hole in the attic."

Instead of answering the inspector, she looked at her nephew. "Lewis, I don't know what this policeman is trying to do . . ."

"Answer his questions," Lewis ordered. "Because if you don't, I swear I'll throw you out of this house with my bare hands."

Her eyes widened and then narrowed as she struggled to hold on to her temper. "Alright, if you insist that I be humiliated in this fashion, I'll answer this man's stupid questions." She turned her attention to the inspector. "It's very simple. I didn't go and look at the attic because I was tired and I didn't want to trudge up all those stairs, so I came home," she replied.

"Why did you need the keys to the outbuildings?" It was Lewis Banfield who spoke.

"I forget; I had a reason but when I got out there, I couldn't recall." She gave him an embarrassed smile. "I'm old, Lewis, and sometimes I forget things."

"Your gardener keeps vermin poison in the garden shed, doesn't he?" Witherspoon pressed. "And it's made to an old family formula containing grains of prussic acid."

"That's right," Lewis responded, his gaze fixed on his aunt.

For a moment, Witherspoon wondered if he had been wise in letting the man stay in here. He turned back to

Geraldine Banfield. "But Mr. Bigglesworth is a very careful man; he keeps the poison under lock and key."

"I imagine he does," she replied coolly. "But that's nothing to do with me."

"Doesn't it, Mrs. Banfield?" Witherspoon spoke softly. "You were the last person to go into the garden shed, the place where the poison is kept. The shed has been locked since you handed the keys back to the gardener. But he went into the shed this morning and discovered something was amiss. The bottle of poison was gone."

"That's impossible, I brought my own bottle—" She broke off when she realized what she'd done. How she'd given herself away.

Fearing that Banfield would go berserk again, Barnes and Witherspoon both moved toward him, but he just stood there, staring at her. The blood had drained from his face and tears filled his eyes. "How could you? How could you? You knew how much I loved her. She was everything to me, everything."

"She was dishonoring our whole family," Geraldine said. "But you were too blind to see it. This is your fault—if you'd been half a man, if you'd told her she couldn't put that disgusting statue out in public so that every bank clerk or jackanapes could leer at a Banfield, I wouldn't have had to do it."

"You were going to let them arrest me," Margaret Bickleton said softly. "I thought you were my friend."

"I was never your friend." Geraldine sneered at her. "And if that simpering mouse of a daughter of yours had been half a woman, she'd have gotten this one to marry her and I wouldn't have had to do anything."

Margaret Bickleton stared at her for a moment and then leapt at Geraldine, raking her across the face with her nails. "You horrible old witch," she cried. She pounded, pummeled, pulled hair, and screamed like a banshee as the two women tumbled to the floor.

It took Witherspoon, Barnes, Banfield, and all three constables to pull her off Geraldine Banfield.

"They arrested Geraldine Banfield," Smythe announced as he and Wiggins came into the kitchen. The two of them had found a street boy from another neighborhood to deliver the forged letter and then paid him well to disappear. They'd kept watch on the Banfield house to see if their ploy had worked.

"And she weren't goin' quietly," Wiggins added eagerly. He dropped into his seat. "She was screamin' and shoutin' and diggin' her 'eels in as they dragged her away. She grabbed on to one of the spokes of the fence, and it took three constables to pry her hands off and get her into the police wagon."

"So I was right." Mrs. Jeffries slumped in relief. "I wasn't absolutely certain it was her, you see. All the evidence pointed to her, but her motive just seemed so ridiculous."

"Alright, the boys are back now, and you promised to tell us how you figured it out," Betsy said. Smythe took his spot next to her and reached for her hand under the table.

"Let's pour them a cup of tea." Mrs. Goodge reached for the pot. "I'm sure they're thirsty, too."

As soon as everyone was served, Mrs. Jeffries began.

"As you all know, I had a feeling our killer wasn't Mrs. Bickleton."

"But so much of the evidence pointed to her," Hatchet said. "Especially her sneaking back into the Banfield house and reading those newspaper clippings."

"That's one of the reasons I was thrown off track, so to speak," Mrs. Jeffries said. "But I was looking at those newspaper clippings the wrong way. What I should have been asking myself was why Geraldine Banfield asked for the trunk to be brought down in the first place."

"She was the one that wanted to read them." Mrs. Goodge nodded her head in agreement. "She was of an age to remember the case but she couldn't recall all the details."

"That's right, and then I remembered what you learned from your friend, that it had been Geraldine Banfield and Emma Stafford who'd sneaked out of the Banfield country house to go watch a trial at the assizes in Aylesbury. It was John Talwell's trial for the murder of Sarah Hart that they went to see. Even though he wasn't a member of the Quakers, he dressed like one. Fanny had told Wiggins the clippings were about 'an old murder trial at Aylesbury'; I suddenly realized that must have been the case that Lady Stafford spoke about."

"So that's where she got the idea of using prussic acid?" Ruth mused.

"Yes, I'm sure of it. But she didn't want to make Talwell's mistakes," Mrs. Jeffries said. "Once I realized that the killer had to be her, it all came together in my mind. It was Geraldine Banfield who went to the country house and she didn't go there to look at a hole in the roof. She went there because she knew there was poison."

"That's why she asked for the keys to the outbuildings while she sent Mr. Bigglesworth off to get the pony and trap," Ruth added eagerly. "Oh, my gracious, thank goodness I overheard that particular conversation."

"Agreed. If you hadn't, we'd never have figured it out," the housekeeper said.

"The poison was kept in an outbuilding," Luty said. "You'd not keep dangerous stuff like that in the house."

"Right, and that's why she intercepted the telegram boy on the day of the ball," Mrs. Jeffries continued.

"I don't understand." Betsy frowned. "What did he have to do with anything?"

"Her excuse for going to the country house was to look at the damaged roof and give instructions to Mr. Bigglesworth about the scope of the repairs. Mr. Bigglesworth was then to send an estimate to Mr. Banfield. Geraldine knew that she had a few days before the gardener would get impatient and start pestering Lewis Banfield for someone to come down and look at the damage. She probably thought she was well on her way to pulling it off when she spotted the telegram boy coming up the drive on the day of the ball. She was planning to kill Arlette that night, so she intercepted the telegram. She didn't want to have to explain to her nephew why she hadn't taken care of business."

"We know where she got the idea and the poison, but I'm still not sure why she did it," Luty admitted. "And neither are any of the rest of you," she charged. "I can tell by lookin' at yer faces that yer just as puzzled as I am."

"I was puzzled as well," Mrs. Jeffries exclaimed. "And when I tell you, you're going to find it difficult to believe. She killed Arlette to save what she thought was the family honor. That was her sole motive and that was the reason she almost got away with murder. She was outraged when she realized that Arlette was going to allow a seminude statue of herself to be mass-produced." She looked at the skeptical expressions on their faces. "I'm quite serious, that was her motive. Think back to the sequence of events. She knew that Arlette was going to sell the production rights to the statue, but she was overheard to say that she hoped Elizabeth Montrose would convince her to drop the project. But that didn't happen and, instead, mother and daughter had a terrible row and when it became clear that Arlette wouldn't be dissuaded, Geraldine decided the woman had to die. She'd already read up on the Talwell case; we know that because she'd made Fanny bring her trunk down from the attic. But as I said, she wasn't going to make Talwell's mistakes. She wanted to make sure that someone else would be blamed for the murder."

"Margaret Bickleton," Hatchet said. "She was the sacrificial lamb."

Mrs. Jeffries nodded. "Mrs. Bickleton had been hinting for an invitation to stay as a houseguest, and Geraldine needed someone to frame for the murder. As soon as she heard Arlette and her mother arguing, she put her plan into action." She looked at Wiggins. "Fanny told you that Mrs. Bickleton was standing there when she ordered the maid to drag that trunk back up to the attic and, later, Fanny saw Mrs. Bickleton up in the attic having a snoop. I'll wager that, knowing how curious the woman was, Geraldine Banfield deliberately piqued her interest."

"But she couldn't have known Mrs. Bickleton would sneak up there that very day," Betsy protested. "No one is that clever."

"Of course not. I think she assumed that Margaret would have her snoop once she came as a houseguest. Mrs. Banfield's only goal was to ensure that Margaret had a look at those clippings and that she knew about the Talwell murder. Believe me, she realized exactly what her friend had been up to when Mrs. Peyton told her that Mrs. Bickleton had come back to the house to search for her earring that day. Providence seemed to have smiled upon her plans. She needed an avenue where it could be proved that Margaret Bickleton knew a few grains of prussic acid could kill. If it came to a trial, Mrs. Peyton could testify to her coming back to the house and Fanny could then confirm she went up to the attic and saw the clippings."

"She played right into her hands, didn't she?" Ruth murmured.

"Yes, and once Geraldine Banfield realized it, she set about doing everything she could to make sure that if anyone was arrested for murder, it was Margaret Bickleton. She put on the woman's distinctive blue jacket and veil and went out into the mews with a jug of cream."

"Why'd she do that?" Wiggins asked.

"She needed it to poison the Millhouse cat," Mrs. Jeffries explained. "Remember, she couldn't ask the gardener how long prussic acid stayed potent and she needed to know that it would work quickly. She knew the cat was old and liked to nap in the sun, so she lured the poor old thing with the poisoned cream and then quite calmly watched it die. She knew then the poison would work on Arlette."

"But she was clever enough to wear her house-guest's clothes so that if anyone saw her or figured out what had been done, she'd not be blamed for it," Phyllis murmured.

"Correct." Mrs. Jeffries gave her an encouraging smile and turned to Ruth. "And, remember, you told us that Arlette complained that Mrs. Banfield the elder had harassed the staff on the day of the ball and made them take all the glassware to be washed."

"Arlette claimed the glassware was perfectly clean because she'd examined it herself."

"And it was. Geraldine Banfield used the supposedly dirty glassware as an excuse to get the servants out of her way so she could get in and out of the butler's pantry undetected. That's when she slipped the grains of prussic acid into the bottom of Arlette's champagne flute. Except for the staff, she would have been the only one who knew that Lewis Banfield's glass had a chip in the base. She would have been the only one of the suspects who knew which glass to poison, and once we learned the poison wasn't in the champagne itself, I knew it had to be her."

"But she insisted the glasses be washed again," Mrs. Goodge pointed out.

"The champagne set was kept separate from the rest of the collection and I'll bet if we ask Michaels or Mrs. Peyton, they'll confirm that she didn't insist that set be cleaned again. Then, of course, there was her chasing the police out of her room with an umbrella."

"I don't get that bit," Wiggins admitted.

"According to the inspector, Geraldine and Lewis Banfield had already had words about her lack of cooperation with the police. But that didn't stop her from raising a fuss and keeping the constables out of her room."

"You think she had the champagne and the poison hidden there?" Betsy helped herself to more tea.

"I do, and that was the moment she was most vulnerable."

"Then, she wasn't doin' it to get the search called off so she could plant the evidence in Mrs. Bickleton's room at a later time?" Luty asked.

"Oh no, but when the search was called off, she took advantage of the situation and shoved the evidence under Margaret Bickleton's bed in the guest room."

"But she couldn't have known the police were going to come back and search again," Smythe protested.

"But she could easily have insisted the maids give the room a thorough cleaning and one of them would have found the box," Betsy pointed out. "And I'll wager she'd have made sure that Lewis Banfield was home when it happened. She wanted that box found."

"Oh, it all pointed to her, but the trouble was, I couldn't understand the why of it until almost too late. Then I remembered that the first thing anyone who knew the Banfields said about them was that they were obsessed with looking honorable, so obsessed that for the last two hundred years they've refused rewards and titles from the crown."

"Not Lewis Banfield—he's not very honorable," Wiggins protested. "Look 'ow he treated Helen Bickleton after promisin' her father he'd ask for her 'and in marriage."

"I didn't say they were honorable, I said they were

obsessed with the appearance of honor—and that's
when the motive made sense," Mrs. Jeffries explained.
"Geraldine Banfield felt the family honor was going to
be completely shattered if Lewis' wife allowed a seminude statue of herself to be produced. It was that act that
sealed the poor woman's fate. She had to die and she
had to die publicly. That's why Geraldine waited till the
night of the ball to kill her."

"Well, I'm glad that Margaret Bickleton escaped the
hangman's noose," Ruth said.

"I don't think she'd have been convicted in any case,"
Mrs. Jeffries mused. "And thanks to Phyllis' excellent
talents, the inspector has now caught the real culprit."

Phyllis blushed. "I'm glad I can help. I'm not very
good with people and I can't do what the rest of you can,
but at least I could do this little bit. I must say, it's ever
so exciting working for justice."

"It is very rewarding," Hatchet agreed. "Madam, now
that we know the guilty party has been apprehended
and how our Mrs. Jeffries figured it out, I suggest we
take our leave. If you've forgotten, you've dinner guests
tonight. The Darringtons and Mr. Widdowes, remember." He went to the coat tree to get their outer garments.

Luty made a face as she stood up. "Oh, blast and tar-
nation, I only invited the Darringtons because I thought
they might know something about our case. They are
two of the most boring creatures on God's green earth.
But John Widdowes is a right interestin' fellow." She
looked at Hatchet as he draped her shawl around her
shoulders. "Make sure the cellar is unlocked," she told

him. "If I can get rid of the Darringtons, I want to give John a taste of my best stuff."

"Oh, good gracious, madam, you're not going to give him that awful moonshine, are you?" Hatchet sighed in exasperation. "One of these days it's going to kill someone."

Witherspoon arrived home only a bit later than his normal time and he readily accepted Mrs. Jeffries' suggestion that they have a glass of sherry. He was glad of the chance to unburden himself and by the time he'd finished telling her everything that had transpired, he felt far more relaxed. "It was quite awful, Mrs. Jeffries. Even after she admitted what she'd done, Geraldine Banfield couldn't see that it was morally reprehensible. She kept blathering on and on about family honor and silly nonsense like that. It didn't seem to bother her in the least when Mr. Banfield told her his wife had been expecting. The poor man was in tears, but all she kept saying was that she'd saved the family honor."

"It must have been difficult for him," she replied. "He's alone now. I'm sure he must have felt terrible about the way he treated Margaret Bickleton."

"When we finally managed to pull her off Mrs. Banfield, he apologized profusely. However, I don't think the two families will remain friends. But I did feel terrible for Lewis Banfield. He genuinely loved his wife and he lost her for the most foolish of reasons: someone else's vanity." He drained his glass and put it on the table. He looked at Mrs. Jeffries. "Murder is always terrible, and

I know that the death of any human being shouldn't be taken lightly. But I'm especially glad I was able to solve this one. I have a feeling I'd have liked Arlette Banfield. If she'd lived, she might have made the world a better place. But then again, I suppose you could say that about almost anyone."

Mrs. Jeffries nodded solemnly. "Lady Cannonberry thought highly of her as well. She came by this afternoon and said she'd love to see you this evening if you weren't too tired. She wondered if you could have dinner together. I told her I'd pass along the message."

Witherspoon shot to his feet. "I'm not the least bit tired. I'll pop over now. Honestly, Mrs. Jeffries, when you see how fragile life can be, it makes one very grateful for what one has."

"Indeed it does, sir."